# Mr. Eastwood's Match

# Mr.
# Eastwood's
## *Match*

❧

*Gentlemen of York*

## SALLY BRITTON

*For the Recovering People Pleasers*
*...the consensus has been reached: your needs matter.*

# A Letter

## July 26th, 1822

*Benwaith House, London*

My Dearest Emily,

Your last letter gave your father and me such comfort. York sounds a far gentler place than London, and I am relieved to know Juniper is such a patient and thoughtful guide. I hope you will not fret over the little missteps that naturally occur while we are all adjusting to new expectations. They cannot be of lasting consequence, provided you continue with your usual kindness and good sense. The people who matter most will see you for who and what you truly are.

Your father bids me say that he hopes you will take care to form acquaintances which will steady your new position. Not for ambition's sake, my darling, but because we wish you to have good friends, a home of your own one day, and a husband who will appreciate your gentle nature. You have always been our peacemaker, our most thoughtful child. Anyone who knows you would surely agree.

Do write soon and tell me how you pass your days, and whether there is anyone of particular interest to you. Not that we press you, of course. But we hope to see you content and settled in a happy situation.

Your father sends his affection, as do your brothers and sisters-in-law. I send all my love.

Your Mother,

*Margaret, Countess Benwaith*

# Chapter One

## August 1st, 1822

" I have not always been a lady, as some of you know," Emily Sterling said with the utmost ease, sipping from a teacup with a spray of pink roses painted on the side. "It has only come about very recently, and I am still learning all that it entails."

The four other unmarried young women sitting in Mrs. Frederickson's sitting room all stared at her, two with their own cups stopped midway to their mouths and one with a sandwich pressed to her lips. For a long moment, the patter of raindrops against the window was the only sound heard.

Of course, Emily meant that her status had undergone a recent elevation as she changed from a humble gentleman's daughter to an earl's. Because of her father's unexpected inheritance of a title. Yet something about how she said it had gone amiss, if the wide eyes of the women around her were indicative of how they received her words.

Botheration. Growing up on her family's farm, without any expectation that she would be more than a squire's wife *if* luck favored her, had not eased Emily's entry into Society at all.

"Not that it is all that different from before," she hastened to add, lowering her cup to its saucer with a soft clash that made her wince. She had to restrain herself from looking for a possible chip in the fragile dish. "It is only that there is so much a lady does not do, you see, that I am accustomed to doing."

Two of the other women, nineteen in age and barely out in Society, exchanged a glance and smiles that conveyed more smugness than amusement. At five-and-twenty, Emily ought to have had more experience than the two of them.

"What sort of things do you find give you the most trouble, Lady Emily?" The hostess's daughter, Miss Hannah Frederickson, asked with a cheeriness the question itself did not merit. "Perhaps we could offer some advice. Or commiseration. I know that I have found myself frustrated by more than one instance of behaving helpless in a circumstance that I should rather see to myself."

Emily wanted to give Miss Frederickson an enormous smile but had been told quite recently that showing too much enthusiasm was crass, she settled for keeping her lips tightly pressed together and widening her eyes. Which made her feel silly, but it seemed a good alternative.

"Yesterday, I saw a fine tabby cat walking through an alleyway, with four little kittens trailing behind her. They were right next to a bakery, so I went inside to get a sausage roll. Then went out to feed them. You see, I needed to pass the time waiting for my sister-in-law, Lady Juniper Sterling, to come out of the bookshop across the road. But a woman named Mrs. Henry Rothingham saw me, and she gave me a stern correction."

One of the nineteen-year-olds covered her mouth, but not before Emily heard the younger lady giggle.

At five and twenty, Emily had thought herself well versed in navigating the world. Certainly, she had never struggled in social situations before her father's rise in rank. Country manners were different, the society she had moved in before humbler. She hadn't ever interacted with nobility before that letter arrived that changed their whole fortune. Since then, however, she questioned every step she took. Every ribbon she admired. Every curl in her hair. Examining each of her actions and being to determine whether others would find her socially adequate.

"Feeding poor waifs that are not brushed and bathed, sitting on velvet cushions at home, is simply not done." Miss Frederickson sounded sympathetic, and that was the best Emily could hope for of late. She could do without admiration and praise, but what she longed for in that moment was a single day, just one, in which no one corrected her at all.

Making friends in York was proving difficult, as it had been in London.

The conversation moved along to other things, such as gowns for upcoming assemblies and musicales. Some of the young ladies had ordered several new things for the upcoming Race Week, a staple in York's social world. They talked of bangles, hairpins, ribbons, and slippers with great enthusiasm.

Emily quietly listened, inwardly keeping notes of what the other ladies said sounded lovely versus what they scoffed at as trite or unsophisticated. Frankly, she found the whole of it exhausting. But it wasn't as overwhelming as trying to keep abreast of London fashion, appetites, and gossip.

She had spent most of her spring and early summer in London, in what had felt like a trial by fire, thrown into the world of wealth and nobility because her father had not wanted to wait even a moment before seizing his place as an earl.

Not because he wanted wealth or grandeur, of course. He was likely seated in his London library at that very moment, stubbornly insisting on wearing his favorite suit of clothes from before his elevation, and letting her two eldest brothers handle everything of importance.

Father wanted the best life offered for his children's sake, and for their mother, not for himself. But that had meant a distinct lack of interest in making certain they were all properly educated about the world their titles pulled them into. Without his youngest son, John Sterling, whose experience serving a duke's family gave him insight into that world, they would have made a great mess of things. Or an even greater one than they already had.

"York will be better for Emily," her brother had told the family. "It is far more forgiving than London, in terms of missteps. Juniper and I will host her for a few months. My wife can chaperone and instruct Emily on proper behavior."

Thus, Emily had been bundled up in a carriage and sent to live with her brother and sister-in-law not long after their wedding. And seated, at that moment, with young ladies who knew far more about proper etiquette than Emily could guess at when left to her own devices.

As the gathering dispersed, and Emily waited in the foyer of the large house for her brother's carriage to arrive, she found herself rehearsing some of the things she had learned.

Chartreuse was a lively color that was worn by the garish. Tiny dogs in laps were adorable but not socially acceptable outside of one's own home. Gentlemen who wore brown jackets at dinner were suspect of being careless with the importance of fashion. Bead-work would likely lead to poor eyesight and the horror of spectacles —someone's mother's brother's apothecary had said so. Unless, of course, such a pastime was enjoyed by a duke's daughter, in which case it was something to be praised rather than cautioned against.

On and on the list went.

Feeding hungry kittens felt more in keeping with what Emily wished to do with her time than worrying about everything else. Yet she had learned, painfully, how little it took for a harmless misstep to become a character-damaging story eagerly passed from person to person.

By the time Emily's brother, called Jack by the family, handed her into the carriage, her head swirled with all the details of the seemingly innocuous afternoon gathering.

"You look as though you wish to spend the rest of the afternoon abusing the gardens," Jack said, voice mild and expression as calm as ever.

His years in service to the Duke of Montfort had rendered him the ability to always appear stoic, whether he was met with little discomforts or enormous misfortune. It almost wasn't fair.

"Pulling weeds when one has a great deal on one's mind is not abusive to flowerbeds." Emily folded her hands delicately in her lap. "Although I have had it confirmed today that the removal of unwanted growth is best left to the gardener." She sighed. "Lest a lady damage her skin by unwittingly touching a bramble."

Jack's eyebrows raised. That was the only thing in his expression that betrayed any of his thoughts on the matter. "How did you receive this piece of advice?"

"Poorly," she muttered, looking out the window at the passing countryside. "How do they expect a woman to modulate her feelings at all times, everywhere she goes, if she is never allowed to express them anywhere?" She tugged at the strings of her reticule. "What am I to do, Jack? I cannot even sit on my hands to keep them still. It is uncouth. I have to keep them politely folded in my lap. No fidgeting at all."

At this moment, she saw him bite the inside of one cheek. If he had been sitting next to her rather than across, she would have missed it completely.

"Are you amused by this?" she asked, accusatory tone slipping out. "You must understand how patently unfair it is to throw a thousand rules at a woman at one time."

"You never complained about it in London," he pointed out, but his eyes glimmered with humor rather than annoyance. "It is almost refreshing to see you finally expressing your concerns."

"You were managing our entire family in London," she said, looking out the window again. "I had no wish to add to the weight you carried with my own minor concerns. And I had the companion you hired for us. Or social tutor. Or whatever you want to call Mrs. Regan."

The formidable woman had saved the ladies of the household many times. Mother, both of Emily's sisters-in-law, and herself, had relied upon the woman's guidance. Mrs. Regan was still in London helping the others.

"A former governess turned etiquette instructor is how she styles herself at present." Jack's demeanor changed somewhat, his eyebrows drawing together as he leaned toward her. "Emily. I thought you were gliding through all this as serenely as a Hyde Park swan."

"Even after the trouble with that odious gentleman—who does not warrant that title in the least—during the Season?" Her gaze went from her brother's concerned expression to her lap. "The gossip he stirred up to make all of us appear like backwards country bumpkins distressed you."

For Emily, the whole thing had been a nightmare. Being gossiped about at a ball for turning down a boorish snob, a man who had stalked her from one place to the next and insisted his offer of marriage was the best she could hope to receive, had frayed her nerves to say the least. It had been Juniper's intervention, along with the kindness of Jack's other connected friends, that had saved Emily and their whole family from social ridicule.

"I never once blamed you for any of that," Jack said, his voice soft in the carriage as it left the city roads for the countryside. "Never, Emily. You have always been a kind, graceful, mannerly young lady from all that I have seen. And remember, if you will, I worked in a duke's household for several years."

As sweet as it was for him to say such a thing, Emily doubted him. Jack looked at her as a protective, kindly older brother would. He could not see her defects as clearly as she did. Nor did he understand the lengths she went to in order to maintain a calm, pleasant facade. When he called her a "young lady," she had to bite her tongue to keep from correcting him.

Of all the unmarried ladies gathered in the Fredericksons' house that day, and in every gathering she had taken part in since coming to York society, she was nearly always the eldest. If others present were older, they often appeared rather sad and resigned to remaining without matrimonial prospects.

Five-and-twenty was not ancient. Indeed, her own sisters-in-law were near that age when they married her eldest brothers. But here, in a world obsessed with the size of a woman's marriage portion and her ability to rise higher in rank, she often felt more on the shelf than off.

Of course, her flesh-and-blood sisters, Mary and Anne, had both married at twenty. A double wedding for twin sisters, seven years ago now. The two of them were happy as larks, running households and tending their children. Emily missed them sorely.

She hadn't exactly thought herself desperate for matrimonial happiness. Many a youngest daughter stayed at home as her parents aged, seeing to their needs, and might one day marry a widower or become the favorite aunt. She had never been in a hurry to leave the safety of her father's home, and her parents hadn't encouraged her to do so.

But that had changed, too.

"These are only a few habits you speak of," Jack said when she remained silent. "Small adjustments in behavior. And if you wear gloves to pull a few weeds in our gardens, no brambles will harm you, and no one need ever know about your strategic campaign to eliminate your frustration through aggressive agricultural maneuvers."

"Aggressive agricultural…" She narrowed her eyes at him. "You have been reading aloud with Juniper again in the evening. Without me. Haven't you?"

He chuckled and did not look that least bit repentant. "I have. She enjoys holding the blankets up to her chin and shivering in horror while I read her gothic tales."

"The vocabulary in gothic novels is so much more interesting than what I find in my books. Except for words like 'elocution,' which sounds rather awful come to think of it, there is never creative phrasing. It is all 'propriety this' and 'mannerly that.'"

"I thought the gothic novels gave you unpleasant dreams?"

"They do. I think the etiquette books make for true nightmares, though." She smirked a little. "Horrible dreams of arriving at important events dressed in the wrong gown, for example." Jack chuckled. "But I can still feel as though I am missing out on excellent words."

"You could try Keats."

"Keats? Oh dear. Then I might start sighing over moonlight and dying of love before supper. That would hardly improve my reputation."

Her brother laughed, though it was a brief sound that he swiftly smothered by putting his fist to his lips and clearing his throat. He laughed more of late. Which was good to see. He had spent most of the last several months utterly frustrated as he tried to help their whole family adjust to their new status.

Having their father unexpectedly inherit an earldom, elevating everyone's status to the peerage, had proved the most challenging thing their family had yet faced. As the humblest of gentry, they had been comfortable. Survived well with good manners, polite behavior, and laughter with each other and their friends.

But now? Lady Emily, daughter of an earl, had to behave far differently than she had as Miss Sterling, daughter to a gentleman with a meager farm and no interest in Society.

It took a great deal of self-control to keep in her sigh as the carriage turned into the drive of her brother and sister-in-law's cottage. A home she had heard others call "quaint" even though it was larger than the house where she had spent her childhood with six other siblings.

"Take heart, Emily," her brother said softly as the vehicle rolled to a stop at the front door. "I know you have the intelligence and ability to conquer York society, and then we will meet London's next Season with a new plan of attack."

That was Jack. Always thinking in terms of battle and strategy.

"I am certain you are right," she said, managing not to wince as she spoke the falsehood. Oh, she meant to give it all her best effort. But somehow, she no longer believed her best would be good enough. Perfection was, unfortunately, what her new life required of her. And Emily had little hope of achieving that.

# Chapter Two

Having a dog the size of a small pony launch itself into one's bed was the surest way to startle a man from sleep. Aside from physically dumping him out of the mattress or pouring water on his head. Wake-ups that Lyness Eastwood had experienced on multiple occasions while at school. Which, really, meant he did not mind Apollo's giant paws on either side of his head as the massive boar hound licked his face.

"Roman!" he yelled, rather than scold the animal. It was not the dog's fault that his master had trained him to do ridiculous things like this. "Can you not send a servant like a normal person?"

Roman leaned against the doorway, arms crossed, eyebrows raised. "Can you not rise at a decent hour?"

"It is only ten in the morning."

"It is one o'clock in the afternoon."

"Oh." Lyness finally pushed Apollo aside well enough to sit up. He squinted at the clock on the mantel, but the curtains were half-drawn and cast most of it in shadow.

"And even ten is late. We are not keeping London hours here, Lyness." Roman came into the room. "Apollo, *Komm.*" The large dog jumped down from the bed and circled around Roman to then settle beside him, sharp ears perked up and ready for the next command. The dog was a towering beast, formidable in both size and bearing. Standing nearly to his master's hip, he bore the unmistakable frame of the German mastiffs favored by continental sportsmen. His coat was a warm tan, short and gleaming, his frame all muscle and elegance. Apollo was a creature bred not merely for beauty, but for strength.

"You know it sounds exactly like the English 'come.' I bet he would even respond to that." The German accent seemed entirely unnecessary. "Most of the commands sound like English words, in my opinion."

"Yes, but then there are delightful words like—"

Lyness raised his hands. "Do *not* do that here, when I am the only one for him to P-a-c-k-e-n." The word for *attack*.

"Apollo would not touch you, Lyness. You know that." Roman grinned and ruffled the fur between the dog's ears. "Your pillows, on the other hand, would never be the same."

Lyness climbed out of the bed and shrugged on a robe he'd left slung over a chair the night before. Belting it at his waist, he pulled the cord to summon his valet next. "I take it you came in search of me, and found me happily asleep, for a particular reason?"

"Why were you still in bed?" Roman came all the way in, taking the chair near the cold hearth as his own. Apollo stayed beside him, flopping on the rug at Roman's feet. "You aren't normally a layabout."

That made Lyness pause. "Did I f-f-forget about something? A meeting? Did a letter come from the estate?"

Roman narrowed his eyes, for a moment looking even older than his thirty-two years. "No letter. No emergency. Though it's rather telling that those were your first thoughts."

Lyness rubbed the back of his neck. At only nine-and-twenty, he felt half his age when Roman gave him such a glare. "You sent your hound to assault me, Roman. One assumes urgency."

"I sent him because I was tired of the housekeeper asking whether you'd been taken ill. She didn't say it, of course. Merely mentioned you hadn't requested breakfast or appeared in the dining room. Which I noticed hours ago."

"Oh." Lyness winced. "I was thinking."

"Mm. In your sleep?"

"Restful thinking," he muttered. "I sat up late copying a poem."

Roman gave him one of his looks. The sort that some might call stern, but Lyness knew well enough meant only that he'd been taken off guard. And didn't know how to react. Finally, slowly, his brother said, "You stayed up half the night. Transcribing poetry."

"It was a good poem." Lyness didn't bother hiding his grin, though he felt Roman's confusion keenly. "An older one. But the structure was beautiful. It reminded me of ivy, actually. The way it winds upward around old trees." And he had tried to put that same feeling into his calligraphy, the ascendant and descendant loops of lettering mimicking vines and leaves.

Roman gave him a look. "So, you missed half the day to transcribe verse no one asked for?"

Lyness crossed to the window and pushed aside the curtain just enough to glance out. Gray skies. Rain clinging to the corners of the glass. "I should have told someone I meant to sleep in." Lyness turned back to the room, catching his reflection in the glass. Hair tousled, dressing gown askew. "I will speak to Mrs. Gibbons. My apologies, Roman."

His older brother shrugged and turned his attention to picking up the iron to poke at the banked coals in the hearth. "You haven't caused a scandal. Merely a brief disruption in the kitchen. Disturbing nothing other than Cook's sense of order."

"If I shift my schedule, others must shift theirs. I can see how that would prove disruptive. That is all."

Roman glanced at him briefly, then let out a slow breath. "You have been out of sorts since we returned from Town."

"I haven't," Lyness said, though he had. But for a reason even he knew to be ridiculous. Who grew distracted over thoughts of a woman he had seen only once? "I am always like this."

"Hm."

There was a silence thick enough to imply all the words neither of them had spoken about their mother's mid-season summons. Lady Hartwell's sudden insistence that they return to York immediately, despite the peak of the Season and the vague assurances in her letter that *everything was fine*.

It had not felt fine. It had felt planned.

Roman was the one she confided in, when she chose to confide in anyone. Lyness had not asked questions. He rarely did.

"Was it really Mother who sent you?" Lyness asked, voice low.

His brother's mouth curled at one corner. "She asked if you were awake. I told her I would find out."

"And instead of knocking like a person with manners—"

"Apollo volunteered." Roman gave a brief scratch behind the dog's ear, and the massive hound wagged his long, thin tail. "I sent word to Cook we would eat an afternoon meal together. The two of us. Mother has gone out."

That made Lyness raise his eyebrows with hope. "Oh. That is a good thing, is it not? Do you know where?"

"Not precisely," Roman said, rubbing at his temple. "She said something about the two of us needing to mingle in society more. As though we are the members of the family refusing to leave the house most days. But she seemed to have a purpose of some sort in mind. Given the gleam in her eyes as she left, I am not certain either of us will like what she is planning."

Lyness tried for a smile. "I suppose we should be grateful she's planning *something*. When she has a project, she has less time to notice I'm not being particularly useful."

Roman shot his brother a dark look. "Less time to worry over you, you mean."

"I wish I understood anything that goes on in our mother's thoughts."

They were both silent for a long moment.

Lyness missed the sensible, reasonable woman their mother had been in the years before they lost their father. She had possessed a vibrancy and openness that kept him from despair over his own failings, because she always saw beauty and bright-ness in even the most profound mistakes. Eight years ago, they had lost their father, and not much initially changed in her character. Or they hadn't noticed it, until small eccentricities grew more frequent.

The last two years, she had withdrawn into herself. Devoting more time to her garden, quietly ignoring friendships, hardly speaking to her own sons. But of late, she had shown interest in a variety of seemingly unconnected things. She had recalled them from London on an urgent matter concerning the complete recon-struction of their country estate. A thoroughly unnecessary idea, but one she had already engaged an architect to look over.

Roman had put a swift end to that idea.

"For now, I take her excitement to leave on mysterious errands as a good sign. Even if it will only result in a dozen new rose clip-pings," Roman said, his smile limp at best. "Are you joining me for something to eat then?"

"I will be ready in half an hour," Lyness promised.

Roman rose to leave, crossing the room without hurry, and then hesitated at the door after Apollo trotted out. "Lyness?"

"Yes?"

"Try not to let Mother see you looking like a poet in mourning. She is already dramatic enough without you feeding her fire."

He shut the door behind him.

Lyness scrubbed his hand across his face and went to his desk, ensuring he had left everything tidy after his late night artistry. Roman might not understand, but Lyness found a measure of peace in making simple words take on greater meaning and beauty with no more than the flourish of his pen. He'd give anything to write an entire book as they had done in the years preceding the printing press, illuminating manuscripts with careful handwriting and evocative imagery.

He sank into the chair and picked up his pen, turning it over in his hands. In this modern era, creating such a thing would be a colossal waste of time and resources. He was helping Roman run the estate so his brother could focus on political and civic matters. There were better uses of Lyness's time.

A few minutes after Roman's exit, the door opened again—this time with a polite knock and a pause long enough to be civilized.

"Good afternoon, sir," said Hobson, entering with a waistcoat draped over one arm. Athena trotted in at his heels, as silent and composed as a duchess at tea, despite matching Apollo in size. "I have brought a guest."

"Well, good afternoon, Athena," Lyness murmured. "I was wondering where you might be."

Athena approached with dignified purpose, nudging his hand before settling beside him. Her tail gave one slow sweep across the rug, then stilled.

"I found her in the morning room," Hobson said, setting the waistcoat on a nearby chair. "She made herself comfortable beneath the window seat. Watching the rain. Likely for the last hour."

"She likes the quiet." Lyness scratched behind Athena's ears, and she huffed with pleasure. "Much like you, Hobson."

"She has excellent instincts," Hobson replied. "And finer manners than her mate, though I wouldn't dare say so in front of His Lordship."

Lyness smiled faintly. "He'd defend Apollo's honor with a sword, I think."

"Or a sermon." Hobson straightened the cravat he'd taken from Lyness's chest of drawers, running a practiced fingers over the fabric. "Regardless, the hounds may be Lord Hartwood's by owner-ship, but Athena's made it quite clear she rules the entire house-hold. Cook feeds her scraps. Mrs. Gibbons speaks to her like a person. Even the footmen step over her rather than ask her to move."

"She has *presence*," Lyness said, still absently petting her. "Unlike some of us."

Hobson gave him a dry look. "Sir, if you wished to command presence, you could easily do so with less ceremony than a German hound."

Lyness huffed a quiet laugh, though it faded almost at once. Presence. In school he'd been told he had none, or rather, that he made a virtue of keeping himself unobtrusive. That had never troubled him much. Until lately.

Until York had grown smaller, in a way. Smaller because every walk along the walls or through St. Helen's Square might, by some happy accident, place him in the path of a certain lady.

Lady Emily Sterling had been in the city long enough to be seen at tea rooms, to stroll with her sister-in-law near the ruins of Saint Mary's Abbey, to pause at the bookshop window and laugh at something unseen, and was noted going to visit Terry's for confectionary delights. He knew this because York was not London, and news—especially the sort that involved a lovely woman with a place in the peerage—moved quickly.

He had known precisely where she was staying since her arrival. He could have called. But he had no business to conduct, no errand to fulfill, no task that required his presence. Without one, he found himself standing still.

He had no right to expect to see her again, truly. They had met once, danced once, exchanged no letters, no promises, and no verbalized hopes of seeing each other again. Yet the memory of her voice lingered, unhelpfully precise, and had returned to him last night as he bent over his desk.

Perhaps that was why the loops of his pen had curved upward like climbing ivy. Why he had lost all sense of time.

Hobson cleared his throat, drawing Lyness back. "Shall I bring hot water, sir?"

"No," Lyness said quickly, setting down the pen he'd been turning between his fingers. "We needn't bother, and I told Roman I would meet him in half an hour. I will not keep him waiting."

Roman likely would say he did not mind, but Lyness had already inconvenienced enough people with his late rising. He would be where he said he would, at Roman's side, when he said he would be there.

Dependability was, without question, one of his greatest talents. It had never failed him yet.

# Chapter Three

As Emily kept pace with her brother and sister-in-law on the New Walk, trees on either side and the water lapping the shore, Emily suspected her brother regretted his easy compliance to his wife's request. The rain of the previous day had left the air damp and cool, but Juniper declared it a perfect afternoon for walking, and Jack had agreed. Somewhat grumpily.

Now, he strode with too much purpose for a man out to enjoy the fresh air, his gaze darting toward the River Ouse as though searching for either an escape or an enemy.

"You look as though we have dragged you to the edge of the unknown," Juniper teased, taking his arm. "A stroll along the river is hardly a forced march through hostile territory."

"I have no objection to walking," Jack replied, though his tone suggested otherwise. "I object to walking without purpose."

"There is purpose," Juniper said, amusement in her tone and the way she leaned against his shoulder. "We are parading your sister before York's most eligible gentlemen. Or perhaps the least eligible. I am not certain yet which of them we ought to like."

Emily managed a small laugh, though her cheeks warmed. "You make it sound as though I am a mare to be inspected at market."

"Hardly!" Juniper straightened, all wide eyes and kind sincerity. "More like a jewel in need of the right setting. And York is full of goldsmiths."

Though tempted to mention her lack of success with the "goldsmiths" of London, Emily wrinkled her nose and remained silent instead.

Jack gave an exaggerated sigh. "Is this truly necessary?" He looked over Juniper's head to Emily's, and she wondered if he was trying to take her side or measuring the amount of work it would be to find her a suitable match. It was difficult to tell with Jack, sometimes, whether he saw her as an ally in their sudden rise in rank or yet another obligation to fulfill.

"Yes," Juniper said firmly. "And I am in charge because your sister is far too agreeable to object, and you have nothing better to do this afternoon."

Emily kept her eyes ahead, pretending the exchange amused her, when in truth her stomach had knotted. She was willing to meet new people, of course. Willing to *try*—but each time the subject of her future arose, the weight of how little she understood about navigating such waters pressed upon her.

She would rather not be another weight on Jack's shoulders or another worry for her parents in this world of new worries.

A change of subject was necessary. She looked up at the mature elm trees. "Why is it called the *New* Walk? It seems the trees have at least been here a long time."

"Oh, the New Walk has been here nearly a century." Juniper gestured with her free hand to the River Ouse. "But why rename it if there is not a *newer* place to walk? The name will likely remain until some other path claims it."

"And it leads nowhere," Jack muttered. "There is no bridge, no connecting lane, merely an end that requires us to turn around and come back along the exact path we have already traversed."

Juniper gave a small shake to his arm, a laugh escaping her at his implied complaint. "Because it is a place of leisure, dear husband. And you *will* learn to enjoy such things in time. My campaign to help you conquer this constant need to be useful will continue as long as it takes."

At that moment, Emily caught the slightest change to her brother's expression. A softening in his gaze, the smallest upward tilt of his lips. He *was* enjoying his wife's gentle assault on his practical nature.

If she could find a husband who looked at her the way her brother looked at his wife, perhaps she would not be so daunted by the world of nobility. Certainly, a man who loved her would make all the rest worthwhile, would he not? Or perhaps she should not have picked up the book on Keats her brother had recommended. Romantic nonsense would hardly help her situation.

It was not even the grandness of such affection that tempted her, but the idea of no longer needing to practice constant vigilance in her manner, to simply exist as she was, made her stare at them. How was it done? That sort of ease of belonging?

Then Juniper laid her head against his shoulder for the briefest of moments. Feeling like she had stumbled upon a private moment between the married couple, Emily hastily averted her gaze forward and looked at the benches between trees facing the River Ouse.

A gentleman sat on one of them, his dark coat a striking contrast to the gray-blue background of the river and sky. A large hound lay at his feet, head up and ears pricked as a trio of ducks flew up from water to the grass. The man watched the dog, but as he turned to look toward the path, as though he searched for someone, she came to a stop.

Emily's breath caught.

Lyness Eastwood.

It had been months since they had danced in London, yet the memory of his steady hands and charming smile returned at once.

Juniper, still addressing a lively lecture to Jack, hadn't noticed him yet. But Jack's head had turned in that direction with a steady focus. He looked at Emily, eyebrows raised.

She swallowed and pretended she had not seen anything

unusual. No, of course not. She had not noticed the handsome younger brother of Baron Hartwell, nor had she immediately hoped to change course to speak to him.

Jack glanced from his wife to the man on the bench, gesturing with a movement of his chin. "Mr. Eastwood. We ought to greet him. I paid a visit to his brother when we arrived, but I have not yet seen Eastwood about town."

And their family had not invited Jack's to visit. Nor did Emily know his mother's at-home day, and Juniper had not said anything about arranging to meet the matriarch of their family.

"Yes. Of course we should," Emily said, arranging a sensible smile even as her feet—traitors to prudence—carried her a measured pace nearer.

Juniper turned to see the gentleman, her eyebrows raised with interest. Before her sister-in-law gave her nod of approval, Emily's steps carried her forward. Toward *him*.

Caution caught up with her as she neared the bench. What if he did not remember her? Let alone with the fondness she had for his memory?

Lyness Eastwood rose the moment his eyes found hers, the great hound beside him lifting her head to watch Emily with mild curiosity.

"Lady Emily," he said, inclining his head. His voice was quiet, but not hesitant, and the faintest smile touched his mouth. "It has been some time."

She curtsied, aware of the heat in her cheeks. "Mr. Eastwood. Indeed. We have not seen each other since the ball in London. I hope you are well?"

"I-I-I—*Yes*. Quite well." His gaze flickered toward the path behind her, taking in Juniper and Jack as they approached, before returning to Emily. "And you?"

The presence of his stutter did nothing to deter her from smiling wider in greeting. Then remembering herself, and her lessons, she forced the smile back to an appropriate size.

"I am well, thank you." She hesitated. "I have been in York for some weeks, but I have yet to come across a member of your family."

One corner of his mouth lifted. "I-I could say the same of you, though York is not large enough to k-keep from r-running into people for long."

He took in a deep breath, his chest visibly expanding, and released it with deliberate slowness. A thing that made her think of all the moments in the past several months when she had to fortify herself to face yet another challenge. Did he have to steady himself to speak to her?

No. What a silly thing to suppose. The more likely explanation was that all women made him nervous, or shy, or…whatever it was that made him hesitate to speak. Or even visit.

When he spoke again, it was with a steady, deliberate tone. "It is good to see you again, Lady Emily."

The remark was harmless enough, but it made her pulse quicken. "I am glad to see you again," she said, and the admission made her breathing steady and her shoulders relax. Especially when his response was the upward turn of his lips.

Jack and Juniper reached them at last, and Jack spoke first, his tone brisk. "Eastwood. What an unexpected pleasure, to see you here."

"The p-pleasure is mine," Lyness said, a faint hitch catching on the second word, and gone so quickly Emily barely noticed it. "Is this your first visit to the Walk this season?"

Juniper, hand still slipped through Jack's arm, answered with her usual good humored tone. "We have been remiss. I told Jack we must take advantage of the fine weather today, and now it seems we have been rewarded with a happy meeting."

"I-I should have called on you before now," Lyness said, his gaze settling on Emily. She held it, perhaps longer than was polite, but he hardly seemed to mind. "Are you—" He stopped, a breath catching for a moment, then continued smoothly, "—enjoying York?"

"I am," she said, hoping the steadiness of her tone disguised the flurry in her chest. "Though I have not yet seen all it has to offer."

The dog had risen when he did and sat again on her haunches throughout the greetings. Emily glanced at the large, elegant animal. "Who is this soulful looking creature?"

"Oh." He blinked and looked down, as though he had somehow forgotten the massive dog keeping him company. "Athena. She i-is my brother's dog. A-a German board h-hound." He put his gloved hand down to scratch behind the creature's pointed ears.

"She is lovely," Emily said with a grin at the dog. "I miss our dogs on the farm, though they could not have been half so large as Athena."

"They were shepherds," Jack said, and winced immediately. The Sterling family had the tendency to call Jack their shepherd dog. He looked after them, metaphorically nipping at their heels, protecting them from harm and their own mistakes. Which was why they had sent Emily to stay with Jack and Juniper. They trusted him to see to Emily's well-being in a less stressful situation than what she had faced in London.

Juniper was, Emily realized, being suspiciously quiet at the moment. She cast a curious glance sideways, at her sister-in-law.

The newly wed woman, who was younger than Emily yet had a lifetime more in terms of experience in the world of nobility, was looking at Mr. Eastwood with raised eyebrows and something approaching curiosity.

When she spoke, it was with her usual cheerful politeness. "I understand your brother's dogs are often together, rather like bookends on either side of him or yourself, Mr. Eastwood. Is your brother here today? Or the other dog? I imagine the pair of them are a sight to see when they're together."

"Not today, L-Lady Juniper." He picked up the leash he hadn't been holding before. "I am passing the t-time while my mother walks with a friend."

Emily would have expressed an immediate desire to meet his mother, but she looked at Juniper who slightly shook her head.

Would it be rude to request an introduction in that moment? As daughters of earls, both Juniper and Emily outranked a baroness and could, therefore, solicit an introduction without being perceived as rude. At least, that was Emily's understanding of the peerage and precedence, but... Goodness. There were far too many rules.

"Please give your mother my good wishes, Mr. Eastwood," Juniper said, tone polite. "I have heard so much about her knowledge of gardening. I hope I will make her acquaintance soon."

Before Lyness could reply, a cheerful female voice called his name from farther down the path. Emily turned to see a handsome, dark-haired lady approaching with a parasol in one hand and an expression of unmistakable satisfaction on her lightly lined face.

Lady Hartwell, she realized. Mother of Lord Hartwell and Lyness Eastwood.

Lyness glanced toward his mother, then back at Emily, the smallest crease forming between his brows. "Perhaps my mother would agree to an introduction presently."

"That would be delightful." Juniper added kindly, "Only if she is presently able, though. I am certain Lady Hartwell has many demands on her time. We will wait here. Either way, it was delightful to see you again, Mr. Eastwood."

Jack gave a sharp nod of agreement.

Emily curtsied again. "It was a pleasure to see you, Mr. Eastwood."

"St-Sterling. My lady. It is always good to meet f-friends." He bowed. "And you, Lady Emily."

As they stood there, watching him go to his mother, Juniper leaned close enough for Emily to hear her murmur, "There now. At least one gentleman in York knows how to look at you properly."

"He is Jack's friend. Of course he would be attentive." Emily kept her gaze fixed ahead, but her cheeks betrayed her, growing warm. As much as she wanted to believe Juniper, believe that Mr. Eastwood had given her pointed interest, she would be lying to herself. He had been kind. He had remembered her. That was all.

"Now you have done it. Here he comes, with Lady Hartwell." Jack's lips turned upward. "A woman considered a pillar of York society by some."

That made Emily's shoulders tighten. She cut a quick glance at her brother, alarm stirring in her mind.

"Hush, Jack. You will make your sister nervous," Juniper said softly, her full attention turned to the approaching pair.

Mr. Eastwood and Lady Hartwell reached them with a swish of her embroidered skirts. She wore a gown that had to have been from a modiste in Paris or Austria, so beautiful and precise was the clothing. Emily had only seen such things depicted in fashion plates. It took effort not to look at her hat sporting a plume of beautiful peach colored feathers with awe.

"Here we are, Lyness," the baroness said, as though she had been hunting the three of them through the entire city. "Meeting friends of yours is always a pleasure."

"Mother," Mr. Eastwood said evenly, though Emily noted his hand tightened a little on Athena's lead. "Allow me to present Lady Juniper Sterling, sister of the Earl of Haverford, and her husband, Mr. John Sterling, younger son of the Earl of Benwaith. And Lady Emily Sterling, Mr. Sterling's sister."

Lady Hartwell's eyes brightened as she inclined her head graciously. "How very delightful. York is most improved by the presence of such distinguished company." She glanced at each in turn, her gaze lingering politely last on Emily. "A pleasure to make your acquaintance, Lady Emily."

Emily reminded herself to temper her smile as she replied, "The pleasure is mine, Lady Hartwell."

"Thank you for agreeing to meet us, Lady Hartwell," Juniper said. "I know you have a great deal to take up your time. I have long hoped I might have a conversation with you about gardening. I did not wish to presume upon my limited acquaintance with your son, however, and descend upon you without meeting first."

"Nonsense," Lady Hartwell said with a little flutter of her hand. "I am forever pleased to welcome new friends to York."

"Mother—" Mr. Eastwood began, but she turned to him with mock severity.

"Do not tell me you have been keeping acquaintances from me, Lyness. It is most unneighborly."

"I met the St-Sterlings in London," he said, the faintest stammer catching on their surname. "Last Season. They have not been in York long."

"Merely a few weeks," Jack said, tone as polite and even as ever it was, "and I have kept both ladies busy with decorating our cottage. I am as much to blame for keeping you from new friendships as your son is, your ladyship." Truly, Emily's brother was a master at wearing a mask of neutrality.

"Then we shall have to make up for lost time," Lady Hartwell declared. "I will not have friends of my son wandering York without proper introductions. At present, I have an appointment I must honor. But I will send an invitation to dine with my family very soon." She cast a knowing glance between them before taking Lyness's arm again. "Now, if you are finished sitting on park benches, Lyness, you may escort me home."

Mr. Eastwood inclined his head, his expression unreadable. "Of course, Mother."

After they took their leave, and as they turned away, Emily thought she saw the corner of Lady Hartwell's mouth curve—a small, oddly satisfied smile, as if she had just seen something that pleased her.

Lyness fell into step beside his mother, Athena's lead in hand. The dog's easy gait kept time with his own, a steadiness he appreciated in the face of his mother's brisk satisfaction. She twirled her parasol over her shoulder, the rapid spinning likely matching whatever pace the thoughts in her head had taken up.

"You might have told me," she said lightly.

"Told you what, Mother?"

"All about meeting someone as lovely as Lady Emily Sterling." Lady Hartwell's voice took on a sing-song tone, her delight as complete as though she had discovered Lady Emily herself. "She is the very picture of unspoilt beauty, and yet there is a maturity there not usually found in debutantes. I have heard her name mentioned only once before, from my friend Mrs. Gainsworth. How old is she? More than twenty, I think. But not too much more?"

"I believe she is five-and-twenty," he responded, tone deliberately flat. Trying not to give away that he was completely aware of her age. Perfectly aware, in fact, of every detail he had managed to learn about her in the little time he had such an opportunity. Too aware.

"An excellent age. But unmarried?"

"As you say." The words came tighter than he intended, as though he'd drawn them through too narrow a space. He cleared his throat softly. "Her family was tucked away in the countryside until recently. They only came to the title through a most unexpected inheritance."

"Oh, that is rather marvelous. That means she has few bad habits, in terms of genteel behavior. Five-and-twenty is excellent, too. You know, girls really do marry too young. Their poor husbands must finish raising them when they are wed at eighteen. What eighteen year old do you know who is wise enough to make life-altering decisions, hm? You certainly were not ready for such things before twenty."

"Why does Lady Emily's age concern you s-so much?" He gave his mother a sideways look, his tone sharpening despite himself. Even Athena seemed to catch his tension, glancing up as though curious at his tone. He cleared his throat quickly and lowered his voice. "What does it matter?"

"How well do you know her?" Lady Hartwell asked rather than answer him. Of course. She seemed half in her own thoughts on the matter, barely paying attention to what he had to say.

They were nearly to the end of the path, where their carriage waited to take them home again. They were not precisely in a hurry, but his mother made it clear she had no intention to linger. Meeting with one friend had obviously fatigued her, and still she had a wish to interview a new gardener that afternoon.

"Not well. We danced together in London. Roman danced with her, too. I have met her brother many times. They are all acquainted with the Duke of Montfort."

"Roman danced with her?" His mother's eyebrows and her tone rose, but no one was near enough to hear. Thankfully. "How interesting. He does not usually bestir himself so."

"It was only a polite gesture, Mother. As a favor to the family."

She made a noncommittal sound that, in his experience, meant she had drawn her own conclusions and would not be dissuaded from them. "She is a very pretty young woman. Elegant without being overdone. I approve."

Lyness averted his gaze forward, watching the boats along the Ouse catch the fitful wind in their sails. A boy leaned in one of the skiffs leaned far over the side, his laughter carrying faintly across the water. "I doubt she requires your approval."

"Nonsense. Everyone requires my approval." She tilted her head to glance at him, her eyes bright beneath the brim of her bonnet. "Do you know if she will visit with her family in York long?"

"I did not have time to ask."

"Mm. Then we must find out. York can be so very dull without new faces at the tea table."

He felt the smallest tug in his chest at her words—a flicker of hope, quickly smothered. "If you wish to invite her, I will deliver the note myself." Only because his mother had expressed an interest to know her, of course. He and Roman both worried over the lack of variation in her activities. It was all gardens and gossip. That she showed interest in someone new was the reason for Lyness's enthusiasm, and *nothing* more.

"I said I would extend an invitation, did I not? But you need hardly play messenger, Lyness." Lady Harwell's smile was mild, but Lyness knew her too well. Plans were already forming behind that expression. Plans with direction, purpose, and none declared aloud. But to what end? "You must be there, of course. And Roman. Because she knows you both."

At the sound of his brother's name a second time, the flicker of hope extinguished. If his mother's plans were more for Roman than himself, he had best not concern himself with them.

He cleared his throat, stroking Athena's head when she nosed at his hand. "Did you enjoy your walk with Mrs. Gainsworth? You were looking forward to it for some time, I believe."

Lady Hartwell laughed softly, twirling her parasol so the light flickered through the eyelets along its edge. "Oh, very much, yes. I am always pleased to spend time with an old school friend. She returned from Scarborough with the most outrageous opinions about sea-bathing. She tried to talk me into coming with her next time, if you can imagine such a thing. Me! In the freezing sea water! I thank you, no." She shook her head, eyes shining with good humor for the first time in weeks. "I do wonder what sort of constitution she imagines herself to have, plunging into cold water every morning. But she is excellent company. We passed a full hour together and scarcely touched on the same topic twice."

Lyness allowed himself a faint smile at that, relieved to have turned her thought. "Then I am glad of it," he said with sincerity. His mother's eccentricities had become more pronounced of late, likely due to her seclusion. "You have missed her."

"Mm. I have," Lady Hartwell admitted, though her gaze slide back toward him with a spark. "It is so important to have good friends, is it not? I am truly looking forward to making more." The tone she used told him, though her words did not, that she had no intention of forgetting Lady Emily Sterling at all.

How could he blame her? He had not forgotten her either. Indeed, he had found himself wishing to see her again since their first—and only—meeting in London. Lady Emily's voice had lingered in his memory, precise and lovely, returning to haunt him at inconvenient hours of the night. He had wished—foolishly, yet persistently—to see her again.

But life had a way of keeping him from the things he wanted, and it was likely for the best. The younger brother to a baron had little to recommend him, aside from obligations enough to weigh down brighter dreams. Acting as his brother's steward kept him up to his elbows in ledgers, most days.

Seeing her today, on the Walk... It was a miracle he had managed to speak at all, so overcome was he when the reality of her presence proved far better than his memory. She was lovelier than he remembered, her voice still as warm, eyes still bright with her enjoyment of the moment. Her smile was a touch smaller, but the curve of it still tempted his gaze to her lips.

Now his mother wished to invite Lady Emily to call upon her. With Roman present. Truly, he was overtired if he had not guessed that his mother wanted to observe the two of them together.

Lyness handed his mother into their carriage, smothering a sigh of dissatisfaction. Athena jumped in next, and he wondered what Roman would make of his mother's sudden interest in a newly arrived earl's daughter. He suspected his own thoughts on the subject would not matter.

At least he could look forward to seeing Lady Emily again. Soon.

# Chapter Four

The Black Swan, a handsome three-story building of two-and-one-half centuries, held a most excellent position at the junction of three well-traveled streets. St. Saviour's Place, Peasholme Green, and Stonebow.

Presently, Lyness stood at a window above the ground floor, looking out at the busy world passing by. The diamond-paned casement windows reminded him more of a cage than usual, as he found himself thinking on all the estate work that waited for him on his desk.

Behind him, Roman sat with several of their friends at a table, eating an afternoon meal and discussing the state of things in York. As usual.

"I think we ought to form a club of some sort that does more than sit about discussing politics," Phineas Nelson, as good a man as Lyness had ever met, said with great feeling. He and his older brother frequented all their meetings, and Lyness felt a kinship for a fellow second-born son. "I have been speaking with William Harcourt—"

"The cleric who has an obsession with bones?" Archibald Kettleburn asked with a raised eyebrow.

Roman gave Kettleburn a withering glance, then turned to Phineas with interest. "Go on. What does Reverend Harcourt say about clubs?"

"He wants to form a philosophical society. A group of like-minded individuals who are interested in educating the public in regards to the sciences." Phineas looked around at their group of friends. "I think we ought to invite him to one of our dinners. Have a chat. Let him tell us his plans. He already has some support. But given what you have said of preserving the history of York, Hartwell, I thought it would be of interest to you."

Roman's smile was slight. If it was there at all. Lyness recognized it due to familiarity with his brother, but he wondered if the others knew him well enough to see the amusement there.

"I have no objection to speaking with the reverend on matters of history, especially in regards to our city." Roman lowered his fork to his plate and steepled his hands together in front of him. "I think, with the repairs we have managed on the city walls, it is obvious that our citizens want to know more about York's past. Preserving what we have for future generations is of utmost importance to all of us."

"Best not let the Tories hear you say that," Kettleburn remarked, sipping at his tea. "They may think it an opportunity to turn you to their side."

Known for his insistence on progress, Roman actually chuckled at the remark. "Let them try. I have been arguing for the cause of my party since I was a schoolboy. I have no intention of being turned from my course without evidence that it is the wrong one for the future of England."

That brought Lyness forward to the table. "W-we agreed no politics today." He retook his seat, his plate already empty. "Save it for Etridge's."

"Of course, our quietest member would finally speak up to save us all from his brother's politicking," Phineas said with a grin as the others chuckled.

Etridge's Royal Hotel had become the official meeting place for the city's progressive politicians and their supporters. And Roman, when not in London, tried to remain entrenched in politics at home.

"I cannot look forward to it." Roman groaned and raked one hand through his hair. "Not with the newspapers equating us to radicals who want to see St. James's burn, and all of London with it."

For a long moment, everyone fell silent. Even a whiff of treasonous activity or support would set the government into grim action. The same way it set all of them on edge.

"Perhaps they mistake your generosity for agreement," Kettleburn said. "You've funded more pamphlets than any man in York."

Roman shrugged in dismissal. "I fund thought, not sedition. If reasoned argument offends them, that is their failing, not mine."

Lyness wished his brother did not sound so certain.

Kettleburn waved the subject away. "Everyone knows the papers exaggerate in an attempt to build up whatever position their owner maintains. It is only the Tories reading exactly what the Tories want to believe." He rapped his knuckles on the table. "Eastwood is right, though. We have important things to discuss in terms of the social expectations of our fair city, especially now that everyone who ran off to London has returned. The Knavesmire Races will soon be upon us. The Royal Theatre has put out a bill for their upcoming plays and operas. The Assembly Rooms have posted about their balls and exhibitions. The matrons are even now putting in orders for more of Cupid's arrows."

This time, Phineas sank lower in his chair. "I have no wish to discuss such things outside of learning where you lot will be, so I may stay in the middle of the pack and avoid notice."

"The races begin the nineteenth," Roman said, glancing at Lyness. "Finishing the twenty-fourth. I cannot imagine it will be a quiet week for any of us."

"I have two horses engaged to race," Kettleburn said. "I expect your best wishes, even if you bet against them."

"Remember when one of Kettleburn's horses refused to turn the corner last year?" Phineas said, eyes alight. "The poor jockey went right into mire."

That lead to a round of laughter. Kettleburn had not had a true champion from his stables in the five years since he'd taken over from his father. He bore the brunt of their teasing well enough, and they had all encouraged him to continue with the enterprise. It took time to breed winners.

At length, they settled their bills and went their separate ways. Roman had Apollo with him, though he had left the large dog tethered in the courtyard of the inn. When he collected his dog, Lyness gave a coin to the lad who had watched Apollo and likely spoiled the animal with affection and treats.

As they stepped out into the bright afternoon sunlight, Lyness glanced at his brother beside him, the great dog trotting at their heels. Roman spoke easily of the races and the weather, yet the earlier political conversation lingered. He drew men to him by conviction as much as charm. It was admirable—and dangerous, if he ever lost their faith.

"It is a fine day to be out," Roman said, a near smile on his lips.

Lyness sighed. Letting go of the topic was best. For now. "Indeed. Perfect weather to be out of doors." Even if he would rather enjoy such weather in the countryside, he could appreciate it nearly as well in town.

Together they walked along St. Saviour's Gate, Apollo between them, their strides evenly matched. The street traffic wasn't yet heavy at that time of day, allowing them to converse easily without having to shout over the sounds of horses or crowds. Despite that, Roman remained unusually quiet for several minutes. Lyness let him have the time to think. His own thoughts proved troublesome, given that they kept turning to a lady with soft smiles and eyes that met his with curiosity rather than hesitation. Despite hearing his stutter.

Such things hardly mattered, he told himself. Besides, he had Roman to keep him occupied. Roman and Lyness had always looked after each other. Even now, on this street that they had walked together a thousand times, Lyness knew his brother's step as well as he knew the way home. When they were younger, they had raced along the pavement together, returning to the house from the market with tales for their father and sweets for their mother. Back before responsibility had changed them both.

Roman broke the silence between them abruptly. "I think it is time I look for a wife. In earnest."

Lyness stumbled on the pavement, catching himself with a sharp breath. "You wh-wh-what?" He stopped walking completely. His brother had not spoken seriously of marriage for years. Not since Lady Josephine, the Duke of Montfort's daughter, had turned down his suit. Roman kept himself too busy for courtship. At two-and-thirty, he was not yet an old bachelor.

Uncertain what to say, Lyness stared at his brother somewhat stupidly.

Roman had made it two steps before realizing he'd rendered his younger brother a statue with his words. When the baron turned, his mouth curved wryly. "You thought I meant to remain a bachelor forever, did you? My life dedicated to nothing but this city? I suppose that is a rather dramatic image. Perhaps my ghost would even take it up after my death. Haunting the ancient walls along with the ghosts of the past." He took the lead of Apollo's leash in both hands and bent it, his gaze on the leather strip rather than on Lyness. "Even a brooding baron must consider the future. I have been remiss in my duties to our family and rather unfair to you. Our legacy cannot rest on your shoulders alone, Lyness."

Lyness's throat tightened around words he could not shape. Not without stumbling all over them as he tried to free them from his lips. Which was strange. Roman did not usually cause the stutter to worsen.

As though sensing the statement had come across as more of a shock than intended, Roman tilted his head to the side. "I did not think you would take the matter this hard, Lyness. I cannot think it will change things too much. Certainly not enough for you to wear such a look of concern. Do you think I will turn into a romantic fool overnight?"

Mutely, Lyness shook his head. No. He could not imagine Roman forgetting any responsibilities. Not even for a wife. Which, Lyness supposed, might cause trouble when the baron did finally find a bride he liked. Roman would need someone patient, for certain, and understanding. A woman grown rather than a young lady, as his mother said, who needed to finish maturing.

A woman like Lady Emily, whom his mother already seemed predisposed to approve of. The dull ache in his chest was evidence enough of his feelings on that matter. Feelings he had to put aside, for loyalty's sake.

Swallowing, Lyness tried to force a single question out. "Do y-y-you know who…?" He shook his head, impatient with his tongue.

Roman did not need him to finish the question to understand it. "I haven't anyone in mind yet, no. But Mother has been rather insistent of late, and she has a point. I am turning three-and-thirty in a matter of weeks. Father has been gone nearly a decade. The barony needs to continue to a new generation. Mother needs a daughter-in-law to keep her company. I need someone with me in London to plan for social events and…it is time, I suppose."

None of those reasons sounded particularly appealing to Lyness, and he wondered if an unmarried lady would find any of them compelling. Added to it the complete lack of enthusiasm in Roman's tone, and Lyness had to shake his head at the whole idea.

"You disapprove?" Roman asked, eyebrows raised.

"N-n-no." Lyness winced, then physically bit his tongue for its misbehavior. He released a sigh and spoke with deliberate slowness. "You sound miserable."

At that, Roman barked a laugh, and Apollo grumbled next to him as though *he* disapproved of the sound. "I am not miserable. Merely…resigned."

"Same th-thing."

"Not truly. But come, Lyness. It is past time for me to wed. Had I no title, I could put it off and be a bachelor for another decade."

They both knew why he had yet to wed. Roman had learned the lesson twice over that most women wanted him for his title and little else. If a man with a greater fortune or higher status came along during courtship, suddenly the unwed ladies were not so eager to set aside time to walk with him in the park. The last time he had tried a courtship, before Lady Josephine, the woman had been perfectly lovely...until she realized how much Apollo and Athena meant to Roman. She had demanded he get rid of the dogs if he wanted to continue as her suitor. Roman had laughed in her face and returned home.

Obviously, the dogs were still around and that young lady had married a gentleman from Cambridge.

Lady Emily had liked Athena immediately.

Lyness did not pursue that thought.

They turned onto Castlegate, where the faces were more familiar. The houses settled snuggly against each other. Number 12 waited to welcome them home.

"Does Mother know?" Lyness asked as they walked toward their own front door.

"Not yet. I would rather wait to tell her. Perhaps until I have a few candidates in mind. Otherwise, she might try to take over the whole scheme and play matchmaker."

All Lyness could do was nod. He had the uneasy sense that his mother had already begun to arrange things in her mind, gathering possibilities and setting them in order. Lady Emily Sterling would, he suspected, fit neatly among them.

Roman deserved happiness. He had always put everyone else— the city, their family, every cause that demanded his attention— before himself. If seeking a wife was the means by which Roman finally allowed himself that grace, then Lyness would not begrudge him the attempt. He would do what he had always done: shoulder what he could, take up what was set aside, and make room. It was a familiar position. A comfortable one.

A picture rose in his mind without warning: Lady Emily's eyes lifting to meet his, curious and kind, as though she expected something of him. Lyness did not linger on it. He let the thought pass, as he had let so many others pass, and turned his attention back to his brother. There were, after all, better uses for his steadiness than wanting.

# Chapter Five

Emily trailed her fingers along the cool stone of a fallen arch, the grass thick and uneven beneath her steps. The ruins of Saint Mary's Abbey held a strange sort of peace in the late summer afternoon. Bees drifted lazily among the wildflowers pushing through the broken masonry, and the distant sound of the Minster bells carried faintly across the gardens.

She had stepped away from Jack and Juniper to sketch, or at least that was what she told them before slipping away with her canvas bag over her shoulder. But she had not yet taken out her book. Something about the abbey drew her to wander first, to trace its broken lines and imagine the church it had once been, hundreds of year ago.

There was talk of clearing it all, she had heard. As it was in a part of York proper that would be excellent if turned into more shops or a warehouse. But what a shame it would be to lose such a poignant piece of the past.

She carefully picked her way through the broken stone path, eyes turned upward to the tallest wall still standing.

A flicker of gold caught her eye near the shadow of an arched window. At first she thought it a scrap of ribbon, blown in from the green where children played. But then it moved—a quick flutter, uneven, as though the creature were unsure how wings ought to work.

It was a bird in apparent distress. She bit her lip and looked around to see if anyone watched, then hurried around the stone to find the poor feathered thing. Perhaps nothing was wrong with it. Perhaps it had experienced a clumsy moment, which immediately made her sympathize with the creature.

Another flash of yellow feathers showed her where the little bird had landed.

Emily approached slowly, crouching to peer through a cluster of thistles. The bird was no wild sparrow, no thrush, or finch that she might expect. Its feathers shone too bright, its shape too delicate.

"A canary," she whispered in sudden wonder. "But what are you doing in the ruins of an abbey?"

She inched closer. The poor thing hopped frantically but could not lift itself more than a foot from the ground. Its wings had been clipped.

"Oh," Emily whispered, her heart giving a small, painful twist. "You are a lost pet." She reached into her bag, searching for the roll she had brought from the picnic. "And you cannot manage on your own out here, I should think."

The bird tilted its head, sharp black eyes catching the light. Emily scattered a few crumbs, holding still until the fragile creature hopped closer, hunger overcoming its fear.

She watched it with sympathy and considered her options. "If I leave you here, a cat could find you. York is teeming with them." She sat carefully and spread her skirts, putting a few breadcrumbs closer to herself. "You look healthy. I doubt you have been away from home long." But there were no houses near enough the abbey ruins to account for a bird falling out of a window. It certainly could not have done so and traveled the distance to the ruins unnoticed. "If only you could speak and tell me how you came to be here."

"Lady Emily?"

She blinked at the bird, then up and over her shoulder, where a familiar gentleman left one of the well-worn paths to walk toward her through the longer grass. Mr. Eastwood had found her.

She didn't stand, though she knew she ought to. She raised a hand to halt his quick progress. She spoke softly, hoping he would not take offense. "Mr. Eastwood, do be careful. There is a little bird here I am trying not to startle."

He immediately stilled at her gesture, brow furrowed, but he nodded and slowed his approach. Coming to stand behind her, carefully looking at the animal that did not seem to notice his arrival at all.

The creature had no instinct for survival.

"A canary," he said, lowering into a crouch. And somehow maintaining his dignity. "How st-strange." He gave her a sidelong look. "Your sis-sister-in-law told me to find you."

"Oh? Does she have need of me?" Emily scattered a few more crumbs for the little bird.

"No." His expression lightened, his shoulders seemed to relax. "I am to ensure your safety. And view your drawings."

"My drawings?" Emily felt her cheeks warm. Why had Juniper mentioned her drawings to Mr. Eastwood? That seemed a betrayal of some kind. Which was certainly an irrational thought. "Most of them need a great deal of improvement. I have never had any training, you see. It is only something I used to do for my own amusement, and I am trying to take it up again." Sketching had been a way to favorite way to fill her time before their elevation in Society. And she had been told by the tutor in London not to mention her family's past in genteel company. Botheration.

"M-may I?" He pointed to the book peeking out of her canvas bag, a relic from her days living in a farmhouse, his eyes still sparkling at her with good humor.

"Yes. If you promise not to tease me."

"T-tease you? Me?" His eyebrows shot up all the way to the brim of his hat. "Never."

Emily took the book from her satchel. "I have older brothers, Mr. Eastwood. I know how men like to tease young ladies."

He chuckled as he accepted the book, head tilted to the side as he examined her. "How brothers tease sisters, perhaps. I am *not* one of your brothers."

How thankful she was for that! He was one of the few gentlemen she had found herself comfortable with since her father's became an earl. She wasn't even certain why, given their comparatively short time in each other's company, but Lyness Eastwood did not make her feel small. Not the way some of the other men had.

He did not look at her as though her conversation was somehow amusing, while other gentlemen had remarked on her "quaint" and "country" charm. A thing that felt like a criticism veiled in spun sugar.

Emily turned her attention back to the bird, shaking slightly and ruffling its feathers until it was quite puffy. Then it hopped closer and turned its head, looking at her from one eye, then the other, perhaps waiting for more food.

"Do you sketch plants more often than people?"

The question startled her; she had been so intent on the trembling creature that she had not expected it. Most who looked at her work made some minor compliment of it and moved on. He was the first in some time to ask anything. Emily glanced up briefly to see him studying the pages of the book rather than her, then turned back to the bird.

"When I can. It is easier to draw plants and stones than people. They keep still. Or animals. They are more forgiving if you do not get their noses quite right."

"I should like to see more of your drawings sometime," he said. His tone was even, not merely polite, as though he meant it sincerely. "Some of the flowers look as though I could lift them from the pages."

She shook her head slightly. "You are too kind, sir. Though I admit to laying a flower on one page and drawing its likeness on the other. I know I do not do them justice. Still. I thank you for the compliment."

"There is an honesty in the way you draw—" He stopped, cleared his throat, and shifted his weight. "It shows the world as you see it, I think. Instead of what the *masters* would call proper technique. What many of them really do is train individuality out of artists, reducing everything to a...a simple parlor trick." His voice trailed away as he spoke, but it was one of the longest speeches she had heard him make.

Emily blinked at him, surprised into stillness. Few people paid much mind to her sketches. Her brothers had sometimes teased about her fascination with weeds, and even Juniper smiled at her pages as though they were pleasant trifles. Juniper had even offered to find a drawing tutor for Emily. But Mr. Eastwood spoke as though the drawings mattered, precisely as they were.

The bird gave a sudden flutter, jumping from the grass and vanishing into the folds of her skirts. Emily gasped, fumbling to gather her gown, fearful she would crush the little thing. "Oh—oh, goodness!"

"Hold still." Mr. Eastwood crouched at once, careful not to touch her, his gloved hands hovering above where the bird hopped about in the net she had made with her skirt. "There—do not move."

The bird's golden head poked from a fold of muslin, its small claws tangled in a ribbon tied around Emily's waist. "It seems I have been claimed."

His mouth quirked, though his eyes stayed on the bird. "Then we must find you a way to carry home so bold a creature." He glanced at her bag. "That will not do. The poor thing could be crushed."

"My bonnet?" She put one hand to the top of her head.

"Too shallow a cap, I think. It could hop out again. Here." He straightened and removed his hat. "If you will allow me, this may serve."

"Oh, but it could scratch up the inside. Or soil it." She hesitated, looking down at the tired, frightened little creature.

He took out a linen handkerchief from his coat and put it in the bottom of the hat. "That will serve well enough."

She hesitated, then nodded. Together they coaxed the canary from her skirts, his hands steady as he guided it toward the dark hollow of the hat. The bird hopped inside with surprising meek-ness, settling on the linen with no objection to such lodgings.

Emily gathered the brim against her, holding the makeshift carrier close. "Thank you. I had not the least idea how I meant to carry it home."

"You would have found a way," he said simply. "But I am glad to be of use."

Emily tilted the hat barely enough to peer inside. The bird stared up at her, feathers puffed and eyes blinking slowly. As though it might sleep there. She laughed quietly, unable to help herself.

"I truly did not think how I would manage if it let me catch it," she admitted. "It seems my impulses often outrun my good sense." At least since leaving the countryside, where her impulses had been praised rather than censured.

"Then they are admirable impulses," he said quietly. "Not many would trouble themselves for a creature so small."

Her cheeks warmed, and she was glad to keep her eyes on the hat. "I think there is beauty, even in small things. Animals, plants, the odd mossy stone wall. Perhaps that is another reason I draw them."

"You sketch well," he said at once, then hesitated as though he had spoken too directly. "Forgive me. You have already heard my opinion."

In that moment, she realized she had not heard him stutter much after his initial greeting. Had she missed it, or did his lack of hesitation upon his words mean something? She thought of asking, but would that stand as yet another breech in etiquette?

The bird gave a soft chirp inside the hat, and Emily adjusted her grip carefully. "Do you draw?" she asked, hoping to turn the attention from herself and her too-personal thoughts.

He drew a breath, the corners of his mouth turning slightly. "Not often. Not as you do. My work is with letters. I copy poems, passages of literature, sometimes only words I find beautiful. I try to shape them so the lines of the ink carry the meaning themselves. That is as close to drawing as I come."

Emily's brows lifted, her eyes still on the canary though her interest sharpened. "Calligraphy, then. That is art, surely."

"It is deliberate, if not entirely artistic," he answered. "Every stroke considered. Every curve of the pen chosen." His gaze lowered, as though embarrassed. "Some call it wasted effort, for a gentleman to dabble in such things."

It sounded as though he had a particular someone in mind, and she instantly disagreed with the unnamed person.

"Unnecessary?" She shook her head quickly. "How can beauty be unnecessary? If words are worth reading, are they not worth beautifying as well?"

"I always thought so." For the first time in their conversation, his smile came without hesitation. "I am glad you share my opinion, Lady Emily."

Emily tilted the hat a little, the golden head peeking up at her from the folds of linen. "Then perhaps we are both right to keep at our work," she said softly. "Even if others fail to see the use in it."

The bird settled down, wings tucked in close, as though satisfied it had found safety.

Lyness hadn't any regrets over handing Lady Emily his hat. Each time she peered down to ensure the canary still rested at the bottom, he had to hold back a smile. The wrinkle that appeared at the bridge of her nose when she furrowed her brow distracted him. So when she looked up at him as though awaiting a reply he had to say, "Forgive me. I am afraid my thoughts were elsewhere, Lady Emily. What was that you said?"

"I asked what brought you to the ruins this day," she said, not the least put out by repeating herself. "This is the second time we have run into each other this week, after going several months without crossing paths." Her steps slowed on the walk. They had only one corner to turn, and then they would be within sight of her brother and sister-in-law once more.

"My brother and I often come here in the afternoons. I had a meeting nearby, and he brings the dogs out with a groom this time of day. They need to be out of doors or they grow agitated."

Her lips turned upward in a smile, even as she looked down at the bird again. "They have my sympathies. I often feel the same when kept inside too long." She sighed and wrapped her arms around his hat, shifting to cradle it against her rather than hold it by the brim.

He wondered if any man had been jealous of a hat before.

Then winced at the impropriety of that thought. He barely knew the woman. Thinking of being held by her was far out of bounds of gentlemanlike behavior. Wasn't it?

The afternoon breeze stirred his hair, with his hat no longer keeping it in place. He brushed it from his eyes and made a mental note to have Hobson trim it soon.

"So you happened upon my family and they sent you off to search for me?" she said with a raise of her eyebrows. "How terribly convenient for Jack that he need not give up the company of his wife, and yet he manages to herd his sister back to him."

That made Lyness chuckle. "He seemed concerned that you were out of sight. A common thing for a brother, I would think, when tasked with watching over a sister."

"He worries too much," she said quietly. "I used to walk miles every day, all on my own, before this inheritance business."

That both alarmed and amused him. A woman like her, wandering about without protector or chaperone? It hardly seemed safe. Yet he could understand the craving for such independence. "I cannot imagine if my own steps were shadowed everywhere I went," he admitted. "But I understand the necessity of it for young ladies."

"Indeed. The world in which we live must be a singularly terrible place if a woman cannot walk about as freely as a man, without fear of harm. Or even rumor stirred by the mere act of it." Lady Emily gave him so direct a look, as though waiting for him to challenge her opinion. "It is most unfair."

Lyness would have solicited her thoughts on all manner of things pertaining to that matter, and others, had he not heard Apollo bark. Roman had arrived at the ruins, and he had likely asked the dog to perform that particular trick for someone else's amusement.

He cleared his throat and gestured to the abbey wall. "I have kept you long enough, my lady. I fear your brother will send out a second search party if we do not appear soon."

They were approaching her family's picnic blanket when Lyness finally looked that direction and realized his brother had joined the Sterlings. Roman stood near their picnic blanket, stance relaxed, speaking to Jack Sterling. All three of them watched as Lyness and Emily approached, and with a word Roman dismissed Apollo to come bounding over to Lyness with tongue lolling out and a happy bark of greeting.

Emily wrapped her arms more securely around the hat when the bird emitted a startled peep. Lyness raised his hand and spoke the command for Apollo to come to heel. He gave the lady at his side an apologetic glance.

"He would never jump on you, Lady Emily."

"One cannot know that about a dog without knowing the dog well," she pointed out with a frown. "If I feared dogs, truly, that would have sent me into a...a... Well. I do not know the genteel way to word it. Into hysterics, perhaps."

His lips quirked upward. "How would you prefer to word it?" He bent and scratched Apollo's large head behind one erect ear. "What would you say, even if not genteel?"

Her cheeks flushed. "I haven't the f-faintest," she stammered, apparently flustered.

He raised his eyebrows, smiling—waiting.

"Oh. Fine. I would have jumped right out of my skin and into the next county," she said with a hint of a more countrified tongue.

He covered his lips with his fist, coughing once to keep from laughing at that vivid description. Her lips twitched upward, but she didn't say another word as Apollo fell in beside Lyness. They arrived at the blanket with the others, and her brother and sister-in-law stood.

"Lady Emily," Roman—Lord Hartwell to most—greeted her with a gallant bow. "I see my brother has fared well, being so fortunate as to have your company. Even if it seems to have cost him his hat."

"I have only temporarily borrowed it, I assure you," she said, stepping closer to show him the contents of the hat. "I found a distressed canary in need of conveyance. Or a nest."

Roman stepped forward to look inside the hat, and he laughed. "What a fortunate creature to have you for its rescuer, Lady Emily. And now, thanks to my brother, it will travel in grand style wherever you may wish to take it."

Sterling moved forward and looked into the hat, too, and Lady Juniper Sterling. Sterling frowned, while the other lady crooned softly.

"Poor little thing. Did someone lose it in the park? Or do you think it escaped?"

"It is unlikely it escaped from a house. Even the nearest are too far for the creature to have made it here without a cat or dog catching it," Roman said with a shrug. "An ill-attempt at setting the thing free, I should think." He glanced at Lyness. "Or perhaps someone irritated with its song thought to rid themselves of the bird without getting their hands dirty."

"A true conspiracy," Sterling said with a shake of his head. "And now, I shall be the one to learn if excessive singing was the cause of abandonmen. As it seems the bird will live within my home from this point onward."

Color rose again in Lady Emily's cheeks, though she narrowed her eyes at her elder brother with more fondness than irritation. "Oh, you like animals as much as I do. I heard you asking our neighbor's steward about their next litter of pups." Their ease with one another was unmistakable, and it extended to Lady Juniper as she laughed.

"You have caught him out. He also personally selected a trio of kittens for the stables not long before your arrival, Emily. He will dote on your little rescue, for certain."

"The whole family makes a habit of collecting strays, then," Roman said with the slightest upturn of his lips, which was more emotion than he generally showed when in public. That gave Lyness pause. Was his brother enjoying this encounter? "It seems your canary is fortunate in his rescuer, though must admit that I am torn as to whether to envy the bird for being taken in with such ease, or my brother for being the one to lend what was required."

Merciful heavens. Was Roman *flirting*?

Lady Emily's eyes flicked up to Roman's, her brows raised. "Surely envy suits neither."

Roman tipped his head forward, mirroring her expression. "Perhaps not. But admiration, at least, cannot be helped. So we will settle there. You have mine for your kind rescue."

The lady glanced at Lyness, but he looked away before he could read her expression. Because he did not want to see what she made of Roman's admiration, so directly stated that it surprised Lyness into complete silence. He gave his attention to the ruins. Tracing the fallen stone on the ground with his gaze.

"You are too kind, my lord," she murmured.

Lady Juniper spoke next, quickly and with a determined brightness that made Lyness cut her a curious glance. "We are so fortunate to meet you both here today. Last time we saw Mr. Eastwood, we had the pleasure of an introduction to your mother. I hope Lady Hartwell is in good health and spirits?"

"The very best of both," Roman answered, voice sincere. "In fact, last evening she asked about all of you. She is curious to know the ladies of the family better. A formal invitation will likely arrive at your home today or tomorrow, but my mother hopes all of you will dine with us in two days' time. I believe our other guests that evening will be valuable acquaintances here in York."

"Oh, that sounds lovely." Lady Juniper threaded her arm through her husband's. "We will be delighted to accept the invitation when it arrives."

"Excellent. I look forward to welcoming all of you into my home." Roman bowed once more to take his leave, and Lyness did the same. As he straightened, and prepared to turn, he realized Roman had not finished.

Roman's attention returned to Lady Emily, his expression more friendly than polite. "Until we meet again, Lady Emily. I find myself already anticipating our next conversation."

This time, Lyness could not help looking for her reaction to what was—for his brother—a bold statement. Which meant Lyness didn't miss a flicker of surprise in her eyes before she dipped into a graceful curtsy. "Then I shall endeavor to think of interesting topics upon which to converse, my lord."

The response was light. Perhaps too light. Flirtatious, even. Was she flirting with Roman? And what was Roman doing? And why?

And why did Lyness feel as though the sun had dimmed, though not one cloud occupied the sky above?

Roman finally started walking, commanding Apollo to trot along beside him, but Lyness remained frozen a moment more.

Lady Emily noticed. "Are you all right, Mr. Eastwood?" She took a half step closer. "I look forward to seeing you at the dinner, too."

Lyness looked away—to the ruins, the grass, anywhere but Lady Emily—and wondered when a simple afternoon had grown so complicated. "Yes. Of c-c-course. Until then, Lady Emily." And he followed after Roman at a quick step, needing to get away before he said anything he regretted.

At least he hadn't stuttered much until the end. When his anxiety over his brother's behavior cut through his speech.

After he caught up to Roman, he scrutinized his brother. "What was all of that?"

"All of what?" Roman asked, gaze still ahead, expression bland as it ever was in public.

"Your particular attention to Lady Emily," he said, and then immediately regretted it when Roman's head turned and his older brother stopped walking completely.

"Oh. Was it obvious?"

"To me. Yes." Lyness looked down at Apollo, who sat between them and kept his eyes fixed to Roman, waiting for command or acknowledgement. Like everyone else in Roman's life. Always looking to him to make the decision, to issue the order, to approve or disapprove.

Roman glanced back, but they were at the edge of the grounds the ruins occupied. Far enough away from the Sterling family that they would not be heard or likely even still observed.

"Hm. I had not thought it noticeable. Ah well. It cannot be helped this time." He started walking again, leaving Lyness no choice but to keep up with him. "As I said the other day, I think it time I give more thought to securing a wife. Though I have not shared my thoughts with her, Mother is concerned about the same. She has mentioned it several times, and I have to think it must cause her some agitation not to see the succession of our title and lands secured. She brings it up more often."

"Wh-what has that to do with Lady Emily?" A sinking feeling in Lyness's gut warned him that he already knew.

"Mother took a liking to her when they met the other day. She suggested I get to know Lady Emily better." Roman spoke as though it were all quite matter-of-fact. "Sterling is a fine chap. They are close to other prominent English families now. Lady Emily is an appropriate candidate for courtship. If we suit one another."

Of course she would suit Roman. Roman belonged in the world Lady Emily was struggling to enter.

Lyness swallowed a protest he had no right to make. "Oh." That was the only word he could get out. Did it even count as a word? It did not matter. Nothing in that moment mattered. His brother wanted to court Lady Emily. If they suited one another.

He reached up to adjust his hat, to bring the brim lower over his eyes—but it was gone. Given to the service of Lady Emily and her little canary. Leaving him bare to the sun and the curious glances of passersby. He wasn't certain which made him feel more vulnerable in that moment. His lack of topper, or that his brother had set his sights on the most charming lady Lyness had ever met.

# Chapter Six

The canary had not stayed in Mr. Eastwood's hat for long. Upon their return tot he cottage, Juniper sent a maid into the attic, where she had seen an old bird cage covered in dust and webs. The servant took care to clean it, then presented it to Emily with a curtsy and a curious glance inside the hat.

"I lined it with some old papers the master threw out," Beth, the maid, said with a proud tilt to her head. "Is the wee bird a boy or a girl bird?"

"I have no idea," Emily admitted as she carefully caught the little thing and put it through the cage door. It did not seem to mind the enclosure in the least, though it did begin pecking at the newsprint. "Who would be able to tell us?"

"M'brother's under gardener at Bells Hollow, m'lady. His duties include pigeon keeping, 'e could tak a look. I doubt pigeons nor canaries are all that different in yon respect." Beth peered into the cage. "'e mun know summat to feed the wee thing, too."

After Emily applied to her brother, he sent word to the neighbor at Bells Hollow to borrow their under gardener, a young man named Tom, who arrived quickly with his cap in hand and a flush on his freckled cheeks. He was quite respectful as he looked the canary over, beneath Emily's watchful eye. Jack stood with her, all of them in Jack's study.

His careful inspection made, Tom announced, "Yonder's a lass all right. I'd laik gamble she's bin real quiet-like, ain't she? The lassie birds dinnae sing as much as yon fellas. That's how they attract the ladies." He reached into his pocket and took out a pouch. "I brung some seeds an' dried peas. Reyt wee lot I could find, perfect for ma pigeons. Jist ye try a bit, see what'n she likes. Seeds prob'ly enuf to keep her wick—lively I mean, m'lady. Sir."

"Does she seem healthy?" Emily asked, looking the canary over as she hopped back into the cage and fluttered up to the perch across the middle.

"Aye, Lady Emily, nowt broken. She seems real spritely." Tom gave a firm nod. "She'll be a fine pet. And not too loud, neither."

"Thank you, Tom." Jack took the pouch of seeds and pressed a coin into the lad's hand. "I appreciate your coming, and I will be certain to thank Mr. Nelson for the loan of your expertise."

"It was a pleasure, Mr. Sterling. Lady Emily." The under gardener bowed and went out the door, where his sister waited to show him out.

Emily bent over the cage, brow furrowed. "I am relieved she is healthy. And to know she's a female."

"I suppose you can give her a proper name now," Jack said, putting the pouch of seeds on his desk beside the cage. "And is is a relief to know she isn't as loud as her male counterparts."

"I wonder if that is why she was left at the ruins," Emily mused, her chest tightening at the thought. She opened the pouch and sprinkled some of the seeds inside. The canary went down to peck at them immediately. "I need to find a dish for feeding her. And a dish for water. And a cover for the cage when she needs to sleep. Do you think we could find a book on keeping a canary?"

"Most likely. We can go into town tomorrow to look for one." Jack leaned against his desk, and Emily glanced up to see him staring rather hard at her, not at the bird. "Emily. I think we should talk."

Emily's hand tightened around the seed pouch. Oh, she did not like the sound of that at all. Jack was always serious, it seemed, but this particular tone sounded far more pointed than normal.

She sprinkled more seeds in. "We are talking. About my canary. Maybe I should name her after a flower. Daisy, perhaps. Or a sort of music. We could call her Sonata."

"I am certain you will select the perfect name for your new pet," Jack said with his usual patience. "But I would like to discuss a more serious topic with you. Lord Hartwell."

"Lord Hartwell?" she echoed, careful to keep her tone light. Likely failing. "What of him? Aside from his habit of leaving his dog's leash at home, I did not think anything amiss when we saw him today. Though it was certainly kind of him to extend his mother's invitation to us."

Jack circled the desk to sit in his chair, a sigh escaping him. A rather long-suffering sigh. "Emily. You must admit, his attention to you, though brief, was pointed."

"Was it? As you said, the interaction was so brief, I did not notice." Except she had. And then immediately hoped she was wrong about it. Lord Hartwell had been kind to her family since their ascension to the peerage, but that did not mean that she wished to be singled out by him. Handsome as he was, he was also quite intimidating. A baron. Of course, her father's new rank was higher, but she still knew so little about being an earl's daughter. She felt more at home among the gentry. Titles still fit like garments she wore for others' comfort rather than her own.

"He made a point of telling you he looked forward to speaking with you at the dinner party," Jack pointed out, posture as soldier-straight as ever. "And Hartwell is not known to be particularly sociable. If the Duke of Montfort hadn't brought us to Hartwell's attention at the beginning of the Season, I doubt he would have paid us any mind, let alone danced with you."

Though such a statement might sting another woman's pride, Emily had no illusions as to her ability to stand out in a crowd of equally pretty women. But she wondered, and then brushed away the question quickly, if Lyness Eastwood would have noticed her without the duke's interference.

Crossing her arms, Emily met Jack's gaze evenly. "Lord Hartwell hardly seems like the sort of man who should host dinner parties, then, if he is so unsociable."

"Emily."

"Jack."

He chuckled. "You will not be influenced, then? Not in the least? Even if I tell you that Lord Hartwell expressed concern for you from the beginning? He and his brother were both quick to dance with you, to offer warning about unsavory gentlemen, and to wish you well during your first Season."

"Both of them?" she asked, a small flicker of interest kindling in her mind. "Oh. I suppose that makes them good friends. To you. I hardly know either of them." Though she had enjoyed speaking to Lyness every time they had met. Which was only a handful of times. And the longest they had spoken in private was that morning at the ruins. Yet those moments remained at the forefront of her mind as the most pleasant conversation she had carried on with another in a long time.

"Then the dinner invitation will serve to give you ample opportunity to amend that circumstance," Jack said, the slightest of smiles on his usually stern face. "Lady Hartwell rarely entertains—"

"Perhaps the family's general standoffishness is hereditary," Emily said with a wider grin, unable to help herself.

Jack narrowed his eyes at her. "Perhaps. But the point, dearest little sister, is that going to dinner at their home is an honor, infrequently bestowed, and that Lord Hartwell is a suitable match for the daughter of an earl. In addition to that, I find him to be honorable and a worthy friend. You ought to consider him an option if he asks to court you."

Why did Jack always have to be so direct?

She knew what a match to a respectable, old family would mean to her father and siblings. It would be good for everyone, and then none of them would have to worry about her anymore, either. She would have a husband, and with him, a place that was no longer provisional. A household to keep her busy. They could turn their energies to matters more important than whether she behaved herself in public. Her father and eldest brother could continue to focus on building the family's reputation and seeing to the estate, her second oldest brother could turn his attention to his daughters —now with dowries of their own and approaching the age to come out in Society. Both of her already married sisters were happily ignoring everything to do with the family's elevation, except when it came to hiring more help in their own homes. None of them had heard from the third eldest brother, Arthur, but they all knew he would turn up eventually.

Emily was the family member flapping about like a loose ribbon, likely causing all of them anxiety when they wondered what would become of her.

With a sigh, she voiced her agreement. "Yes, Jack. I will consider it."

But would such an arrangement make her happy? The question pressed in, and she set it aside.

"That is all I ask," Jack said at last. "Now. Put it from your mind. Enjoy your songbird. Tomorrow, we will visit the bookshop. If they have nothing of use, we will check the subscription library. My membership was approved last week." The touch of pride in his voice did not go unnoticed.

"What excellent news! That must make you feel like a true citizen of York, then."

"It does, indeed." He unfolded his arms and rose to open the door for her. "Off with you, Emily. Juniper will want to help you come up with names for your canary."

She picked up the cage carefully. "Thank you, Jack."

Once in the little corridor, she released a soft sigh. Then walked slowly through to the sitting room on the first floor of the cottage.

Juniper sat there, near the window, reading a book with a dark cover. Whatever it was, it made Juniper's expression rather pale.

"Juniper?"

Emily's sister-in-law snapped the book closed, jolting as she did so. "Oh. I did not notice you coming in. The ghost in the hollow is bellowing, you see." She held the book up. "The poor heroine is frozen with fear, standing at the edge of the cemetery."

"Ah. It is no wonder you were not attuned to our world, given the troubles in the book's." Emily put the canary's cage on a table near the window.

"I appreciate your kind understanding." Juniper rose and came to look at the canary. "Have you news?"

"My little friend is a lady bird."

"Ah. Congratulations." Juniper's grin turned brighter. "What shall we call her, then?"

Naming the little bird was a much pleasanter way to pass the afternoon than worrying about Lord Hartwell. She eagerly agreed to draw up a list of names to choose from, and the better part of the next half hour was listing off names, speaking of why one or two certainly would not work, giggling over half a dozen of them, and finally settling on one.

"Miss Honora Feathersby. But we will call her Feathers for short." Emily picked up a little watering can. It was on the windowsill, next to a fern that Juniper wanted to revive through sheer determination and less sunlight. She picked up Juniper's saucer from tea and poured water into it, then put that inside the bird cage. The canary was quick to go to the water and drink.

"Excellent." Juniper leaned against the window, looking out at the modest garden behind their cottage. "Did Jack tell you his suspicions about Lord Hartwell's interest?"

Emily froze as surely as the heroine in Juniper's book. "Not you, too, Juniper."

"We can hardly help ourselves," Juniper said with a crooked grin. "He is a fine man. An excellent catch. And we did promise your parents we would help you adjust to Society while you are with us. What better way to do so than have a courtship with a handsome baron?"

Emily laughed, though the sound caught awkwardly in her throat. "You and Jack both conspire against me, it seems. I am hardly fit to be anyone's object of interest at present." She still made so many mistakes. Only that morning, she had left the house without her calling cards. She had not realized the mistake until Juniper had them stop in, after the park, to leave word for a friend. She had also worn gloves that did not match, but had strived to keep that hidden, lest the maid be blamed.

"Nonsense," Juniper said, smiling. "You are kind, clever, and charming. That is more than enough to draw attention."

"Perhaps. But my lack of social graces may soon cause that attention to wither."

"Like my poor fern?" Juniper tried to tease, pointing at the sad greenery. "Emily, you hardly make any mistakes now. You are being too hard on yourself. In addition to that, you are lovely. Men are bound to take notice."

Emily bent toward the canary's cage, adjusting the dish of water. "I would rather earn regard for my good sense than my face." She had sense in abundance.

"Then you are in luck," Juniper replied lightly. "Men of good character notice that sort of thing. And I do believe Lord Hartwell has an excellent character. I will leave you to think on that for now. I must return to my poor, frightened heroine and the ghost I highly suspect is her wicked neighbor in disguise."

While Juniper went back to her novel, Emily lingered at the window, watching the pale flutter of the bird's wings inside the cage. She forced her thoughts back to that morning, to Lord Hartwell's barely present smile.

Soon enough, one memory insisted on returning. It was not Lord Hartwell's elegant bow or his voice, smooth as polished wood. The memory that she lingered on was softer. The sound of laughter quickly suppressed, the glint of sunlight in unruly hair, and a gentleman's hat cradled in her arms.

She touched the cage idly, eyes on the canary as it hopped on the perch again. "We are both rather out of place, aren't we, little one? You in a cage, me in a title."

The canary gave a brief, bright chirp in reply, and Emily could only sigh. "And both of us expected to thrive."

THE DESK IN THE TOWNHOUSE STUDY FELT CRAMPED COMPARED TO Lyness's workroom at the family estate, near Easingwold. A little over twenty miles separated him from that workroom and the country air, where stewards of Barons Hartwell had balanced the accounts and conducted business for over a hundred years. Perhaps he should give up on York. Take his leave from his mother and brother and use estate matters as his excuse.

As he signed his name to a letter asking about the replacement of an outbuilding's roof, Lyness let his mind wander in that direction.

Surely, they would not miss him. Not if both of them were planning on finding Roman a match. What could Lyness do to help with that? Better he clear the way and make himself useful by preparing the estate for the coming harvest season. Their tenants would likely appreciate having a member of the family nearby. If nothing else, they would save on postal expenses every time someone had a question they sent along to him.

Then he would not have to watch as Roman attempted to court Lady Emily.

A large drop of ink fell from his pen to the desk.

"Blast," he hissed, dropping his pen into the inkwell. He picked up the stained cloth he used in such moment, hastily getting up the black liquid before dropping the cloth, too, and rubbing his temples.

It should not bother him, to know Roman turned his attentions to Lady Emily. Especially given that it was early days, yet. Roman had only spoken to her once since her arrival in Yorkshire, and one time before that during a ball in London. He hadn't formed any special attachment. There hadn't been enough time for such a thing.

Had there?

Lyness had spoken to her on one more occasion than his brother. That was all. He certainly could not claim any feelings toward Lady Emily greater than curiosity. Perhaps some admiration, too. Certainly, some level of attraction…

"I should leave," he murmured aloud, tilting his head back to stare at the ceiling, trying to ignore the ache growing within his chest.

A soft tap at the door preceded the entrance of a footman, holding a familiar hat.

"Mr. Eastwood, this has just arrived for you. There is a note inside, otherwise I would have returned it to your room."

Lyness sat up straight and motioned for the servant to leave the hat on the desk. "A note, you say? Thank you, Thomas."

Once the servant had withdrawn, Lyness tipped the hat toward him to see a small sheet of paper, not folded, and when he lifted it out, he noted something else. Flowers. At the bottom of his hat. Tiny little things. Tied together with a thin ribbon. He took those out to inspect them. Daisies and forget-me-nots, with a little yellow feather at the center.

His heart tripped.

The two flowers together were an interesting choice, if she knew the meanings behind them. Friendliness, affection, remembrance.

He brought the flowers to his nose and inhaled, then chuckled to himself. Not daisies. Chamomile. That changed things, somewhat. "Patience. Calm. Hm."

Lyness looked at the small square of paper, knowing well that whatever she had written had been approved by her sister-in-law or brother. Unmarried ladies simply did not send notes to bachelors without oversight. It would be improper.

To Mr. Eastwood,

I thank you for the use of your hat in my self-appointed quest to save the canary. It may interest you to know that our tiny yellow friend is a female, and I have thus bestowed upon her the name of Honora Feathersby. Miss Feathersby is obliged to you for the use of your hat, too. She has seen fit to gift you one of her feathers with her thanks. As to your hat, I hope you find it in as good a condition as it was when you loaned it to us. I have made certain it is clean, with the help of my brother, and it has suffered no ill effects from its time with us. Please also find with this note a few flowers, gathered by myself, from my brother's gardens. I look forward to seeing you soon, and I will give you more news of our rescued Miss Feathersby at that time.

Most Sincerely,
Lady Emily Sterling

He read it twice more, smiling all the while. The letter was as sweet as it was amusing, and something about it tugged at his heart as much as it did his sense of humor.

He liked her. A great deal. And he wanted to see her again.

Nothing was set in stone for Roman. Perhaps his brother would direct his interest elsewhere. There were other young ladies coming to dinner the next evening. Roman might find himself more interested in one of them than in Lady Emily.

Nothing was said and done yet. He had time and an opportunity to come to know Lady Emily better. Besides, he conducted estate business from York perfectly well.

He folded the note and tucked it into his pocket with a grin.

Then plucked the feather from the tiny flower arrangement, twirling it between his fingers.

"So much for leaving York," he murmured. The ache from before changed. Lightened. Feeling dangerously akin to hope.

# Chapter Seven

The night of his mother's dinner party, Lyness spent more time in front of the looking glass than usual. His valet had made several slight adjustments to his hair, cravat, and stick pin. Finally, it could not matter that Lyness still felt unsatisfied with his reflection. The time to go downstairs to greet the guests had arrived.

"Thank you, Hobson. I am afraid I am out of sorts this evening. Everything you have done is perfect."

"Yes, Mr. Eastwood." Hobson bowed, gathered up the ruined cravats from the beginning of the ordeal, and went out the door to the servants' staircase. Pointedly not saying another word.

Apparently, Lyness had irritated his valet.

Lyness avoided one last glance in the glass and went out the door. He went lightly down the steps to the first floor and into the sitting room adjoining the dining room, where they would greet their guests.

His mother looked elegant, as usual, in a gown of deep blue. A shawl embroidered with her beloved York roses was draped across her shoulders. She sat in her favorite chair while Roman leaned against the mantel.

"Lyness, my boy. You look well this evening," his mother said, tilting her head to receive a kiss on the cheek from him. "I have missed entertaining, flanked by my two handsome sons. Was there ever a mother as fortunate as I am?"

"We are the fortunate ones, Mother," Lyness said, relieved to find her in such fine spirits. She had not hosted a dinner party in over a year. Despite living in York, she had grown more and more withdrawn from Society. Calling her sons back from London for an unnecessary remodel of the estate had, it seemed, brought some life back to her.

Straightening his stance, and tugging at his sleeves, Roman added, "I agree with Lyness. Whatever fine things we offer this world, we can only do so because we have you, Mother."

At that moment, the first guests arrived.

The Nelson family consisted of the father, two sons of similar ages to Roman and Lyness, and two daughters. Twin sisters of two-and-twenty years old. Thankfully, the sisters were not identical, so addressing them by the correct names wasn't difficult. Roman's solicitor, Mr. Holly, also attended with his mother and his widowed sister, Mrs. Elgin.

Then at last the Sterling family arrived. In a gown the color of soft pink Valerians, Lady Emily was a sight to be seen. She wore flowers in her hair, too. Chamomile, he realized, the same as what she had sent him in the hat.

He had to push down the thought that there may be meaning behind such a thing.

After all the introductions were made, Lyness carefully made his way to stand behind Lady Emily. She turned as though she anticipated him, her eyes alight with good humor.

"Mr. Eastwood, I trust your hat made its way safely back into your possession?"

"Indeed, it has. Along with your news of Miss Feathersby." That he did not stutter was remarkable. He counted it a victory, in fact. "How is she?"

The lady's grin, unaffected and honest, drew him closer. "She is well. Though she has yet to sing, I have every confidence in her having a fine voice. Even if she seems shy about using it. You will have to come visit once she overcomes her reticence, to hear one of her performances for yourself."

"Who is performing?" Roman's voice broke into their conversation as he joined them, necessitating Lyness step back to form a triangle for their conversation.

With a faint blush in her cheeks, Lady Emily explained, "No one, really. We were discussing the canary we rescued. I have great hope that she will sing for us soon."

Lyness wasn't certain what he liked best, that she included him as one of the bird's rescuers, or how charming she looked when she blushed.

"I see." Roman's tone was all genteel charm. "I am glad to hear your new feathered friend is bringing you happiness." He wore a pleasant expression, too. One Lyness rarely saw outside of their circle of friends. "Have you ever kept a canary before? Or other birds?"

"No, this is my first pet since I was a child." Lady Emily spoke without any affectation, and she did not bat her eyelashes or attempt to hide her pleasure in the topic. "Though I named the chickens and ducks on our farm often enough, they can hardly count as pets when we eventually ate them. Or their eggs."

That made Lyness chuckle and brought up all sorts of questions he wished to ask. What sort of names had she dreamed up for the flocks of poultry? Did it ever bother her to eat a creature she'd named? Did she miss the farm her family had left behind with their elevation into the ranks of nobility?

But Roman merely raised his eyebrows. "I suppose one does not generally make pets of chickens. Though I did have a cousin who raised a gosling to follow her about for a number of years." Then he changed the subject, to Lyness's disappointment. "Are you enjoying your time in York? Not many think it compares favorably to London."

It took a measure of self-control for Lyness not to groan aloud.

Anyone who knew Roman well understood that this was a test of sorts. Roman detested London, and he had a strong preference for all things pertaining to York. If the lady expressed a contrary opinion, it would be a mark against her. From Roman's perspective, anyway.

Without pause, Lady Emily answered warmly. "One cannot help being dazzled by London, of course, but I find the air here easier to breathe. The people are kinder, and there is time to think. I cannot imagine ever tiring of green things and open skies."

"I feel the same," Lyness said, thinking of the quiet of the countryside, the beauty surrounding their family estate. For a heartbeat, it felt as though she had reached straight into his own chest and borrowed the words from there. *Green things and open skies.*

Did she speak merely of York? Of walks on the walls and ruined abbeys and the curve of the river beneath its bridges? Or did her thoughts stray, as his did, to fields and hedgerows and the particular stillness that belonged only to true country air?

Perhaps she missed the home where she had grown up. Perhaps, if given the choice, she would rather return to it than belong to any baron's household—Hartwell's or otherwise. The notion checked him, cooling a warmth that had no business rising in the first place.

"I quite agree. York is superior in that way. One can hear oneself think," Roman said, and Lyness almost winced at the near-smug tone. His brother would never admit to loving any place as much as he did their medieval city.

His mother swept toward them, eyes on Lady Emily. "What is this I hear? Lady Emily, how refreshing to find a young woman who can appreciate York's virtues. As fashionable as London may be, I have always preferred my beautiful York. We ought to ride through it together, my dear. I should love to tell you more of its history. But for now, I must inform you of the arrangements for dinner."

Lyness, already aware he was not the one escorting Lady Emily to the table, stepped aside with a quiet sigh. He preferred York to

London, too, but hardly saw a reason to turn that preference into a virtue or a competition.

In short order, everyone found their companions for dinner, and it did not take long to go through to the dining room. Roman sat at the head of the table, with Lady Juniper on his right and Lady Emily on his left. Lyness sat beside Lady Juniper.

The arrangement meant it would not be easy for him to converse with Lady Emily, but he contented himself with enjoying the sight of her. She had an expressive face. More so than he usually saw in women raised within the ranks of nobility and upper gentry.

His mother had taken care with the table's arrangement. Silver candelabra positioned in the middle of the table set the crystal wine goblets to shimmering. Small floral arrangements along the walls lightly perfumed the room in scents of rose and Sweet William, a flower his mother enjoyed despite its commonality in cottage gardens. She had always said the flower, like cloves and honey in its scent, encouraged genteel appetites.

Then there were the dishes, carefully prepared, as bright in taste as in color. The best dishware upon the table setting it all off in grand style. His mother was making a good show of her hostessing abilities. From the flicker of the candles to the table linen, Lady Hartwell honored her guests and family alike.

The soft candlelight on Lady Emily's profile made her lovelier than all of it. And he wondered if she realized the splendor was, at least in part, due to her attendance. What would she make of such attention? Of course, the Misses Nelson were also present. Was there a chance, perhaps, that Roman might redirect his attention to one of them? Or at least divide his attention enough for Lyness to also enjoy Lady Emily's company?

He wished he sat nearer. As it was, once the meal began, he could only watch her navigate conversation with his brother and, on her other side, Mr. Phineas Nelson. Mr. Thaddeus Nelson, his elder brother, at farther down the table.

The bright smile from the day at the ruins was nowhere to be seen. Lady Emily pressed her lips together when she was not eating or speaking, and ventured comment only when one of the gentlemen asked her a question. Her gaze darted to him more than once, and each time their eyes met he tried to reassure her with a nod or raise of his eyebrows.

"You are watching Lady Emily rather closely, Mr. Eastwood," Lady Juniper said at his side, her voice low enough that it would not carry beyond his hearing.

His posture stiffened, as did his hold upon his fork. "Oh. Well." He turned his full attention to her. "I beg your p-pardon, Lady Juniper. I have been an inattentive neighbor." He winced. Cleared his throat softly. "What were you saying?"

He knew precisely what she had said, but he hoped she would turn the conversation to another matter.

"My sister-in-law," she said, still soft enough that no one else would hear. "Is something amiss? Perhaps I am wrong, and you are more concerned with your brother?" The lift of her eyebrows combined with the crook of her mouth told him well enough she knew his stare had not centered on Roman.

Coming up with an answer that would satisfy her sisterly concern without causing alarm meant making several quick mental calculations. And forcing a calm smile while hoping his ears had not changed to red.

"You have c-caught me, Lady Juniper. I am aware, of course, th-that the Sterling family is still adjusting to their change in status. As I have great respect for th-them, I am anxious to see each member succeed. I am m-most impressed with Lady Emily's composure. One would think her b-born to her status."

Her eyebrows climbed higher as he spoke, and Lyness doubted it had anything to do with his stammer. She had weighed his words and seemingly did not believe them.

"You are admiring her, then?"

Sensing there was more to question than the innocent way she posed it, Lyness met her stare and said in as level a voice as possible, "Of c-course. As I would admire anyone in her situation."

"Hm. How interesting. Why have you not engaged her in conversation?"

He gestured to the table. Wide, by town standards, full to bursting. "I have no w-wish to raise my voice or draw attention." It was habit, more than anything. When he spoke without first arranging the words in his thoughts, when not completely comfortable in a situation, his stutter came out often. His family had ever been forgiving of that, always showing forth patience, but his tutors had not. School boys in his past had not. Until his older brother either boxed their ears or stared them down on Lyness's behalf.

"That is unfortunate." The lady's gaze flickered from him to Lady Juniper. "As I do believe your mother has rather hoped Emily would draw *someone's* attention. And I do not think she meant it to be Mr. Phineas Nelson's." She tapped one finger on the table, then appeared ready to say more on the matter, when they heard instead that gentleman.

"I have not been in London this Season myself," Phineas said, tone a trifle louder than before. "But I recall hearing of your family's entrance into Society. We heard at least some of the news, even all the way in York."

"All the way in York?" Roman repeated, brow drawn tight. "You speak as though we live in a backwater parish instead of one of the finest cities in our kingdom's history."

Lady Emily glanced between the two with wide eyes. "Yes. I suppose word of our family's experience would travel. It is rather like a fairy story. Of course, London was where we went at first, to see the house there, and learn more of the inheritance. It seemed the right place to begin."

"But why?" Phineas asked, now looking at Roman with a sly smile, more pleased at the idea of teasing a friend than making the lady between them comfortable. Or so Lyness immediately thought and bristled. "When York is so much more comfortable for that sort of thing. Smaller crowds. Less strict adherence to the social strictures of London."

"I do not think London a poor choice," Roman said, both hands on the table flexing, eyes on Phineas. "Though it likely proved more troublesome than a place such as Bath or Ipswich."

Lady Emily's cheeks had turned pink, and no one had noticed.

"The new earl's family managed well enough, thanks to the help of friends," Lady Juniper said, voice raised to carry gently across the table.

Mrs. Holly, on the other side of Phineas, said suddenly, "Oh, yes. I remember hearing something about that. Was there not some unpleasant rumor about your poor family, Mr. Sterling?" She leaned back slightly, the better to direct her question to Jack, who was at the opposite end of the table from his sister.

Lyness wanted to groan. As much as they liked Mr. Holly, his mother possessed a singular talent for asking inappropriate questions. Usually, it was something that amused Roman, but Lyness always found himself wanting to offer correction. But it was not his place, and rudeness ought not to begat rudeness.

Things were getting out of hand, and Lady Emily had turned from pink, to red, to a worrisome shade of white. And he could not stand to see her look as though she wished to disappear.

"That is the w-way of it in London," Lyness said, voice carrying loudly enough that the others quieted to look at him, even those not yet involved in the conversation. All eyes were on him. Including Lady Emily's.

"Whatever do you mean, Mr. Eastwood?" Mrs. Holly asked, voice warbling inconsiderately at that volume. Vaguely, Lyness sensed Mrs. Elgin, sitting next to him, shrink from her mother's ill-mannered tone.

His heart sped up. He forced himself not to wince even as he felt his throat tightening. He avoided this kind of notice on purpose. And generally did not stutter as much when in his own home. But he knew, even before opening his mouth, that this speech would be short and full of repeated consonants. "London is f-f-full of b-bored people. They m-make much from a single word or detail. T-turning story into r-r-rumor, rumor into gossip, and g-gossip into the r-ruin of another's reputation. I sh-should not give heed to any r-rumors from London. B-best to believe only what one can c-confirm for oneself."

It was a painfully long speech for him to make at one of his mother's dinner parties. He dared not glance her way. Instead, he turned slightly to Lady Juniper.

"D-do you agree, my lady?"

Lady Juniper's eyes had turned quite round as he spoke, but she hastily composed herself. "Oh, yes. Precisely my thoughts on the matter. People in London grow bored with the truth and so invent fiction to entertain themselves, with little care for how it might impact the reputation of another person. I find the worst rumors are often started by rivals, anyway." She turned a far-brighter-than-necessary expression to Mrs. Holly. "I imagine you could tell us many a tale of your rivals, Mrs. Holly. Everyone knows you were quite the catch during your time as a single miss."

That comment took the subject in an entirely different direction. Mrs. Holly had no qualms about speaking of her past as a sought-after beauty. Perhaps it was that long-ago status that made her behave as though she need not confine herself to the normal boundaries of conversation.

No one batted an eye in Lady Emily's direction again.

Expect for Lyness. He met her gaze, saw the color return to her cheeks, and her smile reappear in a smaller, meeker form. She mouthed the words *thank you*. Which, of course, left him elated. Warmth flooded his chest, and he found he liked being her champion. In that moment, had she needed an ogre slain or a dragon defeated, he would have asked only to be pointed in the right direction. And, perhaps, armed himself with a sword.

He bowed his head subtly, hoping she would understand his thoughts. *You are welcome. I am sorry for the need, but I would do it again.*

He glanced at Roman to see what he had made of the near disaster to find his brother staring at him with a deep frown. Roman shook his head slightly, but whether it was a mark of disapproval for Lyness's speaking up or confusion, Lyness couldn't say.

Probably it was best to focus on the fact that he had saved Lady Emily from some mild discomfort and the possible re-ignition of London rumors. Rumors that he had heard, too, after leaving London for York. They were not flattering in any way, even if they had died down by the time Mr. Sterling arrived in York with his wife and sister in tow.

Reviving anything negative about Lady Emily while she was under her brother's protection, away from the rest of her family, would not go well for her. And Lyness had no intention of letting anyone within his hearing cast aspersions on her character or reputation. Not when he knew her to be intelligent, witty, kind, charming….

He had to stop adding to the list when his mother announced that the ladies would adjourn to the drawing room. She rose with her usual grace, and all the gentlemen rose, too.

"We will, of course, be pleased to play cards, or perhaps enjoy some music, after we are rejoined by the gentlemen," she announced. "This evening is proving a delight, and I will not have it end too soon."

Lady Hartwell's entire being took on a brightness of expression, and she moved with a grace and energy Lyness had not seen in her for some time. She smiled pointedly at Roman, then briefly at Lyness, then led the women out of the room.

As Lady Emily left, she looked back over her shoulder once. Lyness caught her gaze—or rather, she caught him staring. As did her sister-in-law. Lady Juniper had turned, too.

It seemed he was terrible at subtlety.

And Lady Emily's departure left him somewhat hollow. He looked from the decanter brought forward by a servant to the door where the women had exited. Would it be terrible of him to skip the private masculine conversation and go directly in to sit with the ladies? Giving his attention to one lady in particular…

Roman was already speaking, though. And glancing at Lyness, which meant the older brother expected the younger to take part in the conversation. Which centered on politics, at first. Lyness listened, or tried to listen, to what his brother was saying.

"I think our party has taken on too much in terms of the entertainments for the races. If anything goes wrong, rather than blame one lord or committee, it will all come onto our party's head."

Mr. Holly, the family's solicitor and a man who had gone to school with Roman, stared into his glass as though the liquid inside had offended him. "There is nothing to be done about it at this point. The Tories have practically backed us into a corner. None of them have curried favor with the elite of London. Not for this specific occasion. I would not be surprised to learn they have told members of the opposition to stay away entirely."

"Surely, no one can sabotage the races that way," Jack Sterling said. "I have never attended them, but I have heard of them often enough to know they are an historic staple to all who care for racing. The same track has been used for a hundred years, has it not?"

"And may it continue for one hundred more," Mr. Nelson, the eldest man present, said with a nod. "Cheer up, my lads. I have seen twice as many races as all of you, and I tell you that no one remembers who hosted which balls, unless they were uncommonly good or the site of some ridiculous scandal."

"Well then," Phineas said with a crooked grin, "we can hope for mediocre balls and solemn scandals, if there must be any scandal at all, and it will go well for us. And the party."

"I am more concerned with York as a whole," Roman muttered.

"Of course you are," Thaddeus Nelson responded, eyes rolling upward. "Heaven preserve our blessed York, and Roman Eastwood, Baron Hartwell, will be happy as a lark."

Roman snorted, and Lyness couldn't help a smile of his own. When Roman cut him a disapproving look, Lyness shrugged. "Your mania for our city is well known, brother. It is the easiest place to nettle you or to jest. If you would not have it so, guard your love more."

"I haven't any need to do such a thing," Roman retorted, folding his arms over his chest.

Jack leaned forward, suddenly serious. "You would be surprised, Lord Hartwell, what exposing your heart to the world can do. One would hope it only brings admiration and understanding, but I have seen such a heart become a target instead. Your enemies, political or otherwise, will all know where to strike to see you undone."

The mood immediately turned somber, and even Phineas had nothing to say on the matter. Instead, he looked at Roman with a contemplative frown.

Lyness thought of the pamphlets Roman funded, the speeches he gave in rooms thick with smoke and argument. His brother called it conviction. Others, less kind, called it courting danger. There was more to it than supporting historical preservation. Political enemies could use Roman's love of his city against him. Denying projects. Shifting public opinion. Ruining his carefully laid plans unless he gave way in other areas. Even merely dividing his attention. When one wore one's heart on his sleeve, he made it an easier target.

It fell to Lyness to half-soothe, half-cheer the party. "It would be difficult to hurt the city itself, with as many protectors as it has, and my brother would not know how to speak if he could not declare his loyalty to the place of his birth. I think York in good hands with Roman."

"And I will drink to that," Phineas said with a raise of his glass. The others followed suit. Even Jack.

The conversation turned, and it was Phineas again looking to stir up something. "Mr. Sterling, your sister, Lady Emily, is quite charming. It was a pleasure to be one of her dining companions. Would you not say so, Hartwell?"

Roman lowered the glass he was drinking from. "Yes. Most charming."

"And?" Phineas asked, eyebrows raised as he leaned forward somewhat theatrically.

Lyness wanted to box his ears. A somewhat violent urge, coming on so suddenly it surprised him. He hastily put both his hands flat on the table. Then paid close attention to his brother.

"And…" Roman appeared confused by the question, looking from Phineas to Jack. "She is sweet-tempered. Well spoken. When she does speak. Is she always so subdued, Sterling?"

Jack shrugged one shoulder upward. "No, indeed. But there were new faces in the company. I am certain she is finding her way and will grow more comfortable voicing her thoughts. In time."

"I do not doubt you are right. She does a credit to your family, Sterling." Roman raised his glass slightly. Not a true toast, but a polite enough compliment. His brother's neutral tone lightened the pressure in Lyness's chest.

The baron had not made any public movements to court Lady Emily. Roman may well still consider other options. That made breathing easier, and it made Lyness all the more eager for the company in the drawing room.

Whatever his mother had hoped for or planned regarding Lady Emily, it might come to nothing after all. Giving Lyness leave to admire the beautiful, intelligent, kind woman as much as he wished. Without feeling that he encroached upon something that rightfully belonged to his brother, a thing that he could not ever allow himself to do.

For the first time that evening, he felt truly at ease.

# Chapter Eight

After the ladies withdrew from dinner, they settled happily in the drawing room beneath Lady Hartwell's solicitude. The baroness quickly had the six women in places of comfort. A chair for Mrs. Holly near the fire, the Misses Norman settled at a card table, and Mrs. Elgin and Juniper given the pianoforte and sheets of music for the entertainment of all.

"We have an even number," Mrs. Elgin, the young widow, said with a bright smile. "Perhaps we could have dancing for any who wished to enjoy such exercise."

"Oh, you young people," Mrs. Holly, her mother, said from her chair. "Forever looking for reasons to pull up the rugs and move about furniture. Matilda, dear, let us not turn Lady Hartwell's drawing room into a den of chaos. Listening to music this evening is enough excitement for all of us."

Mrs. Elgin did not seem put out by her mother, which surprised Emily somewhat. The young widow was better practiced at schooling her features than Emily, given that Emily could not seem to keep herself from giving away all her feelings with a look.

Perhaps that had saved her, though, at the table.

"If exercise is wanted, the garden is open for exploration," Lady Hartwell said, gesturing to the doors open on one side of the room, letting in a soft evening breeze. "I had lanterns hung along the paths and above my favorite of the roses. I do hope everyone who wishes to take a moment in the garden will do so."

That tempted Emily. Yet leaving the room so soon after entering might strike some as rude. Instead, she drifted toward a curio cabinet in one corner of the room, the little shelves filled with dainty works of art made with glass, jade, and clay. Many of the pieces were shaped into flowers and painted with delicate patterns.

Lady Hartwell joined her there. "You have found my treasures," she said quietly, her eyes bright and hands folded elegantly before her. "I have enjoyed collecting these. I have only added one or two for myself. The rest have been gathered by my sons or friends when they see a thing they think I will like."

There were tiny placards, folded cards, with information about each piece set before it. The writing was minuscule, but legible. Emily bent to read one.

*Rose of Jerusalem, Olive Wood, Purchased in Greece. Gift from Her Grace, the Duchess of Montfort, August 1815.*

"Oh. How clever. Writing information about each piece in such a lovely way."

"Yes. The place where it was acquired, when, and who gifted it to me," Lady Hartwell said, a small flutter of her hand gesturing to the cards. "It was Lyness's idea and handiwork, of course. He enjoys the intricacy of the miniature signs. And it rather makes me feel like I have a museum in my keeping. Cataloging the information where anyone can see it."

Mr. Eastwood had created the placards? That made her bend again to examine them closer. The writing was neat and tidy, and still somehow elegant despite the size. His penmanship was absolutely beautiful.

"Which do you like best?" Lady Hartwell asked.

It took Emily a moment to realize the baroness meant the roses and not the script.

"Oh. They are all so beautiful. Let me see." One piece looked so thinly sculpted that she could only imagine how brittle it would feel, how careful one had to touch it. "This one," she said, pointing to the delicate rose.

She immediately experienced sympathy for the inanimate object. In that moment, she felt somewhat fragile herself. The conversation at dinner had been difficult to follow, when she understood what was being said. So often, the men on either side of her had spoken of people she did not know and events—such as the upcoming races—wherein she had no experience. The dishes served that evening had all been new to her, and she was certain she had not eaten the main course in the way intended. She likely should have dipped the meat in the sauce that was next to it, instead of mixing them together on the plate. Dipping was certainly the more delicate option.

"Yes, that is a marvelous piece. Lyness chose that one for me. Of course, it says so on the card. He found it in a market, in France, when he visited a handful of years ago."

"He went to France?"

"Of course. He visited as many countries in Europe as he could in a year. I am glad his interest and age corresponded to a time of relative peace for such things. A decade ago, it would have been too dangerous for him to travel in such a way." Lady Hartwell smiled fondly at her display of treasures. "I think he enjoyed the adventure of it. I hate to have my sons far from me, though I think it an important thing for men of distinction."

Looking at the rose again, and Lyness's careful penmanship, Emily said, "I have hardly stirred outside the county of my birth before we went to London. And now I am here, of course. I have not even wondered what other places might hold."

"I think travel is good for the young," Lady Hartwell said, her hands adjusting the shawl around her shoulder as she spoke. "Perhaps I do not encourage it enough. I know Roman has no wish to stir far from York, but with the *right* persuasion, he might travel the kingdom a touch more." She gave Emily a significant look to punctuate that statement.

Jack's guess that Lady Hartwell wanted to play matchmaker for her eldest son seemed more feasible by the moment.

Several feet away at the gaming table, the twin sisters burst into giggles as one attempted to shuffle, only to send the cards scattering to the floor.

"I can help," Emily said, hurrying to assist. And get away from the expectant smile of the baroness. She bent swiftly, and her head rewarded her for the abrupt movement with a sudden dart of pain.

"Thank you, Lady Emily," one of the twins said, her smile tight. Did she not, in fact, want help? Or was she merely self-conscious about the clumsiness of the accident? Perhaps it was Emily herself that was the problem.

Her head had ached even before the ghastly London gossip had come up. She had hoped to never have to think of that awkward occasion again. Nothing terrible had actually happened, of course. Some mean-spirited members of Society had decided to spread rumors about her being a snob, acting above her station, and luring men into courting her for the amusement of breaking their hearts.

It had all been baseless. Fabricated by those who were offended she did not wish to associate with them, due to their mean-spirited nature.

Having high standards for friendships and courtship had spectacularly backfired, and it had taken the cleverness of friends in London to curtail the rumors and leave her—and her family's—reputation intact. She had taken care to limit new friendships until she was certain of a person's character, after hearing numerous warnings about people taking advantage of her state as a new noble. That care had been labeled the snobbery of an upstart, and Society did not forgive people acting above their place in life.

That horrible experience had cemented her decision to leave London for the less strict society of York.

The other sister accepted the deck of cards with hardly a lift of her eyes. Both had been so cheerful a moment before.

What if the London gossip continued to stand in the way of Emily finding friends? Finding a husband? She did not want to think on it, though she craved understanding and friendship. She missed forming acquaintance and deeper connection over simple things, and conversation about more than the weather and fashion.

Though Juniper and Jack tried, Emily found herself lonely and without people to confide in. Her brother and sister-in-law wanted to soothe her, the rest of her family were carrying on in London and had their own problems, and that left Emily with few people to share her true thoughts and feelings. Her worry about the gossip...

Lady Hartwell had not been bothered by the gossip, though. Surely that was a good thing? Jack and Juniper both thought Roman Eastwood a good match for her. Yet they had asked only that she be civil to him—and she had been.

But when she looked toward the door, wondering when the gentlemen would join them, it was Lyness she hoped to see first. His sympathetic expression, warm sense of humor, and gentle way of listening had set her at ease more than anyone else.

That would never do.

She needed to take in cooler air. She stepped closer to her sister-in-law, who examined the musical selection with eagerness to find another piece to play, and tilted her head toward the doors. "May I step outside alone?"

Juniper looked toward the windows. "I think so. The gardens are within full view of anyone in this room. Lady Hartwell said they are well lit. I see nothing wrong with it if you are not away overlong."

Nodding her understanding, Emily slipped between the thin curtains and out into the cool night.

Immediately, she drew in a deep breath. The air was scented with roses, and a soft breeze tugged at her hem in welcome. For a moment, with the heady smells of fragrant flowers and the night air, she missed her home in the country terribly.

It would be ungrateful to admit it, even to herself, so she tried to put the longing aside. Tried not to think of the stone walls covered in honeysuckle, the bright green of the fields stretching in every direction, interrupted by the occasional copse of old trees with broad green leaves.

She stepped deeper into the garden. Nothing within growing higher than her chest made it easy to stay in sight of anyone standing at the doors or windows of the Hartwell townhouse.

If Lady Hartwell wished for Emily to court her son, the baron, that ought to count as a small victory. And an honor, truly. Courting a baron would fulfill her family's hopes and expectations for her. Marrying a man with wealth or a title would solidify their attainment of nobility. Helping their position in Society. A thing her father wanted.

But she wasn't certain she wanted more of what London had offered, when every day left her thinking of green hills and quiet afternoons in a comfortable home. The time before she had worried overmuch about suitors, enjoying local assemblies and balls without the worry over marriage, had not been perfect. But it was easier than this. Back then, she had known marriage would come if it was meant to, that her family expected her to care for the home as their parents aged, that her marrying was of no consequence to anyone but herself.

Bending closer to a rose, to inhale its fragrance directly, she winced when the strength of the scent made her head throb. With a hand to her temple, she walked on. Not about to make that mistake again.

Romanticizing the past would not benefit her in the least. Best to focus on the present circumstances.

Mr. Eastwood had saved her at the dinner table. She could not forget that. Nor could she forget the warmth in his eyes when she first arrived that evening, as though he looked forward to seeing her. His encouraging glances at dinner, even before he put a stop to talk of gossip and rumor, had kept her from falling silent. Lyness Eastwood made her feel welcome and even wanted.

"Ridiculous," she chastised herself. "He is merely kind. A true gentleman."

The memory of his smile stayed with her, though. It eased something in her chest, to know he enjoyed her company.

As though summoned by her thoughts, Lyness stepped out into the garden at that moment. She saw the movement from the corner of her eye, and turned to find him there, already coming down the few steps to ground level, coming to her with an open smile.

Her heart skipped and her stomach dipped, to see him approach with a warmth in his gaze she was not accustomed to.

When he was mere steps away, he spoke. "Here you are, Lady Emily. I hope I am not intruding. I only… needed a moment's peace myself." The air between them seemed to soften, or perhaps it was only her heart. "Will you forgive me for inflicting my company on your quiet contemplation?"

"I cannot think of ever objecting to your company, Mr. Eastwood," she said, feeling her cheeks grow warmer as she spoke. "You are most welcome. Especially given that these are your family's gardens. I would be a rude beast if I tried to keep you out of them."

He appeared happy to hear her welcome, though it did not strike her as the most elegant of speeches.

"I will never object to your company either, my lady." He tipped his head forward, then offered his arm. "Tell me, what do you think of my mother's roses?"

She looked about her as she slid her hand through the crook of his arm. "She has so many. I think roses are beautiful, of course. One cannot find them otherwise. But I have never been in a garden that has so many."

"To the exclusion of most other plants," Lyness said with a shake of his head. "The different varieties cheer her. It means more colors, shapes, and different blooming seasons. At least, a little difference in seasons."

"It is a good occupation, I think, for anyone to garden. Or to work with living things." She looked down the row of rosebushes. "It makes me miss my own garden, though it was not so elegant, as an herbal garden."

That pulled an expression of interest from him, with his head tilted to one side and his eyebrows drawing together. "Herbal? And what did you do with your garden's bounty?"

"I made things. Useful things."

"Such as?" A smile tugged at his lips as he asked. "I am curious."

The genuine interest in his tone and eyes gave her leave to relax. "Simple things. Oils and tinctures. Home remedies for teas and aches. Nothing that would pass for ladylike accomplishment."

"But my lady, you are mistaken," he said so quickly she startled. He chuckled and ducked his head. "Forgive my enthusiasm, but ladies of all stations often devote a part of their time to herbal gardens. They make perfumes, medicines, artwork, all of it from their herbs and flowers. Most have stillrooms dedicated to such things, where they can dry their flowers and sort them into bottles or steam them into droughts. Has no one told you this?"

Her eyebrows crept higher with his words, she slowly shook her head. "No. But then, I suppose they were busy telling me all the things that I did not yet know about behavior. And I never thought to ask. I doubt my brother and sister-in-law even know of my interest, with Jack away so much from the family. I have made quite a show of weeding Juniper's gardens, though."

"We must amend that at once," he said quietly. "You ought to have your own stillroom."

Excitement bloomed in her heart. She had kept a stillroom, which was more the size of a closet, in her father's country house. She had distilled, steeped, dried, and preserved a variety of things for their family's use. The house her family had in London had a stillroom, but it was part of the housekeeper's responsibilities. She had seen it during the tour, and assumed that at her station she was not to bother with it, that only a housekeeper would see to such things in a noble household.

"You do not think it would be presumptuous to ask for one, truly? Or beneath my station to tend to such things?"

He shook his head adamantly. "No. Not at all. And I must confess, my lady, that I now wonder what other things you might enjoy that you have put aside without reason."

That pulled a soft laugh from her. "I cannot think of much else. I still draw, and that is one of my great joys, though I doubt I will ever feel confident enough to paint. Even though I am told watercolors are quite the thing for ladies."

"Watercolors, yes. But drawing itself…I do still wish to see more of your work. If you ever find you wish to share it. I am not a great artist—"

Here she interrupted him, a thing that most would consider terribly vulgar, and yet she could not help protesting. "But you are —I saw the placards in the curiosity cabinet your mother keeps. Your hand is elegant. We also agreed at the ruins that calligraphy is its own art."

Rather than appear put out by her outburst, his smile turned into a broad grin. The first she had seen from him, and she immediately matched it with her own. "I certainly enjoy it, but I cannot call it an art. Roman thinks it a waste of time, and I confess, there is no use for it beyond little things, like my mother's cabinet." He nodded in the direction of the house.

"Making words beautiful could never be useless," she argued immediately. "I would like to see something else you have done, besides those tiny cards for your mother."

"I would be delighted to show you. If you show me some of your sketches," he added with a gleam in his eye. "There now. That is a bargain, is it not?"

"No, that is terrible," she protested, though she could not help coloring the words with a laugh. "Mr. Eastwood, you will find nothing sophisticated in my drawings, I assure you. They are mostly from the countryside. Fields. Hedgerows. And cows, rather more often than I ought to admit. You saw the best of it at the abbey."

His chuckle warmed her. It was the first time she had heard such unguarded amusement from him. "Then you see beauty where others see labor," he said. "I think you will be pleasantly surprised by my interest in your art, Lady Emily. I am often at our country house. Indeed, I prefer it to York. I manage my family's estate while my brother sees to matters in the city and county. I enjoy the work, and it is a somewhat traditional role for younger brothers in my father's line."

"It must be fulfilling," she said, sobering somewhat. "Feeling essential in that way. I rather miss it, at times."

"Essential. That is the right word for it. Knowing I am protecting my family's interests and legacy is something." His smile faded and he looked toward the house. His tone turned wistful. "Sometimes, merely being useful feels like a defense of sorts. It keeps one from being overlooked. Or a burden on the family."

She met his gaze squarely when he looked at her again, her heart going out to him. "I understand that better than you think."

For a moment, they were quiet, looking at one another. She studied his gaze, the depth of his eyes, the sweep of his hair, and she wondered what thoughts filled his mind. If she asked, would he tell her? She was thinking, at that moment, of brushing a curl back from his forehead. Of telling him that he was not overlooked. That she saw him. That she rather liked him, too.

Except there was a sudden sound of boots on pavement, and they both turned to see Lord Hartwell coming down the path toward them.

"Ah, here you are, Lady Emily. Lyness. Mother wondered if you had managed to become lost in her garden." He sounded amused, and when he stopped before the two of them, he looked between them with interest. "Though I admit, it is far nicer out here than in the drawing room at present. There is an argument underway about whether we ought to dance, play charades, or continue in our own pursuits. I think they mean to put it to a vote, and we have need of you both to settle on how to fill the evening."

Mr. Eastwood had grown stiff as his brother spoke, and withdrew his arm from hers, tucking his hands behind his back. Something about his posture struck her as defensive. The tip of his head, when it occurred, deferential. It wasn't something she had seen from him before. "Of course. We will come inside at once. We were merely speaking of our enjoyment of fresh air. Country air."

Lord Hartwell extended his arm to Emily, and she took it after casting a glance at Lyness. "We will have plenty of that at the races soon enough. For now, there is company to keep indoors."

Something about the moment felt wrong. Stiff. And taking the elder brother's arm while the younger walked behind them did not sit well with her. The camaraderie with Mr. Eastwood vanished, and she found herself trying to remember her own polite expression and appropriate posture.

Lord Hartwell's manners were perfect, and he was quite handsome. Yet she already missed the less formal, more relaxed manner of Lyness, and the ease of his company. She never stopped to consider if her behavior was correct when they spoke. Why was that? Why could she not be as comfortable and confident with herself in the baron's company? Surely, she must be doing something wrong, and the guilt of that made her speak in a softer, apologetic tone.

"I hope we were not away too long. I have no wish to worry your mother. Her roses were so delightful, though, I quite forgot myself." A small exaggeration would not hurt, surely. It was better than admitting she preferred his brother's company to an entire party of people.

"You must tell her that," the baron said, a pleasantness to his tone. "She enjoys speaking of them in great detail."

It ought to have been simple to switch from one brother's company to the other. Especially given that both were kind and well mannered. Both intelligent. Lord Hartwell was the one she ought to give her own attention to, in full.

But her heart, foolish as it was, sunk in disappointment as she settled on a couch next to Lord Hartwell. The debate of how to spend the evening went on around her, without her contributing more than a smile and nod of agreement when others set the course for entertainment. A guessing game of sorts.

Emily looked for Mr. Eastwood and found him standing near his mother, head bowed, gaze unfocused toward the fireplace. That sight, the feeling that he had withdrawn in spirit if not in body, made her feel as though something precious had slipped away. And she did not like the mood it cast over her for the rest of the evening.

# Chapter Nine

The private dining room in Etridge's Royal Hotel, well-appointed with a view of Blakestreet broad windows for natural light, served the York Whig Club well. It was a perfect place for their larger meetings.

Lyness had no notion why the hotel had been chosen years ago as headquarters for the Whigs in favor of reform, but he dutifully attended with Roman whenever he was asked. Even if his mind was on other matters.

The evening of the dinner party had ended as most events did, with Roman at the fore, Mother satisfied, the company diverted, and Lyness precisely where no one would trip over him. He had liked being in the garden with Lady Emily better. Besides the quiet, he had enjoyed their discovery of shared pleasures.

But when Roman had appeared, Lyness followed the old, familiar pattern: withdraw, tidy the edges, let the plans of others resume. It was no tragedy. It was order. Still, as the guests debated charades versus dancing and the lamps glowed softly, he caught himself listening for her laugh. But he heard only the scrape of chairs, the voices of everyone else, the cheer of the company and not her individual mirth.

"It will do you good to be seen," Roman said as he joined Lyness at the window, bringing him back to the present moment in the hotel.

Roman had lately made himself a favorite subject of the *York Gazette*, and not for his tailoring. His habit of paying printers to publish essays on reform delighted some and unsettled others, which meant Lyness sometimes could not tell whether the smiles greeting them at such meetings were friendly or assessing.

Though weary from the previous evening and his thoughts, Lyness nodded. As loyally as ever. He would be useful, as he and Lady Emily had discussed. Wherever Roman required him. That, at least, he knew how to be.

Sir George Cayley, baronet and inventor of flying machines no one yet believed in, presided at the head of the table. At eight-and-forty, he was older than most present, and the rarest guest: their president in person.

Lyness liked Sir George a great deal, and he knew Roman admired the man's scientific mind. But Sir George lived thirty miles from York, which meant his attendance at any such events was rare. It left more work to people such as Roman to motivate the club members into action.

He was also, everyone knew, more middle-of-the-road than a true champion of reform. Not long ago, one of his remarks on the matter had been published in the paper. *"I am as firm a defender of the crown and the aristocracy in their proper spheres as I am a determined enemy to all encroachments upon commoners."*

Many in the club felt no man could be both. Yet the statement had drawn more moderates to their numbers, leaving Roman with the headache of feeling both gratitude and despair in equal proportions. Which meant Lyness, of course, had spent a few weeks cheering his brother up and taking up more duties with the estate's management.

This day did not seem as though it would have any particularly divisive topics shared. Roman was in his element, too. Talking trade, the Corn Laws, Catholic emancipation, and the upcoming York Races with practiced ease.

Lyness watched from his chair at the other end of the table from his brother, admiring him. Wondering how one brother commanded the attention of others so easily while the other could not even command his own tongue. Roman could speak for five minutes on any subject and convince a room he'd been born to lead the cause.

Admirable as Roman's abilities were, there were moments that Lyness wished things were different. He loved his brother, of course. Lyness supported Roman's political ambitions, and worked to maintain their shared heritage. Roman would have made their father proud. But Roman was, at times, so busy looking after everything except his own interests. He treated the city as though it were his life's blood, trying to preserve every historical structure and make all the arrangement, personally, for the continued prosperity of York. The growth of his party was his second greatest concern. It was no wonder he had put off marriage as long as he had. He was practically married to the medieval stones of the walls and minster.

And that made Lyness worry for how his brother's heart measured happiness.

The talk was spirited. Lyness did his best to keep track of who said what and who remained silent, the better to help Roman go over the relative success of the evening at a later time. This was one of his duties, though it had never been asked for by his brother.

It was Mr. Cooke, the only other man over forty-five present, who appeared cross that evening. He was irritable and grew more so as the rest of the party turned more cheerful. This Lyness watched with interest until Cooke himself stood to gain attention.

"While all this is very good, to discuss the things we have in common as though they are all that matter, we ought to give more attention to the upcoming races. For one thing, Lord Hartwell, there is talk the Conservatives mean to paint you and your circle of close friends—young members of the gentry and nobility both—as radicals. They say you have made enemies in the Church and are too cozy with the more radical progressives."

Roman kept his neutral expression as calm as ever, and he leaned back in his chair as though this troubled him not a whit. "Let them talk. I have no interest in their mudslinging or musings. York has better things to concern itself with than unfounded claims."

"Indifference is a luxury," Cooke retorted. "They will print it all the same, and half the county will believe you have taken up arms with the radicals."

"Words, not arms," Roman said. "If they mistake one for the other, it says more of them than me."

"What of the committee Mr. Walter Fawkes means to establish, during Race Week itself?" Phineas Nelson, also present with his older brother, asked from mid-way down the table. "He hopes to bring in more people to his committee precisely because of the races."

"Fawkes is more concerned with his bid to be High Sheriff of Yorkshire," Roman said with a coolness of tone that immediately stilled the room. "He has served well as Yorkshire's former M.P., but he has little interest in anything beyond his breeding of cattle and patronage to the arts. He is too tired to lead. And what is more, he plans to only invite those who are gentlemen or of higher rank. Which is completely the opposite of what we wish."

Lyness felt brief unease at his brother's easy dismissal of a man many knew had played a prominent part in ending the slave trade. Fawkes was not a loud man, but he held much respect in the county. And if his committee drew members of rank from the Whig Club, it could cause trouble for the future of their party.

Sir George gave a long sigh from his place at the head of the table. It was almost the first sound he had made since the conversation began in earnest. "Though we do need younger men such as yourself, Lord Hartwell, to lead the cause, it will not do to alienate more established men of greater reputation. You will forgive me for saying it, but you have yet to prove yourself outside of our fair city."

That made Lyness wince, and he saw the slight tick at Roman's jaw that meant the baron gritted his teeth against making a sharp response.

"We have invited Prince Augustus Frederick, Duke of Sussex, to lead our dinner during the race week," Roman reminded everyone present. "He has yet to accept the invitation, but I am certain he will agree. He presided over the Norwich Fox Dinner two years ago, and he is sympathetic to our cause. Having a brother of our king in attendance will bring all the respectability we need."

Lyness considered, for a moment, mentioning his own misgivings about that endeavor. The press for the York Whig Club had not been favorable of late. He kept up with the London papers, and they were hardly mentioned there except with the written equivalent of a smirk.

He did not wish to appear to undermine Roman, however, and so he was relieved when someone else voiced his question.

"What if the Duke of Sussex declines the invitation?" Mr. Thaddeus Nelson asked, eyes steady on Roman. "What then?"

For a moment, all were silent, waiting for an answer. Looking between their president, Sir George and Roman, their most vocal leader.

Finally, Sir George answered, "We will reschedule the dinner, of course, to a time that is more conducive to speaking as a collective body. Perhaps putting it around that the races were too much a distraction from our goals at the present time."

The tension in the room did not exactly dissolve, but a few tight nods made it possible to at least move forward in the conversation.

"The festivities during Race Week," Archibald Kettleburn said, hands steepled together before him, "are of concern to me. Not merely because I have horses racing, as you all know."

Good natured groans followed that statement. Archibald waved a hand to silence them, but with good humor, before he continued.

"It is a time when all our most prominent members will be in town. Gambling. Attending political meetings. Entertainments. I think it important that we stress keeping all our behavior above board. We are already reported in the papers as a club falling into disrepute."

"Only because we have common men as members," Sir George said with a huff. "A man doing an honest day's labor ought not be seen as disreputable. Quite the opposite."

"Nevertheless," Kettleburn continued, "if one of our most distinguished members should bring undo attention to himself, we may find the papers are more antagonistic than usual toward us. Can we at least voice the warning to our membership this evening, Sir George?"

That was not something Lyness had considered. Thankfully, he had nothing to worry about in Roman or himself. They were committed to upholding the family name in honor, doing all in their power not to summon the ire of good Society.

"We will say something," Sir George promised with a brief nod. "It will not go amiss to remind our men to be on their best behavior."

A gentleman on Lyness's other side turned to him with eyebrows raised. "You have been quiet all evening, Mr. Eastwood. You are one of the most level-headed members of our club. Have you anything to add?"

"Silence should not always be taken as good sense," Lyness said, trying for levity. This was not his sphere of expertise. "If you must know, I am considering how much to bet against Kettleburn's horses come Race Week."

Several of the others laughed, and even Roman nearly smiled at that. They had done a great deal of talking without making any decisions. Other than reminding an assembly of men to behave themselves, as though they were schoolboys let out on holiday for a picnic.

"I, for one, would rather speak of pleasanter things. Like the ball on Wednesday of Race Week," another younger, unmarried man said. "The loveliest ladies in the county and outside of it will be present."

"Ah, and speaking of fair ladies," Phineas said suddenly, turning to Roman. "Rumor has it, Hartwell, that you are entering the marriage mart."

Immediately, Lyness went stiff and still as a statue, hand tightening on his glass.

Roman shook his head in calm denial. "You should know better than to trust to rumor. And I would prefer not to have my private affairs discussed. But if it will satisfy the curiosity I can see come alive in all of you, I admit that I do mean to invite a certain lady to join me on an outing tomorrow."

The table hummed with amusement and curiosity.

But for Lyness, the words struck like a blow—he froze, his glass of wine half raised to his lips.

Some asked which lady, but Lyness already knew. Of course, Roman had not given up the idea of courting Lady Emily. Why had Lyness ever thought that he would? As the men's laughter and conversation dwindled, Lyness withdrew slightly, half-listening, his gaze on the fire.

"I heard she has a handsome marriage portion," Kettleburn murmured, arms crossed over his chest. "I have yet to meet her myself. Though her brother is a good chap."

"Lady Emily Sterling is deserving of better than to be discussed by us," Thaddeus said with a small shake of his head. "I would not wish my sisters speculated about in a room full of men who do not know them. We ought to limit our subjects to matters we know more about."

"You would have us sit in silence, then?" his brother Phineas quipped.

That brought about more laughter, but the conversation moved along.

Lyness sat quietly, berating himself. He should have acted sooner. But if Roman made known to Lady Emily that he wished to court her, it would be a betrayal for Lyness to ask the same. And Roman needed someone steady and calm, someone kind and thoughtful, as his wife. Lady Emily would certainly suit. And their mother would delight in teaching her how to be a leader in York society.

He had come to the meeting keep his brother company, supportive as always—and would leave with the uncomfortable certainty that he'd lost his own peace in the process.

# Chapter Ten

## August 14, 1822

A soft, almost hesitant trill came from the canary, and Emily looked up from her breakfast with a startled gasp. "Did you hear?" she whispered, afraid to startle the bird. "Miss Feathersby. She sang. A little."

Juniper smiled into her teacup. "Perhaps she is merely adjusting to her new situation. In time, we may have a delightful morning accompaniment to our breakfasts."

From his seat, Jack looked up at the bird with raised eyebrows. "She is more pleasant than I thought she would be. I caught her watching me as I read yesterday. When I made eye contact, she fluttered as though pleased. I wonder what fool let her free in the ruins." He shook his head slightly. "It is a good thing you were there, Emily."

"I agree," Emily said with perfect satisfaction, then ventured, "And I am glad that Mr. Eastwood happened by with his hat."

"Indeed." Juniper lowered her teacup to the table. "A series of fortunate events that ended with a happy addition to our lives. And speaking of the Eastwood family, I think Jack had word from their household this morning." She raised her eyebrows at her husband. "Or have you already told Emily about the note that arrived?"

Jack reached into his coat to withdraw a folded square of paper. "I nearly forgot. Thank you for the reminder, my love. Emily, this is for you."

Upon spying the square, Emily's hopes raised. Had Mr. East-wood written? Perhaps he had sent her a sample of his calligraphy.

Her brother's next words dashed that idea quickly.

"It came from Lord Hartwell."

"Oh." She accepted the paper from him.

Something of her disappointment must have shown on her face. Before she unfolded the note, Jack said in an earnest, practical sort of way, "He is a sensible fellow, Emily. I have always liked him. He is steady. His life is well-ordered. He commands respect among his peers."

She unfolded the square without giving more than a nod in response.

"You seem determined to speak in favor of Lord Hartwell," Juniper said, tone light. "Emily is not in any great hurry to secure suitors, Jack."

The two continued speaking of her prospects while Emily read the note.

To the Honorable Mr. John Sterling,

If you would grant me the privilege of escorting your sister, Lady Emily, I should like to take her on a drive through York this afternoon. There are many places in this town of historical note and current interest. If Lady Emily is amenable, and with your permission, I will arrive in a gig at half-past two.

Yours in Friendship, etc.,

*Roman Eastwood, Baron Hartwell*

As she read, her eyes grew wider and her fingers tightened on the paper. Why did the baron want to take her on an outing? What had she done to inspire such an idea? She had behaved with politeness, but she certainly had not offered encouragement. Had she?

Before she could guard against the thought, she wished for a moment that the note had come from Lyness Eastwood instead. A notion she swiftly dismissed.

She folded the paper again and looked up at Jack. "Do you think I ought to go on a ride with him like that? In public? A gig is only built for two riders. There will be no chaperone."

If she hoped he would disapprove of the outing, that was quickly dashed.

"You will remain in the open air," Jack noted. "Which is permissible, especially as you are in public, so long as you conduct yourself appropriately. I have never had cause to worry about such a thing with you, Emily." One of Jack's rare, though encouraging, smiles appeared. "I think you will enjoy it. No one knows this city so intimately as Hartwell. He is an honorable, steady, reliable man. He has noticed you, too. Which proves he is a man of sense."

Emily listened dutifully, hands folded, trying to smile at her brother's compliment. Her mind was torn: she wanted to please Jack but felt nothing when she thought of Roman Eastwood. No spark of curiosity. No niggling interest. He smiled less than Jack, and though she loved her brother dearly, she often wondered what went on his thoughts that kept him from expressing cheer more. Perhaps it was merely habit not to, from his time as a servant.

"I think he will court you in earnest, Emily," Jack said when she remained silent, his brows drawn together. "If you give him encouragement."

The bold statement made her blush, and her lips parted, but she could not think what to say.

As though sensing her sister-in-law's discomfort, Juniper spoke with more lightness of feeling than her husband had. "An honorable, steady, reliable man is certainly the sort of things one wants in a husband. But it is not the whole of things. Nor ought it to be, Jack. There is so much more to a happy match than that."

Jack's smile returned when he looked at his wife, the expression softer now, and his shoulders rose in a slight shrug. "We must all begin somewhere practical, wife. Mustn't we?"

"Yes. What every woman wants to hear in regards to a suitor. 'Practical,'" she said with pursed lips as she lifted her teacup again. "Do you think that is why I fell in love with you, Jack? Practicality?"

That made the man blink, his head tilting back as though startled. "Well. No. I suppose not."

"No, indeed. It is a good trait in a husband, but hardly the most romantic one to focus on. I favored your intensity, as well as your honor, and your loyalty toward those you love."

To Emily's surprise, her brother's ears turned pink.

"I am certain, er, that the baron—well. He must have other good qualities."

"Certainly. But Emily must find those for herself. If she even wishes to do so." Juniper tilted her head toward Emily. "Well? What do you think? Do you wish to go on a tour of York this afternoon? With the baron as your guide?"

Emily looked from Juniper's raised eyebrows to Jack's pointed stare. She put the square of paper on the table and lifted her fork to resume eating her now-cold eggs.

She gave the best answer she could. "A ride with Lord Hartwell sounds like a pleasant way to spend the afternoon." Perhaps she needed to know the baron better to feel as at ease with Roman Eastwood as she was with his younger brother. He was all the things a respectable man ought to be, and Jack liked him, and her family would benefit from a match with such an established family as the Eastwoods.

A practical marriage would not be the worst future for her. And such a union began with a practical courtship. Not everyone could have a love match, like Jack and Juniper. Even if Emily wanted such a thing, there was no promise of obtaining it.

"Excellent." Jack's smile melted into something that looked like relief.

A stone dropped heavily into her stomach. Relief? Was he so

eager to see her wed? A glance at Juniper showed her sister-in-law as poised as ever. If only Emily had been born into her position. Then she might have had half of Juniper's ability to remain calm and graceful no matter her feelings.

"I will write to Hartwell at once and let him know you have accepted his invitation," Jack added when Emily said nothing, pushing his chair away from the table as he rose. "Half-past two. Do not forget."

"I do not think I could," she admitted, that stone in her stomach settling deeper.

At the appointed time, she stood on the steps of her brother's cottage, next to Juniper, waiting for the baron to arrive in his gig.

"Your brother means well," Juniper said, hands folded around her gothic novel. "He wants you to be safe and looked after by someone he trusts. And, given your family is still finding their footing in Society, he feels it is his responsibility to help you secure a good match. Whether or not you wish for one, at present."

"I have no objection to marrying. I am five-and-twenty. I do not feel too young to know my own mind, nor too old. I am not yet on the shelf, as they say." Emily fidgeted with the strings of her reticule, twisting them around each other rather than leaving it on her wrist. "I want to make Jack and my parents proud. Everyone else in my family is still coping with our elevation in status. If I marry well, it is one less thing for anyone to worry about."

Juniper's entire person turned toward her at that, her eyes round. "Dear me. Is that what you think?"

The sound of wheels on gravel grew nearer, and both turned to see the gig coming up the short drive from the road to the cottage.

"He is here," Emily breathed, absently tying the strings into a knot that would not come undone easily. "I must go."

"Yes, darling." Juniper touched her arm, pulling Emily's attention back to her. "But listen to me, Emily. You should not court or wed anyone if you do not like them, or do not want to. Your happiness matters most of all."

What could she say as the carriage pulled to a stop? She nodded and leaned forward, giving Juniper a quick kiss on the cheek. "Thank you. I will think on that." Then she went to the gig, where Lord Hartwell waited to help her up, his expression as stoic as always, and he touched the brim of his hat as he nodded to Juniper.

"I will have her back in an hour, my lady."

"I hope you enjoy yourselves." Juniper waved empty hand, though her eyes met Emily's one more time, laden with concern. "It sounds like you will have a most educational drive."

The gig, open to the air around them, was well sprung. Taller than she was used to, it gave her a lovely view of the surrounding countryside. The leather was so polished it shone, and the rest of the vehicle gleamed as though it were new from the maker. Two horses, matching grays, pulled it. For a moment, she worried he might drive faster than was safe. Though the model was not as sleek as those she had seen young men racing down the lane, it was frightfully stylish.

But Roman Eastwood did not startle her with a wild dash down the road. He gave the horses gentle enough direction, and they clipped along at a steady, unhurried pace.

"I am pleased you agreed to this outing," he said as they left the cottage behind. "I confess, I was uncertain you felt you knew me well enough to spend an hour in my company alone. We have not made much conversation between the two of us yet."

"No, I do not suppose we have." Emily put effort into keeping her tone pleasant and light. "I am thankful for the invitation. York is such a delightful town, and it seems I learn of some new piece of history every time I walk down its streets. I admit, after my conversation with your mother on the New Walk, I thought it more likely she would be the one to give me such a tour."

With the mid-afternoon sunlight warming her shoulders, and a cheerful breeze at her back, there was really no reason why she could not enjoy herself. When people passed the gig, they always nodded politely or called out a greeting to Lord Hartwell. He was well known, it seemed, and liked.

A woman could do much worse.

"My mother loves this city as much, if not more, than I do," he said with fondness, and he almost smiled, too. Or she thought he had. At least his eyes were bright with merriment. Perhaps Jack liked him so much because neither of them smiled all that often. "But my mother also prefers gardening to gossip, and what is history, but ancient gossip and fact twisted around each other?"

That startled a laugh from her. "Is your tour to be full of fact or fiction, my lord?"

"Yes to both," he answered, his head tilted slightly to one side as he looked at her. "How can we know what is fact, hear say, or rumor if we were not there?"

"I suppose that would be difficult, without multiple witnesses sharing the same details of the story," she said, surprised that he had spoken with more lightness than usual.

Lord Hartwell cleared his throat. "Ahem. But I will do my best to impart only the most interesting information to you, my lady, that is generally accepted as fact. At least among those of us who love the old city. We will begin, of course, at the eye of the city. Clifford's Tower."

The tower he named had been in position for hundreds of years. Not the exact one that stood at present, he explained, as the whole thing had been torn down and rebuilt several times.

"It is an impressive piece of York Castle, and once it was the heart of the city's defenses. The Normans built it soon after the Conquest, on a man-made mound—steep and surrounded by a moat in its day. The tower itself is an odd shape, formed from four connected circles. On maps, it looks like a quatrefoil."

She winced slightly. "I am afraid I do not know what that is, my lord."

"They are everywhere in medieval architecture," he explained, slowing the horses to a stop. "Here. Make two circles with your hands, like this." He demonstrated, curving forefinger to touch thumb in a circle. "Now, make them touch. Good. Here are mine on either side."

Emily was grateful for their gloves as they created the shape, which still took her a moment to place. The awkwardness of the touch did not escape her, slight as it was. Why could she not feel a rush of affection? A blush from the brush of their hands? A flutter of her heart? But nothing stirred within her except vague interest in the subject they discussed.

"Oh. Yes. I have seen this shape in churches. I did not think to ever give it a name, though."

"I am, perhaps, focusing on irrelevant details." His brow furrowed.

"Not at all." He certainly was, but she tried her best to smile politely. "You obviously know a great deal about the city. And architecture."

That compliment seemed to cheer him, as he continued his explanation with more exuberance. "That mound the tower stands upon was originally much steeper, with a drawbridge leading up to the entrance. Inside, the lower floor served the soldiers, and the upper rooms were for the castellan and chapel. The walls are almost nine feet thick in places—solid enough to have withstood centuries of neglect. As you can see. If you would like, I could one day arrange for a tour of the inside."

"Oh. That would be something." She looked at the ruins with hesitation. "Is it safe?"

"Completely safe. Though the tower has been through quite a bit. Fires, sieges, executions, and even time as a prison. Inside you can still find the royal arms of Charles the Second above the entrance, right beside the Clifford family crest—hence the name." His eyes took in the sight, attention fully on the lone tower. "The rest of the old castle is not as impressive. Henry the Eighth's survey called it 'five ruinous towers,' which seems generous. Clifford's Tower is the last of the taller towers to stand watch. From up there, you can see the Foss and Ouse Rivers and half of York besides. It is not a bad view—though I wouldn't envy anyone who once had to defend it."

She looked at the tower with some measure of appreciation. "It is alarming, at times, how very old the world in which we live can feel. It makes me think myself quite small."

"Really? I find it exhilarating, to be a piece of a long history," he said, driving them onward.

Had she mis-stepped in sharing her own feelings? He passed over them so quickly, she could not be certain. She fixed her smile in place again, adjusted her posture, and kept her eyes ahead of her while he told her of the city.

He singled out other smaller places of note, where a person of historical significance was said to have slept or done business, until they reached a street where he gestured at a large building that looked as old as the kingdom itself.

"The Merchant Adventurers Hall, standing since the time of Queen Elizabeth." He pointed to the long, timber-and-thatch structure with as much pride as though he had built it himself. "A building that has stood the test of time, and is still used for its original purpose. Mostly."

"It is rather impressive," she admitted, and thoroughly wished she knew more about Queen Elizabeth. Or buildings. Or anything, really, that seemed to excite the man at her side.

Next it was the Shambles, where she covered her nose with her handkerchief.

"All the butchers, tanners, and those whose crafts connect to theirs, have been along this little alley since the city was built. Look at the structures at the top. There are two houses down at the end where you could shake the hand of your neighbor across the way, reaching out of an upstairs window."

"It is quite narrow," she said, and felt her stomach turn slightly. "And butchers have always had their business there?" she asked weakly. Though she had not thought herself one to have a sensitive stomach, the sight of blood going down the lane and into the gutter at that very moment made her wince. The smell was potent, too. "Convenient. That they all are in one place."

He glanced at her, then looked again, and his expression changed more dramatically than she had seen thus far. He went from pleasantly neutral in expression to stoically concerned, given the furrow of his brow and downturn of his lips. He leaned toward her.

"Are you unwell, Lady Emily?" He moved the horses along. "I did not think—I apologize. I forget that there are those of a more delicate constitution than myself. I become fascinated by the history and forget the sensations of the moment."

She waved her hand a little. "It will pass. I do not usually possess such sensitivity. Perhaps it is the excitement of the afternoon." Emily felt her cheeks warm from the falsehood. She had not felt any measure of excitement. Not even once. Gratitude, perhaps, and vague interest. But that was the best she could say for it.

In all honesty, she felt somewhat stupid for not knowing enough history to follow some of the stories he told.

"Right. If you think you are well enough, I thought we would continue to the Minster?" He sounded uncertain now.

"Oh. Yes. The Minster," she said quickly. "A beautiful, marvelous place. I have been only once, for Sunday services, with my brother and sister-in-law during my first week in York."

He nodded slowly. "My family attends there as often as we can," he said softly. "Though there are many, many churches in York to choose from. Some only go to whatever building is closest, but… yes. I have been to nearly all of them." He faced forward again, and they arrived at the Minster Yard.

"Here we are. The most beautiful place in York." His voice softened as they drew up before the cathedral, but his whole posture seemed to come alight. The reins slackened in his hands.

For a long moment, they sat and looked up at the spectacular building.

"It always gives me a sense of great awe," Lord Hartwell said at last, "to look on something this large, beautiful, and complex, and know that it was built centuries ago with tools and contrivances that we would now consider quaint."

She let her eyes linger on the building's fine structure, the sweeps of it, and a reverence for such faith-inspired work made her feel, for the first time since climbing into the gig, a sense of peace.

Lord Hartwell spoke quietly as he said, "York Minster. It's been standing in one form or another for nearly a thousand years, they say. The earliest church here was wooden, according to old records, built for the baptism of a Saxon king. The present Minster took centuries to complete—every generation adding its own mark until they finally called it finished in the fifteenth century. Though of course, no one ever truly finishes a cathedral; they only pause between repairs." The corners of his mouth twitched as though he wanted to smile.

She smiled for him. It was a clever quip. A sign of humor in an otherwise serious man. Did he never laugh? She had not heard him emit such a sound.

"Look at it," he went on, voice full of awe. "The windows alone could humble a man. The great east window is the largest expanse of medieval stained glass in the Kingdom. Perhaps in all of Europe, though Rome may have something to say to that. They say the sunlight shining through it can make even a heathen feel devout for a moment."

It was the most heartfelt thing she had heard him say, and she found herself watching him instead of the building. What else inspired a man such as he? And did he ever look at people, at anyone at all, the way he stared at the landmarks of his beloved city?

He cleared his throat and looked down at the ribbons in his hand. He gave them a shake and the horses started moving once more. "The towers rise two hundred and twenty-five feet above the street, and the bells can be heard for miles. If you stand close enough on a still morning, you can feel the sound in your chest. It's difficult not to be impressed, really. The people of York may quarrel over politics or the price of wheat, but on this, at least, they agree—the Minster belongs to everyone."

Turning the gig toward the edge of town, he maneuvered the

horses and vehicle through the half-crowded streets with the ease of a man who had navigated them all his life.

"We did not see everything, of course," he said as they crossed a bridge over the River Ouse, going southwest toward her brother's home. "But I have lived here my whole life and still find new things to enjoy about my city."

"I do not think I have ever met someone who loves the place he lives as much as you do, my lord," she admitted.

He winced slightly, and she wondered if she had said something wrong. "I am rather zealous in my devotion to her. I cannot explain why, exactly. But yes. York is dear to me, in heart and mind. I would stand on its walls this very moment, if necessary, to protect her."

She could not think of much to say to that, though she found it admirable. It was noble, that sort of loyalty. But she suspected she would have spent the same night tending the wounded rather than defending the stones.

Emily let the silence stretch between them for a time, and when they finally passed out into the countryside, where birdsong met her ears, she felt some of the tension in her hands ease. She did not grip the strings of her reticule as tightly.

She also found a new topic of conversation to introduce. "My brother is looking forward to the races next week. I imagine those are important to the city. The merchants must do a vast deal of trade, and the inns are likely all full to bursting."

"Most years, yes," he said, brow furrowed.

Had she said something wrong *again*?

"There are some that say the races are less popular now than they were a decade ago, but I wonder if it is only old men thinking everything was better in their youth." He shook his head slightly. "We will see. The Duke of Sussex often attends, with many of his friends, and that is always a boon for York. Members of the Royal Family tend to scatter their wealth liberally when seeking enter-tainment." He blinked and looked at her with sudden shock. "I beg your pardon. I should not discuss such matters with you, my lady.

They are dull indeed. Conversations about the economy cannot be of any interest. You asked about the races."

She had not minded in the least. It had sounded interesting. But she adjusted her posture. "I understand there will be a ball?"

"Yes. On Wednesday. I hope you plan to attend." Then he cleared his throat. "And I should like to invite your family to join mine in the Grandstand. We always watch from the second tier. I would enjoy your company during the races."

"I am certain my brother will know which day would be best for such a thing," she said without committing herself. And that was the end of the conversation, as they had arrived at her brother's house. He handed her out of the gig, tipped his hat as she curtsied, and then he was gone the moment she closed the door behind her.

She leaned against it and sighed with relief.

He was everything Jack admired, everything a practical woman could want—and nothing about him made her curiosity stir. Her heart was completely unaffected.

# Chapter Eleven

"Completely unaffected?" Juniper repeated as they walked through the back of the garden, where the carefully cultivated flowerbeds gave way to more wild-looking plants before blending in to a stretch of woods. "Oh dear. And you are not ill? No headache? You mentioned the Shambles made your stomach turn, and I confess they do the same to me."

"Not ill," Emily confirmed. "And no headache until mid-way through, when I felt certain I was disappointing him with my lack of enthusiasm for very old buildings." Her shoulders fell. She knelt and turned a leaf over in her hands, checking the stem of the plant. "Chamomile." She used her gardening sheers to take a cutting for her basket.

Though Emily wished she had a better report to give her sister-in-law, honesty seemed best. She ought to have felt flattered, at the least, by Lord Hartwell's attention. Instead, she felt...nothing. Which was a shame. Jack liked him. The baron seemed to be a good person. There must be many ladies who would be flattered by his attention.

She simply was not one of them.

Juniper shook her head slightly. "After you left, Jack spoke to me at length about his concerns for you. They are not unusual, you know. He is trying to be a responsible, caring brother. I warned him he might be pushing you too much to Lord Hartwell, but he seemed certain you would like him the better you came to know him. I thought, perhaps, giving him a chance…" She shook her head. "But no. Oh dear. What will you say if he asks you on another outing?"

That gave Emily pause. Finally, looking down at a knot of clover the gardener had missed, she said, "I will accept his kind invitation, of course."

It was her duty to find a husband, was it not? Alleviating her family's worries over her future.

"But—" Juniper bent with her and put her hand on Emily's wrist. "—you do not like him."

"I do not dislike him," Emily pointed out. "Jack is right about many things. Lord Hartwell is a steady, honorable man. A woman could do worse for herself. Especially given that there are so many who would wed me for my marriage portion. Or think to take advantage of the lack in my knowledge about Society."

The money was something that often plagued her thoughts. She had gone from being a woman with no worries and no funds to being a lady with fifteen thousand pounds settled upon her after marriage. It was a sum she could not even imagine possessing, yet her father's title and estate had enough to settle the same on all his children, including her two older, already married sisters.

With a frown and both fists going to her hips, Juniper spoke in a corrective tone. "Emily. That is not a good enough reason to wed—"

"Mr. Eastwood is here to pay a call to you, Lady Emily," their butler said.

Emily's head came up so fast it nearly cracked against Juniper's. Emily straightened and brushed her gardening gloves off on her apron.

"Oh." Juniper was slightly shaking her head. "We are not fit to be seen. He must call again, when we—"

"I will see him," Emily said in a rush, stuffing her gloves in her apron pocket and untying the protective covering. "I can go right away. I am still mostly put together from my outing with his brother." She heard her words, recognized the somewhat problematic nature of them, and shook her head. "I will walk with him. Down the lane. It will only be for a few minutes, I am certain."

The butler looked from Juniper to Emily without a word or a flicker of emotion. He waited for direction. Finally, Juniper sighed. "All right. You may walk with him."

So it was that she went through the house to where he waited in a small sitting room by the front door. Smoothing her hair as she went, trying not to run. She had to maintain some decorum in the way she walked, lest she appear overeager or uncouth or…some other ill-mannered sort of thing.

As her lungs tightened from excitement, however, and she paused. "Oh dear," she whispered to herself, turning to a looking glass hanging on the wall, right beside the door that hid Mr. Eastwood from view. The excitement of a brief walk down the lane with this brother far outstripped her excitement of an hour's carriage ride with the other.

Something was terribly wrong with her. But she could not examine the problem at the length it deserved. Not presently. She opened the door to where her caller waited.

Lyness Eastwood stood in the room, looking out the window facing the front drive, and he turned when she entered. His smile appeared immediately, and he bowed without looking away from her. "Lady Emily. Good afternoon."

A quick curtsy managed, she came forward with hands tucked behind her back. "Mr. Eastwood, welcome. I did not expect a visit from you today. I hope you are well?"

"Q-quite well. I ought to have asked, I know, but I was reading today and came upon interesting advice for canary keeping." It was then she realized he'd kept one hand tucked behind his back, and now he drew it forward to reveal a small, brown-paper wrapped parcel. "I learned that canaries enjoy their own reflection. I thought Miss Feathersby might appreciate a gift."

She took the parcel and unwrapped it, finding a small framed mirror inside, with a hook affixed to the back, making it easy to hang. "Oh, it will suit her cage perfectly." She looked up at him. "Thank you." She bit her lip, then said, "I told my sister-in-law that we would walk down the lane, since she is unable to chaperone at present. Otherwise, I would take you to see Miss Feathersby right away—"

"A walk with you would be delightful," he said calmly, his eyes on hers, his lips upturned. "You can tell me how she likes it another time."

She put the mirror and its wrapping down on a table beneath the window, then gestured to the open doorway. "Shall we?"

He walked with her, taking his hat from the butler while she accepted a bonnet and gloves. They walked out into the late afternoon light, and she took in a deep breath.

"I am sorry if I seemed out of breath at first," she said finally. "I was working in the gardens when you came, toward the wooded portion of my brother's property."

His eyebrows raised. "Working, is it? What were you up to? Sketching? Attacking weeds?"

"Gathering wildflowers and herbs," she said with enthusiasm, "because I asked Juniper, after our last meeting, if it was true. That a lady could run her own stillroom. I had never discussed my enjoyment of such work with her before, you see. I have been setting one up off the kitchen ever since. It is merely a second pantry with the smallest of windows, but it has shelves and hooks aplenty."

That brought a chuckle from him. "I am glad to hear it. You seemed rather forlorn before, when you thought you had given it up forever. I hope you will find joy in it again." The sincerity with which he spoke made warmth spread from her heart to her chest, in the most pleasant way, until she felt it in her cheeks. "I will need a list of your stores, of course, so I know which tinctures and teas you will have for curing my ills."

"I am hardly an apothecary, Mr. Eastwood," she protested, though the thought pleased her.

Lowering his voice, as though to share a secret, he said, "That means you will offer me your potions at no charge. As a second son, I can hardly resist such an ideal situation."

That coaxed a small giggle from her, and she immediately hid her smile behind one gloved hand. "Very well. I will offer you my cures for stomach ache, nightmares, and eye bruises without asking one ha'penny for them. In return, however, you must help me label my bottles. You have beautiful penmanship, so I believe it is a fair trade."

"Indeed, it sounds quite fair." The pleasure in his eyes, the upward tug of his lips, even the easy way he shortened his stride to walk with her, made her want to thank him. Merely for being him. For setting her at ease in ways she could not explain.

The tension she had carried since breakfast had melted away, completely. He had thought of her—or, sort of. He had thought of Miss Feathersby. But he had remembered Emily's fondness for herbal work and stillrooms. He had even jested with her in a way her own brothers could not manage. She felt more herself when Mr. Eastwood spoke to her, and had from their first meeting in London.

What did that mean about the lack of such ease with his brother? Was she not trying hard enough? Or was Lord Hartwell the problem?

They made it to a curve in the lane when he suggested turning back. Marking that their times was half gone, much to her disappointment.

"Are you attending the races?" she asked him. "Or the ball on Wednesday? Or any of the events? It sounds as though York will be full of things to do and see."

At first, he did not answer. His cheerful demeanor seemed to dim, then turn into an expression she did not have a name for. It was still warm, still him, but he was less present for a moment.

"Mr. Eastwood?" she said softly. Had she given offense, somehow? Or was he trying to form an excuse for not being present? Her mind jumped to half a dozen other possibilities while waiting for his response.

He blinked and shook his head, as though he needed to dislodge his thoughts. "I beg your pardon. You asked if I would attend any of the race week events? Yes, I believe I will. Almost anywhere my brother goes, I will go. And he would not miss the pleasure of seeing York and its citizens truly shine. What about you, my lady?"

"I believe our family will join yours for some of the races," she said, studying him carefully. The strange pause concerned her, but he did not wish to address it. She let it go. "Of course we will be at the ball, and I have hopes of doing so many things. Plays. Galleries. It sounds better than the Season in London, in all honesty. Because the city will be full of interesting things to do, and it will only last a week."

That brought another smile to his face, though his eyes remained somewhat soft. "Your experience during the Season did not give you a high opinion of it, I take it."

"It did not," she said, raising her chin. "The only good points were the few new friends I made. And my brother courting Lady Juniper, of course."

"Of course." He tucked his hands behind his back, focused his eyes on the cottage as they approached it. "I hope you count me among the good points, then."

"I do," she answered at once, and far too quickly to be considered demure. "One of the very best of them." Her tongue had completely run away from her, it would seem.

But he did not take offense, nor did he laugh as though she had told an outlandish joke. Instead, he turned his head to take her in, that same gentle look in his eyes as he said, "I count you a good point in my year as well, Lady Emily. One of the very best."

That warmth spread through her again, beginning deeper,

lasting longer. And she wished in that moment, with her whole heart, that Roman Eastwood stirred half so much feeling in her as his younger brother did at that moment.

When he took his leave not long after returning her to the door, she watched him ride away on his horse. Her heart felt lighter, her body more relaxed, her mind clearer. And yet, after he disappeared from sight, it all turned. Curled up inside her, like all the good feelings he inspired wanted to hide and let disappointment take their place.

Plucking up the mirror from where she had left it, Emily went through to the drawing room where the little bird sat in her cage, quietly watching a maid tidy the room. The canary seemed to perk up when Emily approached and carefully unlatched the door.

She reached inside with the mirror, hooking it just so, letting it hang above the canary's perch.

Miss Feathersby brightened at once, trilling to the brave little bird she found in her reflection. Smiling, Emily eased the door shut and felt the faint catch of the latch beneath her fingers.

It was a kindness, she told herself. Safety for the tiny creature. But as the song rose, clear and sweet, she could not help thinking how neatly a bird with clipped wings learned to love the limits it was given.

THE HOUSE HAD GONE STILL.

It was the kind of quiet that pressed in from every direction. There was no whisper of conversation, no footsteps on the stair, only the soft sigh of curtains moving in the breeze and the tick of the clock upon the mantel. The dogs had long since settled themselves before the hearth, waiting for Roman's return from dinner with a friend. Apollo's massive head rested on his paws, and Athena lay near Lyness's chair, a guardian even in sleep.

Lyness sat at his desk with a single candle guttering beside him, casting a pool of light across the scattered sheets of paper. He had told himself he meant only to write a few notes before bed. A letter, perhaps, to his mother's gardener about the country house's accounts. But the page before him bore no such practical purpose.

At its top, in his finest hand, was a name.

*Lady Emily Sterling.*

The first attempt had been neat enough. Modest flourishes, measured spacing, as though it were merely an exercise. Practice. The second attempt grew more elaborate. The lines of her name lengthened into leafy chamomile stems, the final *g* trailing away into a stem that descended along the edge of the page in a petaled flower. By the third iteration, the letters became something else entirely. Emotion made visible. The ink lines wove upon themselves, too heavy in places, too ornate, until the whole thing turned into a tangle of dark lines that meant more to him than anyone else would ever understand.

He had spoiled the page and not minded at all.

The truth sat there, unblinking, no matter how many times he changed nibs or wiped his fingers clean. He wanted—foolishly, perhaps—to think of her. To recall the light in her eyes when she spoke of her garden, her laughter when she teased him, the way she looked at him without pity when his words stumbled and skipped all over themselves.

He lifted his pen again, almost absently, and began anew. Just her name. Smaller this time. More controlled. Yet his hand shook when he tried to add the finishing stroke. The ink bled where it shouldn't. He pressed his thumb to the blot and left a dark mark there. A stain he could not remove.

It was absurd. He had no right to think of her with such tenderness. His brother had noticed her, spoken well of her, and even called on her. Roman would make an excellent husband for any woman, and if Lady Emily were wise, she would see that. The baron had charm, rank, purpose, and so many other things Lyness lacked.

Though he had the financial means of setting up a modest household, thanks to the competence he earned from the investment of his inheritance. It would never be as much as Roman had, with the family estate and wealth, but Lyness could afford a family. And he had considered the idea several times, though he hesitated to act on it. In part because Roman and his mother seemed to need him.

Perhaps it had been a convenient excuse, or a series of them, to avoid courtship. Because there were things about himself that he did not entirely wish to expose to others. What if a wife grew tired of his stuttering? Or questioned why they spent so much time in York rather than in the glittering ballrooms of London? What if she did not understand his mother's need to keep her sons close?

He rubbed at his chest as the old concerns spilled out of his thoughts. He set down the pen and leaned back, the ache behind his ribs steady and familiar now. To love anything, whether it was beauty, art, or a woman, seemed always to demand the same thing of him. His silence.

He folded the page carefully, though the ink was still damp, and tore it into pieces. Best to rid himself of the evidence of his feelings. If anyone saw what he had done, they would think him absurd. Or ask questions. Or perhaps laugh, not understanding what it did to him to think of her.

He was utterly ridiculous.

Across the room, Apollo gave a low, contented sigh. The fire cracked softly. Lyness rose with the scraps of paper in his hand. He went to the hearth, and Athena lifted her head to watch him. He crouched low and scattered the paper along the embers, then took up the poker to stir up the flames again.

Orange and yellow fire licked at the paper, curling it at the edges, then caught it. Devoured each and every ink-stained shred.

Lyness stared at the wavering flames until his eyes blurred.

Athena came closer to him, sat down, and whined softly. Bringing him out of his depressing thoughts.

The words he would not speak gathered in his throat anyway. Words meant for no one, or perhaps for whatever Fate had decreed his must be born second.

"May my brother make her happy."

He put the poker in its place, then wrapped his arm around Athena and buried his face in her neck. The dog, sweet in her loyalty, did not move as his heart cracked in two and his tears fell on her coat.

# Chapter Twelve

## August 19th, 1822 - Race Week

One of the worst lies Lyness Eastwood had ever told was to himself. He reflected on this as he stood with his brother at the race track, looking out over the crowd, watching for a particular person to arrive.

The sunlight set off the pale stone arches of the Knavesmire Grandstand well enough that he could imagine what it looked like in its heyday, nearly a century before. The murmur of voices echoing beneath the vaulted arcade, the scent of dust and horses carried on the wind, was familiar in a way that ought to bring comfort.

But his own thoughts distracted him.

The lie he told himself was simple. It was that there was no harm in being a friend to Mr. Jack Sterling and his sister, Lady Emily Sterling. As he had determined to believe that lie, he had repeated it when visiting her twice between the night his heart broke and that very day. The first time he visited was brief. He brought her a book on botany. The illustrations were beautiful, the information helpful, and her pleasure on receiving the book made it worth the pain of pretending he had no greater interest in her than friendship. The second time he visited was to give her strips of paper with his writing samples on it, to ask which she preferred to use for her bottled herbs.

He was delighted that she had continued to insist he make the labels for her stillroom ingredients.

Delighted. Like a fool.

Given her obvious pleasure, though, he could not help but smile even as he took himself to task. Her eyes had glowed with excitement, and she had looked over his samples with an attention to detail that no one had given his handwriting since his time at Harrow.

"I have not seen the Sterling party yet," Roman said at his side, glancing down again somewhat casually. He leaned against the rail of the balcony, studying the building behind them. "I am glad someone thought to touch up the old building. The new paint brings her up to date. But something must be done about the chips in the staircases. I have heard some argue for an addition, but perhaps an entirely new building would be wiser."

"And more expensive," Lyness muttered from where he looked over the rail. "Doncaster's races are growing in popularity. And I hate to say it, Roman, but the crowd does not look as large this year as the last."

Roman turned to rest his elbows on the railing and let his clasped hands hang over the crowd below, for a moment looking like a supplicant about to ask the heavens for divine help. "The Duke of Sussex rejecting our invitation to speak at the Whig dinner did not help matters."

Yes, that had been a blow to Roman and all the members of the Whig club. The news had leaked, too, and their political rivals were practically celebrating this mark against more progressive ideas.

Changing the subject seemed advisable. "I am surprised you prevailed upon Mother to attend today with us."

A slight shrug came before Roman's answer. "She likes the indoors for speaking with her friends. I am certain she will witness none of the actual racing." Still, his lips quirked upward. "She seems more herself of late. I had worried her good humor would not return. This is something of a blessing."

"I agree."

Inside the Grandstand, the reception hall hummed with conversation and rustling of fine gowns and paper fans. They were on the first floor, above the ground, but never went so high as the top floor that was open to the sky. It made their mother light-headed, and there was no relief from either sun or rain, should either make an appearance.

From the balcony where they stood, the crowd below moved like a river, though full of color and sound, sweeping across the green of Knavesmire. Carriages lined the nearest roadway, and the officials were having a difficult time keeping them moving so more passengers could step out into the excitement.

"Did they not put a notice in the paper about this?" Roman asked, pointing to the line of carriages. "I saw it. You saw it. Did the rest of York miss the directions for staging their carriages?"

Lyness looked down at the line of carriages as a door opened, and out came Sterling. He was impossible to miss, with his height and bearing so distinct from other men's. Seeing him made Lyness grow still, because that meant after he handed down his wife, he helped his sister next.

Lady Emily. She looked up at the Grandstand balcony, and immediately his eyes found hers. His heart stopped for a long, painful moment. Then she waved, and it started up again at a faster tempo than before. His stomach dropped. He could not help but smile and lift his hand in return.

"There they are. At last." Roman clapped Lyness on the shoulder and moved away from the rail, going inside to the stairs.

Lyness followed, tugging at the sleeves of his coat. Adjusting his hat. And he had nearly caught Roman up when a hand touched his sleeve.

"Mr. Eastwood. A moment of your time?"

He turned to the voice, unfamiliar as it was, and stiffened when he recognized the speaker. One Victor Patchett, son of a magistrate, stood there with a self-satisfied smirk.

"Mr. Patchett." Lyness stepped away, double the distance needed for a stiff bow. Patchett was not someone Lyness knew well. The man was older than Roman, a Tory, and an arrogant lout who fancied himself far more important than he had any cause to be.

He was of similar height to Lyness, broad of shoulder, and some would likely call him handsome. But he was not a gentleman in most of his conduct, from what Lyness knew of gossip.

"You detain me from meeting my party, Mr. Patchett," Lyness said, slowly and carefully choosing words that would keep him from stuttering. The frustration of knowing his brother would welcome Lady Emily first, as well as having her to himself for her first impressions of the Grandstand and racing spectacle, threatened to trip him more than anything. He looked away for a moment, trying to find her in the crowd, but a chuckle from Patchett brought his focus back.

Amusement brightened the other man's expression, and his teeth flashed, like a hostile creature showing off its fangs. "Yes, I saw your brother pass by. I am certain he needs your support at this critical juncture in his party's history. I understand the Duke of Sussex snubbed every Whig in York, and some say the Kingdom, with his decline of the supper invitation. How bleak."

Lyness's eyes narrowed. "I am here for the r-races. Not politics."

"Of course not." The arrogant man placed both hands on his walking stick and leaned his weight upon it on the ground before him. "We are all here to enjoy ourselves. I merely thought I would share a touch of caution with your brother. Everyone knows he is the driving force behind your club. He's made a nuisance of himself lately, with the pamphlets and papers he has sponsored."

The man's rudeness and overreaching arrogance put Lyness out of composure. Which he hated. His irritation rising would mean a more difficult time getting the words out. Best to get things over with.

"Th-there is nothing w-w-wrong with his s-s-sponsorship of opinion pieces."

Patchett smirked. "Not everyone agrees. Some say he is supporting those who hover near treason, when it comes to speaking against our monarch and government. One cannot help but think of recent conspiracies. I do believe there is hope he will be less...hm...prominently displayed by the Whigs in future."

Roman was charming, spoke well, and possessed intelligence. Lyness had witnessed his brother winning any number of debates and humiliating Tories when they could not contradict the points he made.

But the hint about conspiracy made Lyness's ire rise. Two years had passed since the Cato Street affair—when radicals were caught plotting to murder the Prime Minister and the Cabinet. The whole business had left many in politics keenly aware of how swiftly ordinary days could plunge into chaos. When Lyness made no move to answer that ridiculous hint with more than a narrowing of his eyes, Patchett took a small step back.

"It seems you understand me. Your brother's reputation is tied closely with the *radicals* of York. He would do well to separate the two, before one harms the other. A mere piece of advice, from one man of York to another." He did not bow so much as nod.

Lyness turned away and went to find Roman, already escorting Lady Emily to the balcony while her brother and sister-in-law followed.

He had missed the exchange of greetings and was out of sorts besides. So when he also arrived at the rail, he made his bows quick, though his gaze lingered on Lady Emily. She looked elegant in a soft pink gown, her bonnet trimmed in yellow and pink ribbons. The smile she bestowed on him as she said, "I am happy you are here, Mr. Eastwood," made his heart soar.

Then she turned back to Roman. "All right. I am ready to learn all about racing."

Roman chuckled and gestured to the race course.

The balcony of the grandstand overlooked the Knavesmire like a stage set for spectacle. Parasols dotted the terrace, gentlemen leaned forward with their quizzing glasses, and far below, the green sweep of turf.

Lyness stood a pace behind his brother and Lady Emily. Close enough to hear their conversation, far enough to pretend he didn't listen. Roman was in his element, confident as ever, his voice carrying easily above the hum of the crowd.

"You see the white flag at the far post?" Roman gestured. "That's where they'll start. Two miles round, perhaps more. The best of them will keep something in reserve for the second heat."

Lady Emily followed the line of his hand. "I can just make it out," she said. "It seems a tremendous distance for one race."

Why had Lyness not thought to tell her more of racing before? Of course, she would not know how everything worked. She had never had an opportunity to attend a race like this one. Watching the play of emotions on her face, curiosity, interest, understanding, soothed some of the ache of not being the one to help her learn.

"It tests breeding and stamina both," Roman replied, pleased to instruct. "The trumpet will sound when the horses are called to the post. There—listen."

The clear note carried across the field, bright and ceremonial. Lady Emily turned her head toward the sound, her expression calm, attentive. Beautiful.

"It has a fine clarity to it," she said. "No wonder the crowd stirs at once."

Roman smiled, likely admiring her poise. "You will find there is little else that can rouse York so swiftly."

She smiled in return—polite, perhaps even amused—and within Lyness something unnamable in his chest gave the smallest twist. Roman's charm came easily with Lady Emily, and watching them together gave Lyness the faintest ache, as though he stood too near a fire he could neither approach nor escape.

His brother had not had much luck in courtship before. But this time might prove different. This time, when Lyness fought to wish his brother well with every breath he took.

He looked out instead over the course. The horses were being led out now, their coats shining along with all their tack, and their heads tossing in restless movement. Their jockeys' silks flashed like pennants against the green. A stir went through the balcony as men adjusted their wagers and ladies leaned forward to watch.

Roman continued, pointing out the landmarks with confident ease—the turn by the copse of trees, the slight rise near the finish, the white post below the stand. Emily listened with genuine interest, asking perceptive questions about the upkeep of the grounds and ownership that made Lyness's heart lift in spite of himself.

She was no fool, this woman who thought herself unsuited to the ranks of nobility. She listened and observed as though committing every detail to memory.

When the trumpet called again, louder this time, the murmur of the crowd deepened into a single pulse of anticipation. Roman braced his hands on the railing.

"They are starting next," he said. "Watch the far side. The moment the flag drops, you will feel it before you see it."

Lyness fixed his eyes on the distant shimmer of horses, but his thoughts stayed nearer. On Lady Emily and to the way her voice softened when she asked questions, and the quiet steadiness she brought even to excitement.

It was nothing more than admiration. It *must* be nothing more.

The trumpet called once more. The handkerchief fell. The race began.

He turned his attention to the horses, though he had not placed any bets on the outcome of this particular race. Even with Kettleburn's enthusiasm for his horses. Lyness had never been much for gambling on things when he had no hand in the outcome.

The first race ended amid cheers and groans from winners and losers, respectively. And Miss Nelson came to ask if Lady Emily would watch the next race with her group of female friends. After a nod from her sister-in-law, Lady Emily took her leave from their party, promising to return after the second race.

Roman escorted her to them. Of course.

Lyness needed to get hold of himself. Quickly.

He took off his hat to run his hand through his hair, then replaced it, wishing he did not feel like such a fool. If Roman had not expressed interest, had not moved into the early stages of courtship with Lady Emily, things would be different. Lyness would not feel the pressure of impending catastrophe pounding against his heart.

Watching as a woman he admired grew closer to his brother left him at odds with himself.

The crowd on the balcony pressed closer to the railing as the horses were led to the post. The air itself vibrated with anticipation.

Lady Juniper leaned nearer to Lyness, her fan half-raised against the glare. "Your brother seems determined to impress my sister-in-law," she murmured, eyes following Lord Hartwell and Lady Emily where they stood near the edge of the crowd.

Lyness kept his gaze outward, though her direct statement startled him. He had to clear his throat before speaking, or his tone would not sound cordial. "He usually succeeds when he sets his mind to something."

It was true enough. Roman had a gift for charm, for shining wherever he stood. A few disappointments in earlier courtship attempts had seemingly taught him enough for a better go round this time. Lyness had long since learned to step quietly out of that light and let it fall where it would. He preferred that it fall on Roman, in most instances. Most. This one proved more difficult.

Sterling joined them with a glass of refreshment for his wife, his gaze finding his sister before he relaxed at Lady Juniper's side. "She is doing well today. I had worried this would be too much for her." He shared a quick look with his wife before clarifying to Lyness, "Everything about an event like this is still new to her. Though my sister is every inch a lady, there are still facets of the position that flummox us all."

"She carries herself with grace," Lady Juniper said with a fondness that made her husband smile.

Lyness inclined his head in agreement, though the words he would use to describe her caught somewhere behind his ribs. Lady Emily carried herself with grace, without question. Kindness and warmth, too, and an openness that unsettled him.

The trumpet called again. A hush swept through the stands. Then, like the sudden break of a wave, the second race began. The crowd erupted into cheers, laughter, the flurry of exchanged bets, all underscored by the pounding rhythm of hooves carrying across the field.

Roman had returned in time to stand next to Lyness and lean over the railing, calling out odds and opinions to the gentlemen nearby. "That gray of Kettleburn's will never hold the lead—too light for the distance!" he declared, voice carrying above the noise.

Lyness murmured assent, though he had hardly seen the horse that belonged to their friend. His eyes drifted unbidden toward the far end of the terrace, where Lady Emily stood among the other ladies, her gloved hand resting on the rail. The wind tugged at the ribbon of her bonnet, and the crowd's noise dimmed as he watched her.

For an instant she looked his way. Only an instant—quick, almost startled—but their eyes met across the press of bodies.

The moment ended as swiftly as it began. A friend touched her arm. Pointed. She turned to look. And he forced himself to turn back toward the track.

Still, the sound of the crowd seemed distant after that. His chest had gone tight, his pulse uneven. He clapped politely with the others as the winner galloped past.

Roman was already laughing, calling for refreshment to toast the result. Lyness smiled when expected, nodded at the right intervals—but his thoughts had settled irretrievably elsewhere.

He had no right to envy his brother. Nevertheless, the feeling sat in his chest like a stone he could not dislodge.

THE MOOD AROUND EMILY, THE ENERGY AND VIBRANCE OF THE people and movement, made her head spin. Standing with other ladies, she gripped the railing and cast her eyes out to the sky and fields beyond the track. Though she felt as though someone stared at her from behind. She started to turn, but told herself it would be better not to. The last time she had looked, she had found Mr. Eastwood glancing at her only to look away the moment their gaze connected.

The Sweepstakes race busied the track, and a great many of the onlookers, but Emily still found it surprising so many people invested so much interest in a public race. Perhaps enjoyment for such things had to be acquired over time? It hardly mattered. She was not there for the horses, but for the people.

Miss Hannah Frederickson proved good company, and she already knew the two Nelson daughters Emily had met at dinner the week before. That made it easier for Emily to stand among them, letting the three of them speak while she bent her mind toward ignoring the press of bodies around them.

"Miss Nelson, have you told Lady Emily about your rather unique name?" Miss Frederickson asked with a sudden brightness in her eyes. "Lady Emily, I declare, I have never met a family with such distinct naming traditions for their children. I imagine your sister-in-law would know the story."

Miss Nelson, the older of the two twins by mere minutes, lightly smacked Miss Frederickson on the arm with her fan. "You take far too much delight in the burden of my Christian name, Hannah Frederickson. I should not think you would, were your parents more imaginative with what they called you."

Trying to pay attention to the conversation, especially given that she had been dragged into it by name, Emily met Miss Nelson's gaze. She could not join in the teasing, of course. She wasn't close enough to them and may well get it wrong, causing offense rather than amusement. "I must confess that I have never met anyone else with your name, or your brothers' names. Is there a particular reason your parents chose them?"

At this point, the other twin Nelson sister sighed heavily. "Thaddeus, Phineas, Euphemia, and myself. Theodora." She turned when Miss Frederickson giggled. "Yes, yes, Miss Frederickson, astonishingly rare names. Though having possessed mine my whole life, I cannot say that I find it as odd as you do."

Miss Nelson puffed out a breath that made her curls bounce. "Our mother named us after book characters."

"Book characters?" Emily raised her eyebrows. "I am not as well read as my sister-in-law. I cannot claim to know books with those names among them."

"Because they are from Gothic novels," Miss Theodora said without expression. "Both our parents are avid readers of the genre."

"Ah. Yes. Then my sister-in-law would find them of interest." Emily did not laugh, knowing well enough how unpleasant she found being the center of teasing. Especially in public. "I often wish my name were more unique, but at least I am not one of one hundred Marys likely within our sight at this exact moment. Were we to shout 'Charlotte' above the crowd, fully half the women would turn around to see who called their name."

Miss Nelson's lips twitched upward. "That is a most excellent point. Though I should not mind having been given a name of median usage, or even one common upon the Continent now that we are no longer at war."

The conversation drifted then to other things, especially focusing on other entertainments during the week. The Panorama in the largest assembly room in York, the ball in two days' time, the many plays and private parties, and all of it drifted around Emily like leaves in a puddle. Softly, brightly, but not fully pulling her attention to them.

Mrs. Elgin had arrived, and it was she who touched Emily's arm gently and asked, "Would you like to accompany a few of me to the Panorama tomorrow? I think you would like it. I have seen one before, in London, and it is truly an incredible experience. One feels as though one is partaking in actual history."

"I cannot remember having heard of such a spectacle before," Emily admitted, hoping it was not another mark against her in Society's eyes. "That would be lovely."

"Excellent! I will send a note with the particulars to your family." Mrs. Elgin seemed inordinately pleased, and for a moment Emily wondered if the woman had thought her kind invitation would be turned down. Had she been nervous about asking Emily to attend? Surely not.

Her focus returned to making herself appear composed and sociable. This was what an earl's daughter did. They socialized in public and private. Though she much preferred private, smaller settings to grand, noisy things like the races. The warmth of the sun through her bonnet, the hum of conversation, the flutter of fans, and the faint scent of lemonade and horses surrounded her. Each of her senses assaulted on all sides.

She pulled in a deep breath, hand on the rail again. The feeling from a moment before came back.

She turned to see if Mr. Eastwood was there, and her heart sank when he was not looking her way. Twice now she had thought she felt his eyes on her, but it was a ridiculous thought with little reason behind it. Mr. Eastwood was attentive to the races, like everyone else. She was merely part of the greater spectacle.

Lord Hartwell appeared a moment later, his voice carrying easily above the hum of the crowd. "Ladies, I hope you will not mind if I reclaim Lady Emily. My mother wishes our party to reconvene with her and will expect our attendance before the next race begins."

It was said so pleasantly that no one could respond with anything but polite enthusiasm. The baron offered his arm, and Emily set her hand lightly upon his sleeve, falling into step beside him.

Jack and Juniper waited for them, but Emily saw no sign of Mr. Eastwood. Perhaps he had gone inside already, to be with his mother. An admirable thing for a son, to look in on her. Both brothers seemed devoted to her. Given that Emily's own family was quite close, she understood that level of care. Or her family had once been that close, until all the distractions of rank and title overturned their lives.

The shift from the open air to the shaded interior felt like stepping out of a grand celebration into ceremony—the bustle and noise of the crowd replaced by the hush of polished civility. The change in atmosphere was almost startling. The corridor opened into a large reception room, tall windows gathering the hazy afternoon light and scattering it across the highly polished floors. Candles flickered from sconces though the hour hardly required them. Servants wove through the room with trays of lemonade and wine, and the scent of lemon mingled with perfume and wax until it was difficult to tell one from the other.

Lady Hartwell sat near the center of the room, surrounded by a constellation of acquaintances—ladies in feathered bonnets and a few gentlemen of her age and set. Likely husbands to the women giving her their attention, Emily thought.

The baroness was in her element, blooming amid the hum of conversation. She made it look effortless. This was the woman Emily had been told was not sociable? Every time she saw the baroness, the lady was composed and the very picture of elegance.

And where was Mr. Eastwood?

The moment the baron approached his mother, she extended a hand, smiling with serene satisfaction.

"Roman, my dear. I feared the press of the crowd would make you late. Or cause you to forget me altogether. You know how it fatigues me, worrying about where you are."

"I did not keep you waiting long, Mother," he said with an indulgent smile, bowing over her hand. "And you appear to be in excellent company."

Lady Hartwell laughed softly, then turned her attention to Emily and Juniper. "Lady Juniper Sterling, how lovely you look this afternoon. And Lady Emily, my dear, how charming to see you again."

Emily curtsied, offering the expected compliments about the

fine weather and the success of the day. The words came easily, almost mechanically, while her mind struggled to find something more specific to say. Something interesting. The light coming through the tall windows caused a slight throb at her temples.

Thankfully, Jack and Juniper spoke warmly to their hostess, while Lord Hartwell exchanged pleasantries with his mother's friends. Emily tried to listen, to smile at the right moments, and to appear composed. But the room pressed close. The hum of voices and movement bled into one another, becoming a relentless buzz, like bees trapped in glass.

She told herself she must not falter. Not here. Not now.

Grace. Usefulness. Composure. If she could maintain those three things, no one would suspect how unsteady she felt.

Someone asked a question about the races. She smiled and answered, uncertain of her own words. Her neck felt warm beneath her collar, her gloves damp against her palms. The polished floor slowly tilted under her feet.

Lady Hartwell's laughter drifted to her ears again—airy, confident, unbothered. Emily envied that ease. How long would it take her to learn to look so assured, to belong so wholly to this world?

A wave of dizziness passed through her, and she turned slightly, facing the nearest window. The light there seemed cooler. The glass panes rattled faintly as a breeze moved against them. She drew in a slow breath and tried to summon calm.

A shadow fell beside her. She tilted her head enough to look without moving her eyes.

Mr. Eastwood stood there, a glass of lemonade in one hand and a folded fan in the other. His expression was quiet but intent, his gaze steady.

"You looked as though you might wish for one," he said softly, offering the glass.

Her fingers brushed his as she took it. The coolness startled her, and she had to resist pressing the cup to her temple.

"Thank you," she managed to say, her voice soft. She sipped at it, grateful for the cool liquid, for the sweet and sour on her tongue to draw her mind away from everything else.

He inclined his head, nothing more. No comment, no intrusion. But there was something in his eyes...an unspoken understanding. And that made it easier to breathe.

The noise of the room dimmed slightly. The ache behind her eyes eased. And for a moment, amid the elegance and clamor of the world she was still learning to move within, she felt seen.

# Chapter Thirteen

## August 20th, 1822

Mrs. Elgin, as a widow, had more freedom to move about in Society than an unmarried lady did. Unfortunately for Emily, Mrs. Elgin often included her mother in her entertainments and activities. Emily sat across from Mrs. Holly and Mrs. Elgin, facing backward in the carriage, with Mrs. Elgin's brother, Mr. Holly, seated next to her. He kept his arms folded and his gaze on the window, while his mother kept up a steady litany of naming the best families in the county and how many of them she had already seen present for the races.

For her part, Emily's friend sat with hands clasped in her lap and a pained smile upon her face. She tried, several times, to break into her mother's recitation of names, but had yet to manage a change in the subject.

Emily recalled a friend of her own mother's, from the days before the title, who had a similar way of dominating conversation. What was it her mother would do to maneuver the friend out of such monologues?

Ah. Yes. Give the woman something *useful* to do.

Emily slipped her hand into her reticule and drew out the small notebook she had taken to carrying in town, along with a short pencil. She waited for a pause in Mrs. Holly's naming of the local gentry. At last, there was one, very briefly, after the woman spoke of "the utterly insufferable Mr. Godwin."

Emily leaned forward with what she hoped was an expression of earnest appeal.

"Mrs. Holly, you know everyone far better than I. Might I prevail upon your experience? I am forever muddling names and connections. If I give you my little book, would you be so kind as to mark down which families I ought to be certain to remember? Especially those most important to our local society?"

Mrs. Holly's expression brightened at once, her spine straightening. "My dear Lady Emily, of course. It is high time someone guided you properly. Let me see." She accepted the notebook and pencil with the same firm purpose Emily had once seen in the neighboring farmer's wife when handed a basket of tangled wool. This was a problem the woman fully intended to put right.

At once, her attention bent to the page, lips moving soundlessly as she began to write, occasionally muttering a correction or adding a note in the margin.

Freed from the steady stream of commentary, Emily let out a discreet breath and glanced at Mrs. Elgin. The young widow's shoulders had fallen away from her ears; she sent Emily a look of mingled gratitude and amusement.

Mr. Holly had turned slightly, too, his eyebrows raised as he glanced from his mother to Emily. One corner of his mouth turned up slightly before he redirected his gaze out the window. For a moment, that small smile made her think of another gentleman altogether.

Some corner of her mind wondered, for the space of a heartbeat, whether Mr. Lyness Eastwood would be among the crowds today. She dismissed the thought at once and turned to Mrs. Elgin with a small, conspiratorial smile.

"Now," Emily said quietly, "while your mother assists with my education, perhaps you could tell me more about the Panorama. You said you have been to one before?"

"Yes. I have. In London." Mrs. Elgin glanced at her mother, and when no interruption came, she went on speaking. "My late husband, Henry, took me to view one that showed the Battle of Waterloo. There were many soldiers present at the display, and they said it was most accurate of their experiences. Some had to leave when the cannon fire was performed by the orchestra. It was rather loud. My husband had to take hold of my hand, I jumped so when the cymbals crashed together." A smile, tentative and likely drenched in memory, appeared on her face, making her appear nearer Emily's age. Mrs. Elgin could not be above thirty years old. "But the whole of the spectacle was quite clever. They used flashes of light for gunfire, billowing gauze as smoke, and the master of ceremonies gave a most stirring account of the battle. He quoted the Duke of Wellington many times."

It sounded as though this spectacle would be just as loud, given that a battle was also its subject. Emily did not let that deter her from encouraging her new friend. "It sounds quite thrilling. I am glad you thought to invite me today. And I now understand why my brother was reluctant to attend, as he served in the army himself."

The man beside her turned again, his gaze finding hers with a flicker of interest. "I had heard Mr. Sterling's past included time in the army. I can understand wanting to keep personal memories of such things tucked away. But for those of us who did not have the honor of serving, or do so by necessity, may, I hope, learn of those sacrifices through mediums such as the panorama."

"I had not thought of that," Mrs. Elgin admitted with a thoughtful tilt of her head. "I do hope you will stay close to us, Christopher." Her gaze cut quickly to Emily and then back to her brother. "You know more than I do of battles and the military. Your explanations could make the experience more meaningful."

The invitation to accompany Mrs. Elgin and her family suddenly made more sense to Emily. She did not doubt that Mrs.

Elgin wished to be her friend, but a secondary motive was at play. The woman wanted to see if her brother and Emily would show any interest in one another.

Emily could not be upset with her friend, nor blame her for a sisterly action that Emily had taken part in on her own brother's behalf. Only a few short months ago, she had subtly encouraged Jack to pay court to Juniper. She knew now, of course, he had wanted to all along. But she liked to fancy her approval may have made things happen with greater speed.

Now, though, she looked at Mr. Holly and said, politely, "Will any of your friends be present, Mr. Holly? I imagine you would rather keep company with them than with us, and I am certain the guidebook will do a fair job of explaining anything the master of ceremonies does not."

There. Though it was not her most graceful comment, it did give him an opportunity and excuse to spend the time with others. An amused spark in his eyes suggested he was well aware of his sister's setup and Emily's careful redirection.

"Perhaps I can persuade any of my friends in attendance to join us. As it is an attraction without seating, and people move about freely, we need not worry overmuch about who keeps next to whom."

Emily's thoughts drifted elsewhere again to a quiet gentleman with a quick smile and thoughtful eyes. She hoped, absurdly, to see him again before long.

Mrs. Elgin moved the conversation along to the ball, occurring the next evening, and what she had heard of who would be attending. Emily turned to this discussion with delight, having received her dress from the seamstress earlier that morning. They discussed whether they preferred dressing their hair with flowers, feathers, or ribbons, and how relieved they were that the weather had remained mild in the evenings.

"With the ball beginning at ten, one hopes any heat from the day will have filtered out through the windows," Mrs. Holly muttered, still working on a page in the notebook. The third page, it looked like.

"At least you ladies are not wearing coats and cravats," Mr. Holly said, eyebrows raised. "The gentlemen present have more weighted cloth upon them than anyone ought to in the summer."

"Not this ridiculous debate again," his sister said with a slight toss of her head. "Christopher, you will never convince me that gentlemen dress more uncomfortably than ladies. Why, the number of undergarments one must wear—"

Mrs. Holly cleared her throat. "We do not discuss undergarments in mixed company, Matilda."

Mrs. Elgin pressed her lips together, but her eyes still sparkled with amusement. Despite whatever attempts the woman might make at matchmaking, Emily liked her on instinct. When she was not allowing her mother to overtake the conversation, Mrs. Elgin was quite pleasant in conversation and manner.

They passed the remainder of the ride speaking of the races, though none of the ladies intended to go to the Knavesmire again that week. They arrived outside the largest of York's Assembly Rooms, on Blake Street. With half an hour remaining before the seven o'clock exhibition began, there was time to buy their guidebooks and enter the large assembly room before it grew too crowded.

The moment Emily stepped into the assembly room, the movement of bodies and the warm hum of voices closed around her. The large hall was already filling, people drifting in loose currents between the tall windows and the raised platform where the panorama would soon be unveiled. Heat gathered beneath the high ceiling, carrying the scents of starch and perfume through the air. The military band, promised in the newspaper article, were warming up in the orchestra balcony above the platform.

Emily paused to take it in, steadying herself, then caught sight of Lady Hartwell.

The older woman sat along the far wall in one of the few chairs provided for those unable to stand through the whole exhibition, her elegant posture unchanged despite the crowd shifting around her. Lady Hartwell was studying one of the beautiful floral arrangements displayed on a small table beside her.

Emily's breath stalled. If Lady Hartwell was here, then Lord Hartwell must be somewhere nearby. And if Lord Hartwell was attending…

Her heart gave an unhelpfully hopeful little lift.

Lyness Eastwood could be present as well.

Before she realized she had moved, she had taken several steps deeper into the room, her gaze skimming the faces of the gentlemen present. She searched for the familiar figure of broad shoulders, quiet manner, and the composed elegance that made Mr. Eastwood stand out to her even when he seemed determined to blend into corners and shadows. She spotted a dozen dark coats with dark hair above them, none quite matching the picture in her mind.

"Oh, Lady Emily, the flowers," Mrs. Elgin crooned from beside her, stepping forward as well. "I heard the arrangements were lovely, and look how clever the laurel is woven in frames on the wall."

Emily straightened, recalling herself to her role as guest, and smoothed her gloves against her skirts. It was rather silly to feel so flustered. She was not here to look for *him*. She was certainly not here to be looked at *by* him, either. Even so, her pulse fluttered with a mixture of anticipation and nerves.

If he was here, she hoped she would not disgrace herself with some ill-timed blush or awkward greeting. They were supposed to be friends. And friends did not make each other blush. And if he was not present—

Well. That thought disappointed her far more than it should have.

Still, her gaze wandered once more through the crowd, stubbornly, quietly hopeful.

A familiar, deep voice spoke near her shoulder, and for a

moment her heart leapt. "Are you looking for someone, Lady Emily?"

Her smile faltered. It was not Mr. Eastwood but his brother.

"Lord Hartwell," she said, turning and offering a curtsy. "I caught sight of your mother and knew you would be nearby. Good evening."

The baron met her gaze evenly, his not-quite-a-smile in place as always. "Lady Emily. I am glad to see you." Then his eyes flickered to her friend. "And Mrs. Elgin, good evening. Your brother told me you would be present this evening. I have heard every showing of the panorama has had a large turnout, and I decided I must see it for myself at last." He nodded toward his mother's position in the room as he made eye contact with Emily again. "I have promised to attend upon my mother for the spectacle, but perhaps afterward we could all discuss it together?"

"That would be delightful," Mrs. Elgin answered with a slight smile.

"Indeed," Emily added when he continued to hold her gaze. "Yes, of course. I look forward to it." The intensity of his regard made her far too aware of Mrs. Elgin watching them, and of others near enough to see it. Why would he not look away?

The military band's peculiar-sounding tuning session quieted, and a man stood in front of them, leading them into something that sounded softer. A prelude to the evening's events.

"I had best take up my station," Lord Hartwell said with a brief bow, then crossed the room to his mother's side.

"Let us move somewhere toward the middle, but not behind any of the taller men," Mrs. Elgin said. "I understand why they do not seat people for these events, but it would be far more convenient to order people by height."

"Yes," Emily answered, somewhat distracted. Her attention kept tugging back toward the door, as though her thoughts might pull Mr. Eastwood into the room by force of will. She shook her head and tried to pay more attention to the people around her, not certain the middle of the crowd appealed to her. The room grew warmer as more bodies pressed together near the platform. But the panorama would soon hold all her attention, and that would help.

Servants went around the room to dim the lights in the sconces while lamps behind the platform were lit and turned brighter. The conversations in the room hushed.

Mr. Holly appeared behind his sister, leaning forward a touch to say over her shoulder, "Mother is still in the foyer, speaking with friends. I doubt she will come in at all, but I am here if you have need of me."

"Thank you, Christopher," his sister answered.

"Oh, and look who I found before the lights dimmed," he said, and Emily half-turned to greet she-knew-not-who, and found Mr. Eastwood standing directly behind her. Close enough that her thoughts flushed and took wing, leaving her rather bereft. His dark eyes held hers, a smile on his handsome face as he made an abbreviated bow.

"Lady Emily. Mrs. Elgin." He looked up at the platform and then at Emily again. "This exhibit is quite a spectacle. I hope you do not mind sharing it with me."

Her breath tightened. Mind? She could hardly think, but she certainly did not *mind*.

Though her friend said something polite, Emily did not understand it. She was too busy forming her own response, which was not entirely complicated, but certainly too close to the truth. "I cannot think of anyone better to share it with."

A flush crept up the back of her neck the moment she heard herself.

His eyebrows raised, but no one else marked her words, as they had already turned their attention to the front of the room, where a deep, booming voice took up a well-performed narration.

"The age of chivalry is not gone! When we behold, through the mist of distant ages, the valorous knight of the feudal times going forth to succor the widow, the distressed lady, and the oppressed—wherever and whenever he might find them—we feel, as it were, instinctively, a glow of enthusiasm warm us at this high generosity of soul, at those noble employments of knighthood; and cannot avoid wishing that all such enterprises might be crowned with success."

The warmth Lyness Eastwood's breath brushed the back of her neck as he spoke near her ear. The sensation stole her breath for a single, treacherous moment. "I hope you are not easily startled, my lady. I have seen this once already, to make certain it would not harm my mother's nerves. There is nothing of horror in the art, but there are many, many crashes of cymbals and drums."

She swallowed and turned her head toward him to whisper, "You will likely see me jump in fear then, Mr. Eastwood. I hope it proves amusing."

A soft chuckle breezed by her ear. "Why would I find your distress amusing? I would rather prevent it, if I could."

His sincerity was disarming. She had to turn away. Why did she have the terrible urge to lean backward to brush his shoulder with hers? Such a point of contact would hardly be appropriate. The knowledge that he stood there already distracted her enough without adding such a temptation.

The master of ceremonies was still speaking of feelings and honor, victory and virtue, as the first scene of the panorama rolled out before them. The City of Algiers. She kept silent as the crowd paid attention to his narration. The city was situated upon a lofty hill, a thousand feet above sea-level. The houses were painted as descending from the hill all the way to the edge of the water. There was a thick wall surrounding the city, with towers placed at regular intervals. Light was cleverly directed to shine brighter on each feature of the city as the man spoke of them. He also recounted the number of people stolen and put into chains by the Algerians.

His voice suddenly thundered, making her body startle for the first time that evening.

"Nothing, therefore, but the arm of power, assisted by the thunder of the British Navy, could arrest the havoc of the spoiler! Nothing but the loud-mouthed cannon could shake the despot on his throne!"

A warm hand gently took hers where she had closed it into a fist at her side, wrinkling the booklet she had purchased for greater insight into the evening. Heat unfurled in her palm at the contact and raced up her arm, through to her chest, until she blushed. Gently, Mr. Eastwood's fingers moved to instead circle her wrist.

His voice in her ear said, "I will warn you, his voice is nothing to the cannon fire, my lady." A soft squeeze. Then his fingers withdrew.

Emily found herself hoping the cannons began firing quickly. Because, perhaps, he would reach out to calm her again. It was foolish, but she longed for any excuse to feel his hand on hers once more.

LYNESS HAD NOT COME TO THE EXHIBITION INTENDING TO PLANT himself at Lady Emily Sterling's side. Truly, he had not. He had meant to accompany his mother and brother, make himself available should need arise, and stand somewhere unobtrusive.

Unobtrusive, however, proved impossible the moment Christopher Holly murmured that Lady Emily was among the company.

His feet changed direction before he consciously made the decision, before Holly had even invited him to join them. A poor showing of restraint, but he could not bring himself to regret it. He joined their perfectly respectable little party. Respectable enough that no one should question his presence.

Except himself. He questioned a lot of things about himself.

He bowed and murmured his greetings, and she looked at him with that gentle, incandescent smile that undid his good intentions quicker than any artillery barrage. When she answered that she could think of no one better to share the spectacle with, he thought he might never recover his wits.

He ought to have stood several inches farther back. He ought to have kept a careful, gentlemanly distance. He *ought* to have stopped himself from leaning near enough that his breath stirred the loose curls at her neck when he warned her about the cymbals.

But he did none of those things. He stood too close. He spoke too softly. He indulged himself shamelessly.

And when the first crash of cymbals split the air, sharp enough to rattle the floorboards, she flinched—only slightly, but he saw it.

Before he could think better of it, his fingers closed warmly around hers a second time.

Too familiar. Far too familiar. And yet stopping himself felt impossible. His entire life had been governed by restraint and measured behavior; he could not recall a single moment of impulse that had ever rewarded him. Besides those that had made her smile, such as offering his hat for the canary, his calligraphy for her bottles, and now this.

This felt like stepping into sunlight after standing in shadows.

"Forgive me," he murmured near her ear, barely a breath of sound. "Perhaps a warning was not enough."

She turned her head, eyes wide, lips parted slightly in surprise. The soft lamplight caught against her lashes, and for one reckless heartbeat he imagined lowering his lips to hers.

Madness.

Though he released her hand at once, his palm tingled with the memory of her warmth.

He folded his hands behind his back where they could do no more mischief, and he stared straight ahead at the rolling canvas of Algiers. He heard none of the narration. His entire awareness remained fixed on the woman standing barely in front of him—the slight tremor she tried to hide, the way her shoulders stiffened at each loud report, the delicate brush of her curls on the back of her neck.

He was too familiar by half.

And yet... If another crash came, he knew, with a sinking certainty, he would take her hand again. Unless he put distance between them. The crowd around them made such a thing difficult. He could see no easy way to slide through the audience without drawing attention or causing irritation.

Somehow, Lyness had trapped himself in a position of blissful torture.

The panorama canvas continued to move before him, the mechanism employed wrapping the already viewed scenes to one side while the other uncurled to present new images of ships firing upon each other in a harbor. People around him gasped and exclaimed at the brightly painted water and smoke rising from the ships' guns.

Lady Emily's hand reached back at the same moment his reached forward, and he held on to her, gently, as the drums rolled and cymbals punctuated the narration of the battle. Others in the crowd covered their ears. A few stepped backward. Mrs. Elgin had squeezed her eyes shut and covered her ears when mirrored light flashed across the audience.

Aware of it all, Lyness's focus remained on Lady Emily's slender fingers in his grasp. His whole focus narrowed to that touch of their gloved hands. He wished he had the right to hold her hand always, and not only here, where no one would see in the dimly lit room and between the press of bodies.

Somewhere behind him, along the wall, Roman stood with their mother. Lyness knew this. Roman could likely see Lyness's head and shoulders, his position relative to Lady Emily's, and his older brother would suspect nothing amiss. He would never think that Lyness harbored feelings for a woman Roman wished to court. And how would it be, if Roman made a formal request of courtship? And if he succeeded in drawing Lady Emily's affection, how would Lyness stamp out his own attraction to her?

"This is incredible," she whispered over her shoulder to him, eyes wide with wonder.

"Yes. Incredible." That one word meant something entirely different to him as red lamplight shone, the canvas moving to bring the flicker of fire to mind. He barely heard the final words the master of ceremonies spoke.

"When Lord Exmouth considered that he had accomplished the objects of his mission, he ordered the ships to retire as before mentioned, which, from their crippled state, they did with great difficulty. The enemy, upon their withdrawing, opened, with fresh vigor, a tremendous discharge of shells, which was answered by showers of rockets from the boats. At this moment a violent thunder-storm began, accompanied with lightning, which swept along the ships in vivid streams; whilst the pealing of the thunder far exceeded in loudness the 'cannon's deafening roar.' The combined effect of the thunder, the lightning, the noise of the loud-mouthed cannon, and the arsenal and the ships, now in flames, was at once terrific, overwhelming, and sublime."

The roar of the imagined cannon fire died away, leaving the room in a vibrating hush. Lyness exhaled, slow and quiet, as Lady Emily's fingers slipped from his. He let his hand fall, let his shoulders return to their proper posture, let the mask of polite interest settle once more across features that felt far too warm.

What was he doing?

He should have stepped back long ago. He should have moved across the room. He should have remembered that Roman had told him—plainly, earnestly—that he had decided to take a bride, and Lady Emily was a most obvious choice. A baron's younger brother had no right to hover behind her like some besotted schoolboy.

And yet he had done exactly that.

Blasted hypocrisy. He prided himself on temperance and good sense, and here he was indulging every impulse simply because she looked a little startled in a darkened room.

He shifted, meaning to put a safer inch or two between them.

Then she glanced back—only briefly, eyes seeking reassurance—and his breath tangled again.

"I am glad you were here," she said quietly. "I did not expect to be shaken by this event to such an extent."

He wondered, absurd fool that he was, whether she might have wanted to stand with him from the beginning. Whether she had been pleased to see him arrive. Whether her soft intake of breath when he took her hand had more to do with him than it did the cymbals.

For one wild instant, he let himself imagine she might choose him instead of Roman, if he asked.

Then he dismissed the thought so sharply that it stung.

Lady Emily Sterling deserved a man with rank and presence and confidence—not a second son who communicated best with ink and paper and lost every trace of composure the moment she smiled at him. She would be far better matched with Roman, who carried a title, a commanding manner, and the important members of Society standing behind him.

Roman would never hesitate. Roman would never be undone by a pair of gloved hands brushing his.

No. Lyness knew precisely where he stood. And more so, where he *must* stand.

At a distance.

He straightened, folding his hands behind him once more, the only safe place for them. The painted ships glowed on the canvas before him as the exhibition drew to a gentle close, but he saw none of it. Holding within him the knowledge that wanting more than his lot was folly of the worst kind.

When the panorama finally ended and the lights rose, he told himself he would make a polite farewell, return to his mother's side, and forget every reckless impulse of the evening. Never to repeat it.

He already suspected he would fail.

Lady Emily straightened, blinking as the brighter lamps returned shape and color to the room.

Mrs. Elgin turned to her at once, cheeks flushed with excitement. "What an astonishing display! My dear Lady Emily, you endured it beautifully. I jumped nearly every time the drums sounded, yet you held yourself with such composure." She put a hand to her throat, her eyes wide and bright. "How did you fare? Truly?"

Lady Emily's composure had returned, though Lyness thought her voice carried a faint tremor. "It was louder than I expected, but quite extraordinary. And I did well, I think."

Lyness felt the words settle in his chest, part relief, part guilt. *She did well,* he repeated silently, as if that might excuse his behavior.

Mr. Holly stepped beside his sister, looking at each of them with an air of pleased approval. "I daresay you handled the affair with admirable grace, Lady Emily. Many of the gentlemen in this room ducked at that first cannon blast." His amused smile deepened. "Though some of us had the advantage of foresight."

His gaze slid pointedly to Lyness—not unkind, but with a curious lift of his brows.

Lyness resisted the urge to tug at his cuffs. Holly *knew.* Or at least suspected more than Lyness wished anyone to notice. He inclined his head in a polite acknowledgment, schooling his expression into something mild. If he attempted a verbal response in that moment, his words would trip all over themselves.

Mrs. Elgin gave her brother a playful nudge. "Christopher, do not tease. Lady Emily may well have been startled, but she recovered splendidly."

"Yes," Mr. Holly agreed, eyes flicking again between Lady Emily and Lyness. "She did."

Unaware of the silent exchange, Lady Emily looked up at the platform and the scenes being rolled backward for the next showing. "I am glad to have seen it. Though I certainly do not believe I will attend a second viewing."

Mrs. Elgin laughed. "Indeed not. My nerves could not withstand another barrage."

"This is certainly a unique way to learn of significant events in our time," Lady Emily said, turning to look again at Lyness. Her lips curled upward. "Experiencing the display with others makes it more enjoyable than solitary study."

Lyness swallowed down the warmth rising in him again—warmth and something precarious, something dangerously close to hope. He willed his breathing steady.

And then Roman appeared.

"Lady Emily." Roman's baritone cut smoothly through the chatter as he stepped up beside them, bowing to the ladies with polished ease. "Mrs. Elgin. Mr. Holly." His gaze shifted last—and longest—to Lyness. "I am glad to see my brother found good company for the exhibition. I wondered where he had gone."

"As you see, I found th-the very best of c-company," Lyness returned, keeping his tone as steady as possible, his words unremarkable.

Roman looked to Lady Emily again, his expression brightening in a way Lyness had learned to interpret far too well. "I trust the spectacle did not overwhelm you? It is rather more dramatic than a play or art gallery."

Lady Emily offered him a more polite smile than she had bestowed upon Lyness. "It was rather dramatic, yes, but I found it impressive. I enjoyed myself fully."

"I am pleased to hear it." Roman's gaze sharpened, intense and direct. "Mother found it enlightening as well. She will want to speak with you before the evening ends."

"Of course. I would be happy to hear her thoughts." She sounded as though she meant it.

Lyness felt something cold and familiar settle beneath his ribs—the faint tightening of a vise he had put around his own heart long ago. To limit his wishes and desires, to better serve the family.

Holly made a soft, amused sound under his breath. When Lyness glanced at him, the man's eyes held a flicker of sympathy, or understanding, before he engaged again in the general conversation.

Mrs. Elgin chattered on about the painted canvas and the cleverness of the lighting, drawing Emily with her to examine one of the colorful lamps near the platform. Roman followed after, listening attentively. Lyness followed two steps behind his brother, exactly where propriety dictated.

Exactly where temptation could not reach.

# Chapter Fourteen

## Four Months Previous, London

The night in London had started as many others. Lady Emily Sterling had no way of knowing how low her spirits would sink. Only an hour before the ball began, she had reminded herself that she ought to enjoy the evening. It was not the first ball she had attended since that night in Town when a certain gentleman with a crooked smile and quiet steadiness had asked her for a dance. She had not looked for Mr. Eastwood tonight—he had been called away to York weeks ago—but she had wished, foolishly, that someone of his character had been there nonetheless.

Especially when her hopes came crashing down upon her.

Emily had fled the ballroom as gracefully as she could manage, though she feared anyone watching closely had seen the tremor in her steps.

The ladies' withdrawing room was mercifully quiet. The door closed behind her without a sound, muting the music, the hum of voices, the rustle of ballgowns. For a blessed moment there was stillness and the faint crackle of the fire in the grate.

She moved deeper into the room, past the tall mirror with its gilded frame. One glance at her reflection—eyes over-bright, color too high in her cheeks—was enough to make her turn away. She did not wish to see herself. Not when the echo of those words still rang in her ears.

Mr. Waldegrave, a suitor she had tried to dismiss when she realized his nature was selfish and cruel, had found a way to speak to her. His verbal attack had been brief, but effective.

*Country manners...*

*...no true notion of how to behave...*

*...an earl's daughter in name only...*

*...you will disappoint your family...*

Of course, she knew she should not give heed to his words. He was unkind. Arrogant. Angry that she had spurned him. Yet his words were the exact fears she harbored in her heart.

*I will make you sorry. Already, people are talking and seeing you for what you are.*

She tried to recall something pleasant. Anything to block out the sting. That made her mind reach again to that brief dance with Mr. Eastwood. He had spoken so gently to her, stuttering once before offering an apology that made her laugh despite her nerves. He had made her feel seen without being judged. That memory felt far away now.

Emily swallowed hard, her throat tight and sore. Her father's title, the new consequence attached to their family name, her sisters' careful efforts in teaching her how to curtsy, how to speak, how to move—none of it mattered if one careless remark revealed how she did not properly belong.

Her steps carried her toward one of the tall windows as if of their own accord. Heavy curtains framed the glass, the folds deep enough to hide inside. It was childish, perhaps, but she could not bear the thought anyone discovering her, sitting openly and weeping like a silly girl.

She slipped behind the curtains and sank into the corner, her pale blue skirts crumpling around her. The fabric brushed against the wall and floor, then all fell still. The enclosed space felt oddly safe, dim and muffled. She drew her knees close and pressed her face into her hands.

She tried—truly she did—not to cry. It was foolish. Overly sensitive. A *proper* lady would have brushed off a cruel comment with a laugh, or answered it with a clever remark. A proper lady would not be hiding, holding herself together by sheer force of will. But the words had lodged into her chest like thorns, scraping with every breath.

A small, ragged sob escaped her before she could stop it. She bit her lip, willing herself to silence.

*Do not make a spectacle. Do not give anyone reason to look.*

Another sob trembled out, quiet but impossible to entirely swallow back.

"Emily?"

Emily's head jerked up at the sound of her name—without the ill-fitting title of *lady*—spoken in a voice of true concern. She blinked against the blur of tears as the curtain shifted, lamplight spilling into her refuge.

Juniper stood there, the rich colors of her gown a blur of jewel tones above Emily's hunched form. Her expression was all kindness and worry, those dark eyes warm rather than critical.

Emily's cheeks burned. She dashed at them with the back of her gloved hand, trying in vain to wipe away the evidence of her shame. "I—I am sorry," she whispered, her voice breaking. "I did not mean… I did not intend for anyone to see me like this."

"There is nothing to apologize for," Juniper said, her tone soft as she lowered herself into a crouch beside Emily. The rustle of her skirts, the faint scent of rosewater and something bright and citrus, wrapped around them both. Juniper took Emily's trembling hands in her own and gave them a reassuring squeeze. "But you must tell me—what has happened? I saw you not ten minutes ago, and you seemed perfectly well."

Emily shook her head, fresh tears stinging her eyes. She did not wish to repeat the words. Saying them aloud would make them feel truer somehow, giving them weight enough to crush her completely. "It is nothing," she managed to say, though her voice wavered. "Someone said something. Something...unkind."

Juniper's mouth tightened, though her touch remained gentle. "What did they say?" she asked quietly. "Who was it?"

Emily couldn't meet her gaze. Shame curled in her stomach, sharp and twisting. "I have no wish to talk about it." Her words came out small, a little broken. If she spoke it, Juniper will know how foolish Emily was. How unfit for all of this. "I only... I want to leave. I cannot face them all again, not after—" The rest dissolved into another sob, her throat closing around it.

Juniper's hand moved to Emily's back, stroking in slow, comforting circles. The kindness of the gesture made Emily's eyes sting all the more. "You need not explain if you do not wish to," Juniper said. "But you are not alone, Emily. I will not let you face this without someone by your side."

Whatever she was supposed to be, she did not feel equal to any of it. Tears spilled over again despite her effort to hold them back, but she nodded all the same. It was a strange mixture of humiliation and relief—that someone had found her, that someone cared. That *Juniper* cared.

"I will find one of the ladies in your family," Juniper said at last, rising gracefully to her feet. "They will know what to do, and they can take you home if that is what you wish."

Home. That word did not mean to Emily what it did to Juniper. Her friend meant the townhouse where the Sterling family resided at present. But that was not home to Emily. It hadn't felt like home even once. She missed the country home, humble in size with barely enough room for all of them, and simply furnished but filled with the memories of easier times.

Away from the music, the bright lights, the watchful eyes weighing every word she spoke, every step she took. Emily nodded, unable to form a proper reply. The tightness in her chest eased just a fraction. Juniper believed her distress mattered—not because of her father's title, not because she ought to be useful or accomplished, but simply because she was *hurt.*

"Thank you," Emily whispered, a little hoarse, wiping again at her cheeks. "I... I am very grateful."

Juniper offered her a small, encouraging smile and gave her shoulder a gentle pat before letting the curtain fall back into place. Emily listened to the soft retreat of her footsteps, the distant rise and fall of the music beyond the withdrawing room door.

Alone again behind the curtain, she drew in a careful breath. Her eyes still burned, her heart still ached, but a fragile thread of steadiness wound through the pain.

Perhaps she was not quite as alone in this glittering, unforgiving world as she had feared.

# Chapter Fifteen

## August 21st, 1822

Pacing in agitation while wearing a ballgown was not something Emily would recommend to anyone, though she practiced it herself the evening of the ball. Her thoughts raced and tripped and grew muddled. All because of one man. She couldn't believe how completely her thoughts had tangled themselves around Mr. Lyness Eastwood.

How had he become such a presence in her life in so short a time? When had he begun to occupy so many of her thoughts, so much quiet territory in her heart?

With him, she did not have to watch herself.

All she could think of was the panorama the day before: how he had stood so near her that she could feel the soft tickle of his breath at the back of her neck, the subtle heat of him close enough to steady her without a word. And when he had taken her hand... she doubted she would ever forget the sensation. His fingers had wrapped around hers with such gentle certainty, offering both comfort and strength.

It was silly to have startled at the lights and noise. Nothing truly frightening had occurred. But she had leapt all the same—her heart thundering in her ears—and he had been there at once to soothe her. And she had let him.

She had not hesitated to offer him her hand again, and again. Until he held it for nearly the entire performance.

What was she to do?

It was his *brother* who acted as though he meant to court her. His brother who invited her on outings. His brother who held the title. His brother whom her family would expect her to favor. That was the match already forming around her.

Emily paused at the window. The sky remained bright, though the hour crept steadily toward the start of the ball. Why must assemblies begin so late? Ten o'clock felt far better suited to settling into a comfortable chair with a book and a cup of tea.

Yet she would not miss this ball for the world—not for any book or any tea.

*Lyness would be there.*

She corrected herself hastily. *The baron* would be there, and it was the baron she ought to focus her attentions upon. The thought sat like a weight at the base of her throat.

Lyness was only a friend.

*Mr. Eastwood.* That was what she must call him. When, precisely, had he become "Lyness" in her thoughts? When he held her hand? Before? She did not know—but it was entirely inappropriate. Mr. Eastwood was his name, and that was what he must remain: a friend, a gentleman, the brother of a man who seemed poised to offer her courtship. Perhaps tonight.

She drew in a slow breath, her stays tightening comfortingly around her ribs—holding her together when her thoughts threatened to fly away with any semblance of calm she possessed.

A cheerful trill sounded from the birdcage, and she turned. Miss Feathersby bobbed on her perch, bright-eyed, hopping from one end of the looking glass to the other.

Emily smiled. "I am thankful you are part of my life now, Feathers. You are a bright spot in the evenings. And during difficult moments like this one." The last words came out on a sigh. She could not help it; looking at the bird made her think of Mr. Eastwood. That made her wonder if he thought of her. And if he did, what his thoughts about her were like. Did he see all her hesitations in a world where she did not belong?

Miss Feathersby was small and unremarkable. But Emily cherished her without hesitation. Why, then, was she unwilling to grant herself the same gentleness? Why did she demand perfection from herself when she did not require it of anything she loved?

Smoothing her gloved hands down the front of her gown, she redirected her thoughts. She *needed* to stop thinking about him.

Lyness was a friend.

Ladies in her position did not indulge fanciful hopes. They behaved properly. Perfectly. Her father's new station demanded as much. She pressed her lips together.

Blessedly, Juniper entered the room, and Emily turned with a practiced smile. Grateful for the distraction from her thoughts.

"Oh, Emily," Juniper breathed, "that gown is absolutely dazzling. Every time you put it on, from the first fitting until now, I'm grateful we found such a skilled seamstress. That shade of pink truly becomes you. It is not a color every woman can wear."

"Thank you," Emily said, adjusting the neckline again. Then she glanced down at the many ruffled lace flounces at the hem. "It all seems rather excessive. I cannot believe how fashionable these ruffles have become. I constantly fear they will catch on something and tear."

Juniper's eyes lit with humor. "That is fashion. Rarely practical, always spectacular." She crossed to the table where a slim volume lay waiting and lifted it with triumph. "Ah—this is what I was searching for. I shall slip it into my reticule and hope for a quiet moment to read a page or two."

Emily laughed. "Only you would bring a book to a ball and expect time to read."

Juniper placed a hand to her heart, raising her eyebrows as high as possible. "How could I *not*? The story is just becoming interesting. Putting it down to dress for the ball was agony."

Jack entered then, adjusting the cuffs of his jacket. "I hear the familiar debate: 'Which book shall accompany me to the ball? Which volume shall I smuggle into my social calls?' My love, why must you forever be attached to a book? Surely we can find reading materials in the places we go. There must be a stray volume lurking in the ballroom somewhere."

Juniper shot him a disgusted look—a moment later softened by sticking out her tongue like a gargoyle. Their affection was unmistakable.

Emily had never thought to describe a relationship as *adorable*, yet the word suited them perfectly. Jack with his stoic reserve, Juniper with her bright laughter—they complemented each other effortlessly.

She wondered, not for the first time, whether such easy companionship was meant for someone like her. Someone who spent every day striving not to disappoint. Someone who feared that, if she faltered even once, everything around her might crumble.

"Now, I have come to escort my wife and my sister to a ball." Jack held his hand out to Juniper, and she placed her own in his with a look in her eyes that made Emily blink in surprise. They had turned from banter to something else, something softer that had her turning away to spare herself, because seeing it made her heart ache.

They were perfectly in love. And neither of them seemed to be trying. That was why they teased one another, why they laughed together, and why they looked at one another as though they could speak with their eyes and hearts alone.

And Emily…Emily longed for that, too. But love matches were rarities. Weren't they?

It was a foolish hope to carry into a ballroom. She followed as Jack led them out the door to the waiting carriage. The short drive became an exercise in restraint. Emily kept her gloved hands folded tightly in her lap, while Juniper chatted about books and fashion and Jack answered in his dry way. Emily heard very little of it. She sat beside Juniper, both of them across from Jack, surrounded by their easy companionship. However, she could not enjoy it, as she spent the ride trying to smooth her own unruly hopes into something neat and sensible. Hopefully, before the doors of the assembly rooms opened upon her.

They arrived, stepped out of the carriage, and walked between tall columns and were swept along by the crowd into the assembly-room-turned-ballroom

Emily drew in a steadying breath as she absorbed the spectacle around her. The crowd had already swelled—gentlemen in handsome frock coats, ladies in shimmering silks and lace—milling about with bright anticipation of the evening and of the entertainments already enjoyed that week.

Yet none of it held her attention for long. Her pulse thrummed loudly in her ears, drowning out the conversation around her, her focus on her own silent search of the room.

Where was he?

Juniper laid a reassuring hand on Emily's wrist, startling her. "Once the dancing begins," her sister-in-law murmured, "everything will be much better. Far less overwhelming."

Juniper had noted her unease. Emily had never been troubled by crowds before her father's unexpected elevation to nobility. She had danced at many a country assembly without growing faint, and she had sat packed into church pews without the slightest flutter. Yet in the months since everything changed, her tolerance for bustling rooms had dwindled.

What was it about becoming a titled lady that made everything about her conspicuous? The constant worry of mis-stepping, the fear of reflecting poorly upon her family, coursed through her mind in a constant stream. She missed the unselfconscious girl she had been before her father became an earl.

There was also that memory of the ball in London that stung every time it came to mind. Anxiety strangled her heart, and she took in a deep breath to settle it. This was not London. She had Jack and Juniper as her support. She was making friends. And this time, she would see Lyness Eastwood.

Jack stepped between his wife and sister. "As the evening goes on, things will calm down," he said confidently. "And Emily will be distracted from the sound and noise by pleasant conversation. Several acquaintances assured me you will have a full night of dancing, Emily. Should you wish it."

She shot him a sharp look. "Jack, have you been soliciting dances for me? I would much rather gentlemen ask because they *want* to, not because my brother hinted I needed partners."

Jack lifted his brows. "I beg your pardon. I believed myself rather clever for ensuring you had a list of options."

Juniper exhaled sharply. "Securing partners for one's female relatives is hardly unusual, but one generally does not *announce* to the young lady that one has done so." With a commiserating glance at Emily, she added, "And we like to think we are sought after for our own merits. Not our relatives' meddling."

Emily folded her arms. "Precisely. I should like my partners to enjoy my company—not merely your friendship." It was absurd, really, that the only gentleman she wished to see was the one she worried would not seek her out. Her stomach tightened at the thought of it.

Jack looked between the two women. Juniper nodded pointedly. He sighed. "Very well. I made a poor decision. Forgive me. Truly, Emily, I wanted you to enjoy as many dances as you please. You loved dancing once. I remember."

That wistful thought softened her irritation with her brother. After Jack joined the military, he returned home perhaps once a year, usually to fulfill family obligations. But the winter before their elevation, he had taken a week's leave from his post as a footman and attended a country dance with the family. She had not lacked partners that night—her brothers' friends, local gentlemen, all were happy to take a turn with her. She had laughed nearly the whole night. The contrast of those simpler evenings with the London balls was extreme.

This York assembly, however, was entirely different from both.

"Unfortunately," she said quietly, "I am not as confident here. Everyone looks so resplendent. I hope I remember the steps well enough not to disgrace myself."

"You will be wonderful," Juniper assured her, as though bolstering Emily for an ordeal. "More than wonderful. By the end of the evening, I daresay many here will speak of your grace."

Emily laughed. "I would rather they did not speak of me at all—unless to merely say that I attended and had a pleasant time."

Juniper gave Jack a pointed look. "Do you hear her? She has no desire to stand out."

Jack—who had spent years in service, accustomed to the edges of grand rooms—only shrugged. "Sensible, if you ask me. Who wishes to be the center of a crowd's notice?"

"Exactly." Emily gestured with a flick of her fingers at him. "If Jack may stand at the periphery and enjoy himself, why should I not find my own wall to prop up?"

"You will not be on the periphery," Juniper said, tone brooking no argument. "You will be dancing."

Jack offered each lady an arm. "Come—let us make a circuit of the room and determine where we would most like to be. Walls or no walls."

They set off together. Jack leaned slightly toward Emily. "I have it on good authority that Lord Hartwell intends to ask you for at least two sets."

"Two?" she whispered. "Jack!"

Two sets with Lord Hartwell—and yet the thought brought none of the flutter she felt wondering whether Mr. Eastwood might claim even a single dance.

"The ball will last into the early hours," he reminded her. "Do not be surprised if he claims the supper dance."

Emily winced but quickly arranged her features into polite serenity. "If he asks, I will accept." That was the bargain every lady made when coming to a ball. To deny a dance with one gentleman meant forgoing that pleasure the rest of the evening. Unless one was clever enough to work around that social constraint. Something she wasn't equal to this evening.

No sign of Lord Hartwell's party caught her eye yet.

Truly, she needed to take more control of her thoughts. From the moment she had entered the assembly rooms, her gaze had searched for one man alone: Mr. Lyness Eastwood.

Would he still think of the way their hands had fit together the day before? Had it meant anything to him? Would he ask her to dance? She dearly hoped so. And if he did not, she would find some graceful way to hint that he ought. One set with him—two, if she were fortunate—would make the anxiety about attending, would make even the crowded evening, more than worth the effort.

"Oh! Lady Emily!" called a familiar voice. Miss Nelson and her twin sister, Miss Theodora, approached in gowns of deep blue and green, both looking thoroughly pleased with themselves.

"Is this not marvelous?" Miss Nelson asked. "The splendor of the room cannot be overstated."

"And the evening is perfect," Miss Theodora added. "Not too warm, and the air is circulating nicely. I have very high hopes for tonight."

"Have you seen Mr. Holly?" Miss Nelson went on. "He has a cousin with him this evening I have not met yet. I simply must determine whether he is worth flirting with."

Emily gasped softly, glancing toward Jack, who appeared entirely unmoved by such candid scheming.

"Do not worry after him," Juniper said, eyebrows raised and a smirk playing upon her lips. "My husband is well acquainted with the mischief young ladies whisper before a ball."

"Indeed," Jack agreed without so much as a flicker of humor. "But to put all of you at ease, I shall leave you ladies to your private conversation." He bowed and withdrew.

"Oh, my lady," sighed Miss Theodora, "you have such a wonderful husband. I hope I find one exactly the same."

"You think my brother wonderful?" Emily asked, unable to hide the surprise in her tone. "What convinces you of that?" She liked him well enough, of course, and she rejoiced that Juniper did, too. But Jack was so somber, and determined to see the danger in every situation.

Miss Theodora blushed prettily. "Well, he is handsome, is he not? And so polite. And though reserved, he observes everything. I always feel he is quietly attentive."

"As do I," her sister agreed. "One should hope for a handsome, attentive, *and* silent husband."

All four ladies laughed softly, Juniper included.

"I assure you," she said, "he speaks quite enough at home. But the true secret to a happy marriage—the sort that lasts beyond courtship—is finding a gentleman who stirs not only your heart but your mind. Jack and I speak of books, nature, politics, and history. I am fortunate he appreciates my intelligence as well as my domestic accomplishments."

"Indeed," said Miss Nelson, "one might say a woman's intellect is her *finest* accomplishment."

Before Emily responded, a movement at the entrance caught her eye. The baron had arrived with his mother, Lady Hartwell, on his arm. He did not waste time in approaching their group, nodding to acquaintances he passed until he stood before them.

Where was Lyness Eastwood? Why was he not in company with his mother and brother?

"Good evening," he said, bowing deeply. "We have not missed the opening set, I hope."

"One is never late," Lady Hartwell chided gently, "so long as one arrives before the supper dance."

Juniper tilted her head. "Or perhaps a gentleman is only late if he arrives after all the eligible ladies have already secured partners for it."

Emily restrained herself from casting a glare at her sister-in-law.

"An excellent point," Lady Hartwell agreed. "Dancing—and

discussing the dancers—is the entire purpose of the evening. I hope you young ladies give us something delightful to gossip about over tea tomorrow."

Everyone laughed except Emily. She had endured enough gossip in London to last her a lifetime. She simply needed to make it through this evening without providing the rumor mill anything new.

"My lord," she said, picking her words with care. "I understand my brother has been arranging partners for me. I hope he did not coerce you into asking."

A flicker of surprise lifted his brows. "I assure you, my lady, there was no coercion. I was present when your brother mentioned that he hoped you would enjoy a full evening of dancing. Several gentlemen assured him you would not lack for partners. He was thoughtful—not intrusive."

"That does sound rather less dreadful than he made it seem," Emily admitted. "Very well. I shall forgive him."

Juniper relaxed somewhat, too. "I am pleased to hear my husband has greater tact than he lead us to believe. You have defended his honor, my lord."

Roman's lips curved, never quite into a full smile, but nearly so. Why was it that he never truly smiled? What lay behind that carefully controlled composure she had come to expect from him?

It occurred to her that if he continued in an earnest courtship, if it concluded the way a courtship ought, then she would one day know.

The thought did not soothe her in the least.

"Oh, there is my friend, Mrs. Pew. If you will excuse me, Roman. Ladies. I hope all of you enjoy the evening." Lady Hartwell nodded graciously to them before snapping her fan open and gliding away with an elegance that Emily could not help envying.

Lord Hartwell watched his mother with concern in his expression.

"Is everything all right, Lord Hartwell?" she asked, keeping her voice quieter as the Nelson sisters engaged someone who had drifted near in a conversation. Juniper had stepped aside, to study a flower arrangement along the wall, giving Emily and Lord Hartwell some semblance of privacy.

"Yes, of course," he said, his features smoothing back into his usual pleasantly neutral expression. "My lady," he continued, "I hope you will not mind if I secure your supper dance now, before another gentleman claims it. It would be my honor to enjoy your company for both the waltz and the evening meal."

Emily inclined her head. "The supper dance is yours, my lord."

His eyes warmed. "Thank you. And having secured your hand for one dance, I hope you will allow me another request. The reel is one of my favorites. I should enjoy the second reel more so with you as my partner."

"How gracious of you," she replied, keeping her tone even. "Yes, of course."

"Excellent." He started to take his leave. "Then I look forward to claiming your hand for that dance." He took a step back, ready to leave her side, his gaze already to where his mother stood among several other matrons.

As his brother still had not appeared, Emily raised her hand to stop him, nearly taking his arm. She caught herself before committing that impropriety, but hastened to speak.

"My lord, I have noticed your brother is not in attendance this evening. Does he plan to arrive later or...?" If Lyness—Mr. Eastwood—was not coming at all, she would rather know in that moment than spend the entirely of the ball looking for him in the crowd.

"My brother?" He blinked at her, then looked back over his shoulder, as though he had realized in the same moment that his younger brother did not shadow him. "He arrived with us. He must have been delayed by someone. I am certain he will appear at any moment. I will tell him you asked after him, if he finds me before he speaks to you." He returned to his bow, then walked toward his mother.

Her heart tripped as she looked toward the doors again. He was here. She would see him. Dance with him. And, hopefully, decide what to do about the pull she felt every time he came near.

Juniper rejoined her, standing directly at Emily's side. "That conversation seemed to go well." She studied Emily, her eyes curious and kind. "Are you looking forward to dancing with the baron?"

"Yes. Of course." Emily checked the buttons on her gloves. "I am. I have not danced with him since that first ball in London."

"No. You have not. Nor have you danced with Mr. Eastwood." Juniper raised her eyebrows slightly. "I heard you ask after him."

Oh. Emily forced her smile to shrink to a more neutral expression. "It seemed polite. Was it wrong?"

"No." Juniper's brows drew together. "Not in the least. But I do wonder, my dear, if—"

Miss Nelson returned at that moment, and relief made Emily greet her with greater enthusiasm. She did not know what Juniper wondered, but she could guess it had something to do with Juniper's curiosity toward Mr. Eastwood. A thing Emily couldn't discuss at present without heat coloring her cheeks.

"I am eager for the dancing to begin, Miss Nelson. I can understand the appeal now to arriving late to a ball."

"Oh, but you did find one benefit," sighed Miss Nelson, using her fan to tap Emily's arm, "to have one's supper dance secured so early in the evening, and by one of the most eligible bachelors in York, is quite an accomplishment. You must feel very grand indeed, Lady Emily."

"I feel…" Emily searched for the right word. *Trapped* would not do. "I feel aware, painfully so, that I must not tread upon Lord Hartwell's toes, either literally or figuratively."

Miss Theodora laughed. "I am sure you will do no such thing. You looked perfectly at ease while speaking with him."

"That is different," Emily said. "I will have to keep up a conversation for a quarter of an hour, at the least, while going through the steps of the dance. I hope no one thinks poorly of him for any ungracefulness on my part."

"Nonsense," Miss Nelson declared. "He seemed pleased when you accepted his invitation. And what does it matter, what anyone else thinks? Everyone is far too occupied with themselves to notice others. Well. Almost everyone."

The younger Miss Theodora leaned closer, her eyes sparkling. "Speaking of being occupied, I do believe Mr. Holly is about to occupy my full attention. Look—there he is. With Mr. Eastwood and a stranger. That must be his cousin from Town."

Emily turned around at once. Mr. Holly made his way toward them through the throng, offering polite nods and smiles to others as he came. On one side of him was a man Emily had never seen before, nor had much interest in. Beside *that* man walked another gentleman, taller and more soberly dressed, his expression distinctly displeased.

Her breath caught.

Lyness.

Lyness Eastwood lingered on Blake Street after his mother and brother disappeared into the Assembly Rooms ahead of him. The lamplight glowed warmly through the tall windows, music already threading faintly into the night, but he made no move to follow.

He was not eager to do more injury to his heart.

Even so, the desire to go inside tugged at him relentlessly. To see Lady Emily again. To assure himself that she was well, enjoying herself, not overwhelmed by the noise and movement of the evening. He could scarcely think of the panorama exhibit without his pulse quickening—those quiet moments when she had leaned into his presence without hesitation, when she had placed her hand in his as though it belonged there.

Stolen things, those moments. Not meant for him.

He had lived his life accustomed to standing behind his brother.

Roman stepped forward; Lyness supported him from behind. Roman spoke; Lyness ensured the details held together. He waited in the wings, ready to step in only if his brother faltered. It had never troubled him before. He had never wanted anything for himself that Roman wanted.

And while Roman did not yet possess Lady Emily's affections—or her hand—he had marked his interest plainly enough. An interest their mother approved. An interest the world would understand.

So Lyness remained where he was, weighing the loyalty to his brother against his longing to see the lady. Something in him rebelled against that loyalty when he thought of Emily.

The thoughts were not merely of her sweetness, though she had that in abundance, nor her kindness—but the way she spoke, thoughtfully, of people and plants and the life she had known before her title. The careful honesty with which she spoke of her fears. The canary they had rescued together, cradled gently in his hat as she trusted him to treasure what she had found worthy.

He admired her intelligence, the spark that lit her eyes when she spoke of her sketches or her herbs. He understood her unease with society's expectations because he had lived beneath those expectations all his life—measured, assessed, found wanting in ways no one ever understood.

Her struggle was achingly familiar.

And somewhere between reproaching himself for holding her hand and longing to do so again, he had realized the truth he most wished to deny:

He wanted to know her heart.

And his own wanted—foolishly, dangerously—to be known by her.

Was there anything more extraordinary than being seen as one was, without judgment? She did not hear his stutter and look away. She did not regard him as Roman's lesser echo. She saw a man with interests, with purpose, with worth.

He wanted more time with her.

The thought settled heavily in his chest.

They had met months ago in London, danced once, exchanged nothing but pleasantries—and yet she had occupied his thoughts ever since. Had the circumstances been different, had he not been summoned away to York so abruptly, perhaps he might have found the courage to ask for more. In London, surrounded by countless eligible women for Roman to notice, Lyness might have—

A hand landed on his shoulder.

He turned sharply, breath caught, irritation rising—then exhaled as he recognized Christopher Holly.

"Holly," he said. "You startled me."

"My apologies." Holly smiled faintly. "I called your name twice. I have never seen a man glare at a building with such intensity. Though I grant you, the matchmaking matrons inside are enough to inspire dread in even the bravest souls."

The jest landed poorly. Lyness shook his head. "I am reconsidering my attendance this evening."

Holly's brows rose. "That is unexpected. Has a dragon taken residence inside the Assembly Rooms? I cannot imagine you being frightened by anything less."

"You mistake me for my brother," Lyness replied, the words dry. "I am not the bold one."

Holly studied him, his expression thoughtful. "That is an odd assessment. You have always been willing to step forward when it mattered—especially when it would be easier to remain silent."

Lyness adjusted his coat, avoiding his friend's gaze. "Why are you still outside?"

"I am waiting for my mother and sister," Holly said, nodding toward the arriving carriages. "My cousin is with us tonight. And you? Why do you skulk about out here?"

"I am *not* skulking. My family is already inside." Lyness hesitated. "I cannot recall the excuse I gave for lingering—only that no one questioned it."

Holly's expression sharpened. "Lyness Eastwood, I believe I

understand what troubles you. I suspected it at your mother's dinner. The panorama confirmed it."

Lyness said nothing.

"You have an interest," Holly continued calmly. "A romantic interest, in fact. In Lady Emily Sterling."

Lyness swallowed again an outright denial. "You confuse me with my brother. He is the one in a position to have such interests. Not I."

"What does your brother's position have to do with your happiness?"

"He is the baron. He holds the estate. He intends to court her."

"And?" Holly asked, voice lowered as a party of several ladies walked by them to enter the ball. "What if she prefers you?"

Lyness shook his head. "You cannot know that."

"Nor can you—unless you give her the chance to choose. Ask her, Eastwood." Holly's voice softened. "What is the worst that could happen? She is a kind woman. She would not wound you deliberately. But by remaining silent, you deny her agency in her own future. Is that truly what you wish?"

The words struck deeper than Lyness liked. He recognized the truth in them—and rejected it all the same.

"It is not so simple," he said. "I have neither title nor fortune to offer."

"So?" Holly countered. "Her father is an earl. She is not seeking advancement. And if she were, she could do far better than your brother."

Lyness had no reply.

Holly sighed. "A woman like her deserves to know when she is loved."

Before Lyness responded, Holly stepped away to greet his family as their carriage arrived. Moments later, he returned, his manner composed once more. He had his mother on his arm, his cousin escorted Holly's sister.

"Mr. Eastwood," he said, extending an implicit invitation, "will you join us inside?"

Lyness hesitated only a moment.

Then he followed.

The noise of the ballroom struck Lyness at once—the swell of voices, the scrape of shoes against polished floorboards, the bright shimmer of fabric and jewels beneath the chandeliers. The air inside was warmer than outside, heavier, filled with motion and expectation.

He reminded himself to breathe.

Holly guided his family forward, exchanging greetings with acquaintances, and Lyness followed a half step behind, his attention undirected.

Until he saw her.

Lady Emily stood near the edge of the room, her pale pink gown catching the light with every small movement. She was not at the center of any gathering, nor was she withdrawn entirely— simply present, poised with a few friends around her. Her gloved hands were folded with careful precision, her posture composed, though something in the angle of her shoulders betrayed her tension.

She looked… luminous.

Not in the way fashion plates depicted beauty, nor in the manner of women trained from girlhood to command a room. It was subtler than that. She looked as though she belonged to herself, even here. As though she carried a quiet gravity that did not demand attention but drew it all the same.

The air left his lungs.

This—*this feeling*—was the cost of coming inside. Part agony, part longing.

She turned toward then, and for one unguarded moment her eyes swept the room with an openness that startled him. Not assessing. Not performing. Searching.

Looking for someone.

The realization struck him with sudden clarity, and the next instant her gaze collided with his. As his steps ate up the distance between them, covering the marble floors too slowly for his liking, he knew. But the knowledge he dare not yet name lodged in his chest, heavy and insistent.

He had told himself he could stand aside. That he could be content with usefulness, with restraint, with doing what was proper. But seeing her there—brave in her composure, vulnerable in her stillness—he knew the lie for what it was.

He did not want to be useful tonight.

He wanted to be *chosen*.

# Chapter Sixteen

When Emily finally laid eyes on Mr. Lyness Eastwood, the tension in his jaw and the set of his shoulders gave her pause. Was he unhappy with the ball? With Mr. Holly? His mouth was set in a firm line, his gaze fixed somewhere past their little group, as though he would rather have been anywhere else than dragged along in Mr. Holly's wake. For one terrible moment she thought he did not wish to be there at all.

Then her eyes met his.

The change was immediate. The stiffness about his mouth eased; familiar warmth lit his features. He inclined his head, the tiniest of smiles touching his lips. Emily's heart gave a startled skip.

"Ladies," Mr. Holly said as he reached them, bowing. "May I present my cousin to you? Lady Juniper Sterling sister to the Earl of Haverford. Lady Emily, daughter of the Earl of Benwaith. Miss Nelson, Miss Theodora Nelson. This is my cousin, Mr. August Booth. He is visiting from London, for the races."

Mr. Booth was fair of features and wore an amiable expression as he bowed and expressed his pleasure in meeting all of them. But Emily's attention darted from him to Mr. Eastwood immediately. She found him glancing at her, too.

Miss Nelson's fan fluttered. "Oh, it is a pleasure, indeed, Mr. Booth," she said with a lift of her brows and leaning toward him. "And have you made the visit here alone? Or do you have family as eager to enjoy the entertainments as yourself?"

It was, of course, a polite way to ask after his marital status. Emily's lips twitched, and she saw Lyness's smile do the same when she met his gaze. He moved to her side subtly, not drawing attention away from the newcomer. Indeed, Mr. Booth seemed quite happy to give a full explanation of having parents in London, brothers in another part of the country, and younger sisters.

Emily scarcely attended to a word. Not with Lyness shifting to stand nearer. He bent slightly nearer her, a warmth in his eyes that made her pulse thrum a reassuring rhythm in her ears.

"Lady Emily," he said, and his voice was perfectly courteous, but she heard something more beneath it. Something tender. "I trust you are well this evening?"

"I am very well, Mr. Eastwood," she replied, hoping Juniper was not paying attention to this conversation. Her sister-in-law saw too much as it was. "It is a great deal to take in and I cannot help but feel rather lost, but I am determined to enjoy it."

Their eyes held for several insistent heartbeats. Long enough for the clamor of the ballroom to recede a fraction. His gaze stayed kind and steady. She was not lost in the crowd after all. Not if he saw her so clearly. Then the Nelson sisters' laughter rippled outward, breaking the moment, while Mr. Booth wore an unrestrained smile.

Reluctantly, Emily gave her attention back to their conversation. But a rustle of movement swept through the room as gentlemen and ladies drifted toward the edges of the floor. The first notes from the musicians rose above the hum of conversation, bright and inviting.

"Oh," Miss Nelson breathed, turning toward the music with obvious delight. "The dancing is beginning at last."

Mr. Booth offered his arm at once. "Miss Nelson, may I beg the honor of this first set? If you are not already engaged."

"I am not, Mr. Booth. Fortunately," she replied, cheeks glowing as she placed her hand on his sleeve.

Her sister was claimed almost as quickly by Mr. Holly. Who looked once, pointedly, over his shoulder as he escorted her to the floor. Right at Lyness Eastwood.

Juniper gave Emily a quick glance. In the flurry of movement, Emily's breath had caught and her body stiffened. Surely, this could not be more anxiety? She was among friends. And York was not London. Everything would be all right.

"Lady Emily."

Lyness's voice drew her attention at his steadying presence again. He stood closer than he had a moment before, his expression composed but his eyes full of an understanding she immediately appreciated. He bowed.

"If you have not yet engaged yourself for this set," he said, "may I ask if you would do me the honor of partnering with me for the first two dances?"

Relief loosened the growing tightness in her chest. She let out a breathless, "Yes." Then to cover the awkwardness of the answer, she spoke with more calm. "Yes, I would be glad to."

His lips curved upward in a way that left no doubt of his pleasure. Not at all like his brother's careful expression. Lyness offered his arm, and when she laid her gloved hand upon his sleeve, she was struck once more by the quiet steadiness of him. Nothing about him was pompous, or demanding, or arrogant. He was calm. Being near him was comforting. She did not find herself worrying about anything other than enjoying the moments in his company.

He led her onto the floor, guiding her into their place in the set with easy, unhurried movements. The figures of the dance were familiar, but the crowd, the heat, the possibility of misstep had all seemed so overwhelming moments before. Now, as the music swelled and they made their first steps, Lyness matched her with such ease that she barely felt the old panic stir at all.

They met in the center and parted again. "Do you enjoy the exercise, my lady?"

"I do," she answered, her lips tipping upward. "I only wish my nerves were more reliable."

He blinked, then gave a quiet huff that was almost a laugh. "I have never yet seen you falter when it counts, Lady Emily."

"That is because you did not witness my first London quadrille," she said, emboldened by the rhythm carrying them along. "I crossed at the wrong moment entirely and collided with a viscount."

"Then I regret not being there to claim responsibility for the error," he replied, tone dry but eyes twinkling. "I am very good at taking the blame for dancing mistakes. As any gentleman should be."

The corner of her mouth lifted at that, and as they wove through the pattern—hands touching and parting, turning and casting off—the tightness in her lungs eased. Somewhat strangely, the noise of the ballroom faded to a manageable hum. His hand was always where it ought to be, never grasping too tightly. When the set called for a brief touch, his was gentle, no more than was needed to guide her.

Somewhere between one turn and the next, she realized she was smiling—truly smiling, not the careful, measured expression she had practiced in the mirror.

For the length of the dance, it felt as though the floor beneath her feet had steadied. As though the eyes around the room had turned away, leaving her to breathe freely. The same lightness kept her feet moving happily through the steps of the second dance, more lively than the first.

All too soon, the final chords of the set faded away. The couples bowed and curtseyed. Lyness stepped back and gave her a formal, if slightly reluctant, inclination of his head.

"Thank you, Lady Emily," he said. "You dance beautifully."

"Thank you, Mr. Eastwood." She dipped in return, wishing the music might begin again at once. "You are a very patient partner. I quite forgot to worry over where to place my feet."

"I am glad to hear it," he replied as he took her gloved hand, tucking it through his arm. "Let me return you to your friends."

For a perfect moment, on his arm and near enough to enjoy the warmth of him, Emily did not want the night to end.

As the dancers couples rearranged themselves on the floor, the swell of voices rose again, and the shifting crowd pressed at the edges of her awareness. The sense of calm she had borrowed from his nearness slipped away by degrees. By the time they regained the company of the Misses Nelsons, also returned from dancing, the ballroom had regained its full, daunting immensity.

Her earlier unease crept back in, though thankfully quieter than before, but present all the same. A stark reminder to her that dancing with Lyness, however steadying, could not entirely shield her from the weight of the evening's expectations. Even if most of those expectations were in her own mind.

As Lyness led Lady Emily away from the dancing, he admired her elegant profile. She was beautiful, but more than that, every time they met, he experienced a connection to her that made him feel more himself than he had in ages.

While they danced, every time their hands met, a comforting warmth spread from his heart outward.

"Would you like some refreshment before I return you to the Misses Nelsons? There is punch and lemonade, I believe, in the next room." The suggestion meant keeping her at his side for precious minutes more.

Her gaze met his, and she winced as though the light bothered her. "I think that is an excellent idea. Yes, please."

Lyness redirected his path to go through the crowd at the edges of the long room, making his way to the crowded corridor and across to the tea room. His attention divided between keeping her safely with him and his own thoughts.

Perhaps Holly's advice had been good for Lyness after all. Perhaps he could advocate for his feelings this once. Roman did not yet behave as a man in love. A true attachment to her wasn't likely.

The way she smiled at him that evening, as though all the world was better when they were together, made him think it possible she would say yes to a courtship. He treasured her friendship, and if it lead to more, his gratitude would know no bounds. Leading her from the dancing, her hand on his arm, a sense of rightness settled in his chest. He would do it.

After speaking to Roman. He owed his brother that much. When Roman gave his blessing, Lyness would speak to Lady Emily. Lovely, kind, intelligent Emily. Asking her for the opportunity to truly win her heart.

And he dearly hoped she would say yes.

As they stepped through into the designated tea room, where tables with light refreshment waited, Lyness looked down at her again and his alarm grew. Her features had turned pale.

"My lady," he said, stepping to the side with her. "Are you unwell?"

"I think I would like to speak to my sister-in-law," she said at a level Lyness barely heard over the music and hum of the room.

He studied her carefully, brow drawn. "Does something trouble you? May I be of some help?"

The tension in her posture eased enough for him to see her quiet need beneath the composed exterior. "If you can bring me to my sister-in-law, I will be grateful. I need a moment to speak with her, that is all."

In that moment, he would have escorted her to the North Pole and back. Anywhere she wanted, anything she wanted, he would give it to her if only to see her well again. "Of course, my lady."

Roman appeared as if from nowhere, a glass in hand, looking at Emily with a frown. "Is something wrong, my lady? Lyness?"

Lyness met his brother's concerned gaze. "Lady Emily needs to speak to her sister-in-law. Have you seen Lady Juniper Sterling?"

Immediately, his elder brother shook his head. "She is not in this room. She must be in the main hall."

If that was so, he would have to take Emily through that ordeal of pressing bodies a second time. That did not seem wise at all. Especially given how pale she had grown, and the way she placed her free hand at her temple made his alarm leap higher.

Lyness met Roman's gaze and gave the slightest shake to his head. She was unwell. That much was obvious to both of them. "She needs something to drink." He nodded to the cup Roman held.

"Of course. I have not had any myself, yet. You are welcome to this lemonade, my lady." Roman gently pressed the cup into her hand. "You look ready to swoon. It will cool you."

"Thank you." She took the cup and pressed it to her lips. She made a face as she swallowed, and Lyness spared a moment of sympathy for the notoriously low quality of refreshment at balls.

Lyness put his hand on Roman's shelter, lowering his voice as he spoke to his brother. "I will find her sister-in-law and bring her back here. Roman, will you stay with Lady Emily?"

With a lift of his brow, Roman said, "Of course. I will see to her every comfort."

Relieved that his brother looked after her, Lyness turned to make his way out back to the crowded assembly-room-turned-ballroom.

Lyness stepped back into the current of the crowd, the noise of the people swelling around him like a tide. He moved quickly, threading through gaps between men's broad shoulders and the ruffled skirts of women, intent on finding Lady Juniper Sterling or her husband and bringing them to Emily's side as swiftly as possible.

He had taken scarcely a dozen steps when he glanced over his shoulder. A foolish thing, really. Stemming from his need to protect her, to be certain Emily had what she needed. Completely unnecessary, of course. Roman was with her. Roman was always dependable in a crisis.

But what Lyness saw made his steps falter.

Roman was no longer standing with Emily at the refreshment table. He was guiding her toward the nearest set of open doors. No, not merely guiding her. Supporting her. Emily's hand clutched at his sleeve. Her steps faltered beneath her as though her slippers could not find purchase on the floor. Her head dipped, the white blossoms in her dark hair brushing Roman's shoulder, and she leaned heavily upon him.

A sickening jolt went through Lyness, forcing him to move. This time toward Lady Emily and Roman rather than away. He saw when she stumbled. Roman caught her fully, his arm sweeping around her waist to hold her upright.

She looked...wrong. Too pale. Eyes mostly closed. Her lips parted on a sound Lyness could not hear across the room, though he saw the shape of it: confusion, or apology, or fear.

Roman bent to murmur something to her, then lifted his head, looking for help. He saw Lyness and lifted his chin in silent command. Completely unnecessary. Lyness was already wading back toward them, hoping no one else saw what was unfolding. Roman's gaze swung back to the open doors, he adjusted his grip and guided Emily in that direction with urgency.

Lyness lost his patience, pushing aside the gentlemen blocking his way, ignoring the startled looks cast after him. His heart hammered in his throat.

Something was terribly, terribly wrong.

Yes, Emily had been pale before. Nervous and possibly overwhelmed. But this... this was different. This was not nerves. This was not merely a lady in want of air or calm.

He had seen a cousin swoon from heat once. He had seen his mother go glassy-eyed after one of her stronger draughts for her nerves. He had never seen Emily like this.

And Roman—serious, unshakeable Roman—appeared alarmed.

Lyness's jaw clenched. He stepped through the door and into a corridor where servants moved quickly to and fro. He caught the arm of a young footman. "A man and woman came through here. The woman was ill. Which way?"

The youth pointed to another door. "Out into the air, sir."

A few decades before, a Medieval Catholic church had stood to the south of where the Assembly Rooms now took precedence. Saint Wilfrid's. The building had been removed when the Catholics opened a newer church across the road. Now the site was the back of the Judges Lodgings' gardens and made into a patch of greenery and cobblestone, with little purpose. It was there that Roman had taken Lady Emily, and there that he lowered her to sit on a large crate when Lyness arrived.

"What happened?" Lyness asked, hurrying toward them in the semi-darkness. The only source of light was what spilled from the windows of the buildings around them and the moon, which was not even at a quarter full. "R-R-Roman," he said, kneeling on the ground as she swayed where she sat. He put his hands up to hold her steady by her forearms, looking into her eyes. Or trying to.

"Lady Emily?" When she blinked without seeming to see him, he repeated her name with more firmness. *"Emily,* can you tell me what is wrong?"

Her eyelashes fluttered rapidly, like she was trying—and failing —to focus on him. Her fingers, which had clutched Roman's sleeve a moment before, lay limply in her lap. Her temples shone with sweat.

Roman sat beside her, arm going around her shoulders to steady her. "She said she felt unwell," Roman said, "and that she could not catch her breath. Had you not brought her to me, were I not the one to hand her a drink, I would have thought her drunk. Her cheeks went red. She could not walk."

"Dizzy," she whispered and fell forward. Roman caught her against him as Lyness lunged forward to steady her. The single word she whispered sounded wrong in her mouth, soft and slurred, in a tone that made it seem to belong someone else entirely. Her lips moved again, as though she meant to say something reassuring, but no sound other than a sigh escaped her.

The brothers exchanged a glance.

"Wh-what was in your-your c-c-cup?" Lyness asked, trying not to panic even as his words tripped and repeated themselves against his will.

"Lemonade. I thought." Roman's glare was a powerful thing, even in the dark. "A servant handed it to me when I entered the room. I did not even ask for it."

Without a word, Lyness leaned close enough to inhale the scent of Emily's breath. She smelled faintly of lemons and something… wrong. Too sweet. Almost medicinal.

"T-t-tampered with. L-l-laud-laud—," Lyness bit off the word he could not speak. His words were tangled, and he gave Roman a look that he inwardly begged his brother to interpret with haste.

"Laudanum." Roman growled and then muttered a curse beneath his breath. Lyness shut his eyes briefly, grateful Roman gave the word he himself could not force out. "We need to get her away from here. Without anyone seeing."

Lyness glanced to the Stamp House directly beside the Assembly Rooms, then farther away, to an alley that would lead them out to Blake Street. He stood. "Y-you re-re-retrieve the c-c-carriage."

No one would understand a word Lyness said if he attempted to command such a thing at present.

"I will bring it to the alley's exit on Blake Street. Meet me there. Stay in the shadows as much as you can. I will send someone to find her brother without returning to the ball myself. Hopefully, no one paid attention to our exit." Roman stood, maneuvering carefully so Lyness could trade positions with him to support Emily. Her hair was mussed where it had rested on Roman's shoulder, and the chamomile flowers barely clung to the dark curls. A tiny, involuntary sound she made, a whimper from clenched lips, cut straight to his heart.

Someone had meant for Roman to drink the lemonade. Instead, an already distressed Emily had taken what was meant to make the baron look like a fool. Lyness's anger threatened to intrude in that moment, but he cast it aside and instead tilted his forehead to rest against the softness of her curls. He had to take hold of himself and the situation. For Emily's sake.

He wanted to speak. To reassure her. But he knew his tongue would not obey, though he fiercely wished it would. All he had were his actions, and he did not know if her mind remained fully present. He wanted to tell her that he would lift her in his arms and carry her to safety. Instead, he pressed his lips briefly to the curls above her ear. Not a kiss. Not truly. Only the ghost of one. And the closest he dared come with his intentions still undeclared.

He inhaled deeply, stealing himself for what came next. Carrying her through the dark. Keeping her safe from stumbling and prying eyes both.

He slid one arm beneath her legs, the other around her shoulders, and he lifted her into his arms. She tried to take hold of him with one hand, but it slipped down the front of his coat. Her head fell against his shoulder. She made barely a sound, and he hoped she had fallen into a faint. Better that than awake and frightened of what was happening.

He picked his way through the darkness toward the alley, determined to spirit her away without anyone being the wiser. His hopes from earlier in the evening, not even an hour past, resurfaced in his heart. He hated seeing her helpless and harmed by another. It troubled him that he felt steadier with her weight in his arms. But being the one to hold her, to cradle her close to his heart, felt right.

# Chapter Seventeen

Voices, muffled but not distant, crept into Emily's awareness. She turned her head, pressing her cheek against the raised texture of an embroidered cushion. She shifted, her legs caught in too much fabric. She blinked several times but everything around her was smudged red and gold firelight.

Where was she? She tried to sit up and barely raised her head before everything spun. Closing her eyes hardly made it better. She groaned softly and lifted her hand, which was heavier than usual, to her forehead. It ached, terribly.

Since she could not move or open her eyes, and she had no idea where she was, Emily put all her effort into listening to the people speaking in the next room. They were agitated. Both men. One of them was softer than the other.

Lyness. His was the voice she could barely make out. His words were catching terribly, too. More than she had ever heard. It took her a moment to make out that he was speaking to his brother. About her?

The baron's answer was louder and clearer. "I have every intention of hunting him down and finding out!"

Finding out? Finding out what?

Why was she somewhere listening to the Eastwood brothers argue?

Then there was a woman's voice. "I know it may not seem like it, but bringing her here was the right thing to do. I only wish I had been with you in the carriage."

"There was not time, Mother—" The baron's voice cut short when a door opened. She heard quick, heavy footsteps.

"Where is my sister?" That voice she knew well.

"Jack." And that was Juniper. Trying to sound calm. "You need to take a moment to steady yourself. We do not know—"

"I want to see Emily at once," Jack snapped out, and Emily's eyes flew open in surprise. She had never heard him use that tone of voice before. And interrupting Juniper? It was not at all like him.

A particularly sharp pain went through her head, from temple to temple, making her wince and close her eyes again.

A soft, firm response followed. "She is resting on the couch in the next room. The doctor is on his way." The baroness this time. "If you will excuse me, I will see to it there is tea."

Heavy footsteps, then a door opening, then a rush of clomping steps to her side. Her head made everything sound unpleasant.

"Oh, Emily." It was Jack. She opened her eyes the barest amount and found him staring at her, his face half in shadows and half revealed by the orange glow of firelight. Candles? Lamps? A fireplace? She did not know, but the way the light painted his face made him look heartily unliked himself. His large hand was on her forehead. Ungloved. "Can you hear me?"

She blinked at her brother and opened her mouth to speak, then made a face. Her mouth felt dry. And unpleasant. As though she had stuffed wool in it and spat it out again. But she managed at last to say, "Jack. What happened? Where am I?"

His hand on her forehead moved slowly, stroking her hair back. The gentleness of it startled her. Jack had not touched her with such care since her childhood. The look on his face, his brows drawn together, his eyes wide, made her heart drop.

"Jack, I am all right. I am only a little dizzy. And I have a headache. And there is this feeling in my mouth…" The crease in his brow went deeper, and she added quietly, "I am so sorry to be a bother."

"You are the furthest thing from a bother." A smile that did not look quite right appeared on Jack's face. "I imagine you feel terrible, and you do not need to reassure me when you are the one who is ill."

It finally occurred to her what was wrong with Jack. Worry had drawn his features, his eyes too wide and the rest of him too taut. And perhaps a little sad. Two emotions she had not seen on his face at such intensity before.

"You are at Lord Hartwell's house in York," he explained to her, hand still resting on the top of her head. It was quite nice. Rather like when she had a cold, just before he left to fight Napoleon. He had sat with her then, talking nonsense to her about her dolls. "It is past midnight. We were all at the ball. Do you remember anything?"

Movement behind his shoulder made her adjust her gaze, and she saw Juniper standing behind him. Her gloved hand on his shoulder. Juniper appeared even more distressed than Jack. That was not a good thing.

Emily pulled her focus back to her brother's probing stare. "I remember the ball. But…" She winced and closed her eyes again. Thinking backward. Which was an odd thing to do. And everything felt strange. Like ribbons running through her hands while she tried to grasp at them.

"It is all right if you cannot remember," Juniper said, and she moved closer. Kneeling beside Jack. Why were they kneeling? "We can ask Lord Hartwell for more details. And the doctor is coming."

"No. No, I can try." Emily swallowed, the dryness in her mouth making the effort unpleasant. "I remember dancing with Lyness." Heat rushed into her face. She hastily corrected herself. "Mr. Eastwood. It was pleasant. Calm." Her brow furrowed. "I felt anxious. But the dancing helped."

Jack didn't speak. Neither did Juniper. Thank goodness. She was already having a difficult time keeping her thoughts ordered.

"Afterward, everything pressed in upon," Emily continued softly, her eyes half-closed as she chased the ribbons of memory through the fog in her mind. "The room was so warm. And the crowd louder. Closer." She winced. "Mr. Eastwood asked if I wished for lemonade. Or perhaps I asked him. I am not certain."

She lifted a hand weakly, as if brushing aside smoke. "Then we went to the refreshment table. Lord Hartwell was already there. I think." Her eyes squeezed shut.

Juniper's hand found hers. She smiled at her sister-in-law, hoping it reassured her. Then she swallowed again. Her stomach turned. Too much swallowing. Did she need something to drink?

What had she had to drink at the ball? "Lemonade. I remember that. After… everything is strange. Like it has been smudged or lost."

For the first time since he arrived at her side, Jack took his gaze off her, turning it to Juniper. His jaw went tight. She knew that look. She had seen it before. In London. When that horrid man had started nasty rumors about her. At a ball.

"I hate balls," Emily whispered to no one.

Jack rose and walked away, and Emily tried to follow him with her gaze, but then Juniper was there. Still holding Emily's hand and wearing a reassuring smile, her gaze assessing as it flicked across Emily's features.

"Everything will be all right, darling. Lord Hartwell sent us a message that said you were ill. He brought you to his home, since it was nearer than ours, and sent for a doctor, too. We will solve this mystery together, and I am certain you will be put to rights in no time."

There were voices speaking again in the other room. But they were no longer muffled. The door stood open still.

"We believe it was laudanum. Intended for me," Lord Hartwell's deep voice said. "I hold the blame for handing the draught to Lady Emily without knowing what was in it. A servant passed it to me."

"We must return at once to the Assembly Rooms and find that servant." Jack sounded as though he were issuing a command.

Something he should not do, since he was the son of an earl and Lord Hartwell was a baron. Or did Jack outrank Lord Hartwell? For a moment, she could not remember. It was one of the first things she had learned. Or relearned when she became the daughter to an earl rather than the daughter of a gentleman so poor they learned order of precedence without thinking they would have need of it.

Why were her thoughts all tumbling over one another?

"He will not have lingered," Lord Hartwell said. "After putting the cup in my hand, whoever it was likely vanished to report the deed done."

"Would you recognize him again? If you saw him?" The frustration in Jack's tone made Emily and Juniper wince at the same moment.

"Perhaps. But...I hardly paid attention. He was only another servant." The baron sounded as resigned as he was frustrated. All this fuss because someone wanted to do him harm?

Emily winced up at Juniper. "Was I poisoned?"

"It certainly seems that way." Juniper stroked her hair back as gently as Jack had a moment before. "My poor Emily. I regret that I was not beside you in that moment to offer comfort and advice." She released a soft sigh, and her shoulders drooped as though a heavy burden rested upon them.

The headache thudded with greater rudeness against Emily's temples, and she squeezed her eyes closed again.

"The doc-doctor is here." Lyness. She lifted her head to see if he was within sight, but he spoke from the doorway, as though held there by some invisible boundary. When his gaze found hers, she wanted to offer some reassurance to him. At least a smile to let him know she was all right, and that she certainly did not blame him or his brother for her predicament. But he looked away too quickly for her to even attempt it, and then disappeared into the shadows.

The baron took over from there. "Doctor Garrett, here is your patient, Lady Emily."

The physician stepped forward, bowing briefly to the room at large before addressing Emily herself. He was a tidy man of middle years, his coat brushed and his cravat immaculate, and he immediately gave her the impression of someone who valued order above all else.

"Lady Emily," he said briskly, "may I ask you a few questions?"

Emily blinked at him. "Yes, of course," she murmured, though her voice scraped unpleasantly in her throat. She glanced up as Jack circled behind the couch, taking up a position that looked rather as though he meant to stand guard over her.

The doctor did not touch her. Instead, he clasped his hands behind his back and studied her with a practiced, assessing eye. "Can you focus on my face? Right here." He angled his head slightly. "Very good. And do you find the light troubles you?"

"Yes," she whispered. "My head aches."

"As expected when one swoons." The doctor nodded once, clearly unsurprised. "Do you feel any chill, my lady? Any trembling in the limbs?"

Ordering her thoughts was not precisely easy with so many people staring at her and waiting for an answer. Emily hesitated. "I…do not think so. Only a great heaviness. And this dryness in my mouth." Her own mind tried to put the pieces together. Though not a doctor, she had prided herself on herbal remedies for various illnesses over the years. Small things that every household had to manage. And her symptoms tumbled over one another in her head without making much sense.

Jack made a tight sound from behind her, but the doctor continued unruffled. "Tell me, have you been ill recently? Any fevers? Faintness before this evening?"

"No," she said. "I was somewhat anxious during the ball. Only a small discomfort, I thought."

He pursed his lips thoughtfully, then turned slightly toward the brothers standing nearer the doorway. "I am given to understand," he said in a voice easily heard by everyone present, "that the young lady drank from a cup handed to Lord Hartwell by an unknown servant. And that she soon after exhibited flushing, confusion, weakness in the limbs, and disordered vision."

A sharp exhale escaped Jack. Juniper squeezed Emily's hand.

"That is what happened, yes," Baron Hartwell stated, standing with something more like his usual poise. Lyness stood among the others but slightly apart, shoulders rigid, eyes on the floor. Every line of him was taut with something she could not decipher.

The physician returned his attention to Emily. "My lady, do you recall the taste of the drink?"

Emily swallowed again and closed her eyes to think. Did she remember? Vaguely, perhaps. As she opened her eyes to focus on the physician again, she said, "I think it was odd. Overly sweet. Medicinal. Not quite right."

Doctor Garrett nodded once, decisively. "These symptoms, combined with your present condition, strongly suggest that an opiate tincture—laudanum, most likely—was mixed into the lemonade. Which would be an efficient way to hide it if one was not already familiar with the distinct scent and taste of that particular narcotic."

"I have never had reason to take laudanum." And that suddenly seemed like a failing of some sort. Emily looked up as Juniper leaned closer, ready to apologize for all the trouble again, but the doctor continued calmly.

"The dose does not appear to have been sufficient to endanger your life, Lady Emily. But it was unquestionably strong enough to befog your senses and overcome you in short order." He raised his brows slightly, speaking to the room now. "She will recover. The worst has passed."

At last, some good news. Emily's shoulders loosened a fraction.

The physician went on, brisk but kind. "She must be kept warm, quiet, and under watch until the remaining effects fade. Small sips of cool tea as she is able. No excitements, no bright lights, and no further exertion." His gaze swept briefly over Jack's tense form. "And absolutely *no* distressing conversation."

Jack folded his arms and did not appear the least chastened.

Emily at last managed to ask one of the questions that troubled her. "Will I...should I remember more of what happened?"

"Perhaps," the doctor replied. "Perhaps not. The mind shields itself during such incidents. You are not to trouble yourself if the recollection remains unclear. You have had a bad time of it, my lady, but you seem healthy in all other respects."

"Thank you, Doctor Garrett," Juniper said, rising from the floor at last to curtsy. "I will need to write her parents about the situation at once, and I am glad I can offer them the comfort of your diagnosis. She has said her head aches, and given that my sister-in-law is slow to complain of such things, it must be rather severe. If you might leave us something for that?"

Though Emily was tempted to protest, Juniper was right. So she kept her lips pressed together this time.

He inclined his head. "I will leave a draught for the headache, though it will subside on its own before tomorrow afternoon. If she becomes nauseated, let her expel whatever is in her stomach. Some of the drug may remain. But if her breathing grows shallow, send for me immediately. Otherwise, she will mend." He bowed and went to speak with the baron. Juniper turned all her attention to Emily.

Then the baroness came into the room, a servant with a tray keeping pace behind her, but Lyness appeared from the shadowed corner of the room.

"Mother," he said, tone firm and quiet. "Lady Emily's troubled by a s-severe headache. I think it best the men leave the room to let her recover. Her sister-in-law will stay, of course. And she will want the tea." He looked at Juniper for her nod of approval, but his gaze did not seek out Emily.

It was terribly disappointing to be near him, in distress, and not even have the opportunity to smile at him, let alone speak with him. Had she done something shameful while under the influence of the laudanum? Why did he seem reluctant to even look at her? It made her chest ache in a manner completely different from the pounding in her head.

"Oh, of course," the baroness agreed readily. "Doubtless, the gentlemen will wish for something stronger. But I will have tea sent to the study for you."

"I must take my leave," the physician said as he left the room with the Eastwood brothers.

Before Jack followed them, he looked down at Emily and offered her a tight smile. "I must join the others. But I leave you in good hands." As he walked by Juniper, he brushed her arm with his hand, and Emily found that the ache in her chest increased. "Ladies." He bowed and exited the room, closing the door behind him without a sound.

The baroness settled in a chair across the rug from Emily, serving the tea. She spoke in a soft tone as she poured out. "I know precisely how you feel, Lady Emily. Poor girl. I have nervous complaints of my own, and my personal physician suggested a laudanum tincture a year past. Trying that odious concoction once was enough for me. It is all very well and good to have it for something serious, and to sleep away grievous injuries, but it caused more discomfort than it cured in my circumstance."

"Thank you, my lady. Your kindness is of great comfort to me," Emily said with as much gratitude as she could manage.

"Here, darling. Let me help you sit up enough to try the tea." Juniper took her by the hand and together they managed to put Emily in an upright position, though she leaned back against the furniture. Her posture rather terrible. And it made her stays pull uncomfortably at her ribs in a way they normally did not. Women's undergarments made for balls were not as suitable for lounging.

For a moment, she thought she saw Juniper and Lady Hartwell exchanging a troubled glance. But when she focused on them, the baroness gave a shake of her head to Juniper and turned a calm smile to Emily.

"All will be right, my dear." Lady Hartwell passed a cup to Juniper, who handed it carefully to Emily. "Roman and your brother will see to it, I am certain. The miscreant who harmed you will be brought to justice. You must try not to worry, and put all your efforts into recovery. You have been through enough tonight."

That made Emily's brows come down in a way that pulled unpleasantly at the pain inside her head. How as that even possible? She did not know. And she did not want to know what the baroness thought worried her. All she wanted was a sip of tea to clear the horrid taste from her mouth. And perhaps the tincture the doctor had mentioned for her headache.

Everything else could wait. Including her concern for Lyness Eastwood, and the way it hurt when he completely ignored her, even though everyone else clustered around trying to be helpful.

Juniper's attentiveness was compassionate. Lady Hartwell's voice was soothing. Jack had hovered like a sentry. She was surrounded by people who cared, protected and safe.

And yet... The one person she had hoped might care for her, truly comfort her, had not met her eyes once. A fresh sting warmed the back of her throat. She had hoped their friendship meant something more to him. Even now, even helpless, she could not banish one quiet, pitiful thought: that in her most vulnerable moment, Lyness Eastwood had not spared her even a single look.

AFTER LYNESS AND JACK ENTERED THE STUDY, ROMAN SHUT THE door with more force than necessary, the latch clicking sharply into place. He strode to the sideboard without a word and poured three measures of brandy, his movements spare and precise as the crystal decanter clinked softly against each glass. Jack stood a few feet from the door, jaw tight, hands balled at his sides. Lyness crossed the room to the hearth, caught between wanting to fade into the corner and needing to hear every word.

The dogs both picked up their heads, watching Roman move across the room but unmoving unless he commanded them. They had been commanded to the study when Lyness carried Lady Emily into the house.

The room felt too close. Too warm. Too still for the agitation growing inside Lyness's mind. He tried to take in a slow breath, the scent of beeswax polish and books doing nothing to settle him.

Before speaking, Roman took a glass to Jack. "Sterling."

Jack accepted it, though his expression suggested he would have preferred a weapon and a battle plan. He swallowed the first mouthful like a man fueling fire rather than quenching it.

Never had Lyness felt as helpless as he did while everyone stood in the room listening to the doctor. Everything in him had wanted to go to Emily, to sit beside her, to take her hand while the room held its breath and the doctor asked his questions.

Every second standing there, he forced himself to practice restraint. He had not even been able to look at her, to offer that much comfort, for fear she would read the pain in his eyes. Pain because he lacked the right to sit by her side.

When handed his own glass, Lyness held it in both hands. Not drinking. Turning it around and around as Roman walked to his desk with the final glass. Lyness would much rather keep his mind sharp. He settled the glass on the mantel instead.

Roman exhaled slowly. "She is out of danger. The doctor said as much."

Jack's answering laugh was low and humorless. "You think her *physical* danger is what concerns me most at this moment?"

The words landed like blows on Lyness's heart, and he winced beneath them. Roman's jaw flexed. Athena's great head turned from studying Roman to looking up at Lyness, while Apollo whined softly and lowered his own to his paws. The dogs wanted to be of use, of course. But they were as helpless as Lyness in that moment.

Jack stepped farther into the room, his tread heavy on the carpet. "My sister was practically carried from a public ballroom. In your arms." His voice remained low, but the strain beneath his words was unmistakable. "And she did not return. Neither did you.

And neither did my wife nor myself once we were summoned away."

Setting his glass down with a soft clink, Roman turned to fully face the distraught gentleman. "What choice did I have? I could not leave her senseless on a bench for all the world to gawk at."

"I am not criticizing that," Jack snapped. "I am criticizing what comes *after.* What the world will say." He looked between the two brothers, eyes sharp and pained. "My sister has been the subject of gossip before. You do not know what that cost her or how it shook my family. Her position in Society is already delicate."

Roman's shoulders stiffened as though absorbing a blow. Lyness had to curl his own hand into a fist to keep from speaking too quickly, too defensively.

Jack drew a breath that sounded torn from him. "We all know it will not have gone unnoticed, the way in which you left. How could it? A baron leaving with an earl's daughter—unattended—will not be excused. Men will whisper. Women will murmur behind fans. And the story repeated tomorrow morning will not resemble truth."

For a long moment, Roman stared at the floor before lifting his head. "I take responsibility."

"Responsibility will not silence the whispers," Jack said bitterly. "The reputation of an unmarried woman is more fragile than any of us care to admit."

A silence fell. Lyness felt it tighten around his throat. His pulse pounded in his ears. He knew what was coming. He had heard of such things, and they were the fodder for many a novel, but here it was. Happening before his eyes.

At last, Roman said, quieter, "If you are implying what I think—"

"I am not *implying*," Jack said, voice edged with anger. "I am telling you plainly: if this is spoken of unfavorably, the only way she will recover is if you offer for her."

Lyness's breath caught painfully. He kept his face still. Neither of the other men looked at him. As far as they were concerned, this moment was theirs alone. Athena kept low to the ground and moved closer to him, dropping her chin onto his foot when she laid down again. Sweet soul.

"I will do so if required." Of course he would. Roman never hesitated to act with honor.

The former soldier's eyes darkened and his frown was something to behold. "Required," he repeated. "Not the most charming beginning to a marriage."

"Forced by circumstance," Roman agreed, voice strained. "Circumstance I regret more deeply than you can imagine. Your sister deserves better, Sterling. Lady Emily is a wonderful woman."

Pacing to the sideboard, Jack put his glass down. He did not face them as he bent his head, his posture stiff with defeat. "I cannot bear the thought of her name dragged through ugliness again."

At that, Roman moved to him, lowering his voice. "Jack. I admire your sister. I do. She deserves someone honorable. And if the burden falls to me, I will carry it with the upmost respect for her."

A burden? Lyness winced at the idea of anyone thinking marrying Emily, no matter the situation, a burden. Marrying her due to honor? Respect? Both virtues, but Emily deserved more. Lyness's heart twisted, a knot of emotion rising in his chest. He stared into the fire, trying to steady his breathing. His mind scrambled for a plan.

But he heard Jack, in a low voice, murmur, "Then we are in agreement." Lyness's gaze came up at that, watching the two of them intently.

Roman swallowed the last of his drink, then stared at his empty glass as though he held it in contempt. "Yes. We are."

A long, weighted silence followed before Jack spoke. "For now, I will give the ladies a gentler story. And tomorrow, we will discover what the people of York noticed. After determining what is being said, we will know how to act."

Lyness watched as Roman nodded, his brother's confidence to set matters right on full display. "I will craft the explanation carefully, and I will repair as much as I am able."

When he spoke, Jack's voice was hoarse. "Thank you." He looked at last at Lyness. "Both of you. For being there. For protecting her when I had not the slightest idea of my sister's vulnerability."

The guilt in the man's eyes sank deep into Lyness's heart. Both men in the room with him were being driven by different motivations. Guilt and honor. Protectiveness and righteousness. Neither of them were acting without reason, and saving Emily from censure was a strong motivation.

But their solution did not sit well with Lyness.

Jack straightened. "Now, we must ensure we choose a path that preserves her." He turned toward the door.

Roman's voice stopped him. "Sterling…"

The man paused.

Quietly, staring at the former soldier's back, Roman said, "This is not how I would have preferred to announce an engagement."

Jack's eyes closed a moment. "Nor I." Shaking his head as though to clear the misery from it, he said, "We will take our leave as soon as Emily can manage the walk to the carriage."

He left the room, closing the door behind him.

Lyness stared at Roman's slumped posture across the desk. Standing there, the shape of a decision formed in Lyness's mind—sharp, daring, and terribly clear.

Roman lifted his head. "This is not at all what I wanted to happen. I had no even asked for a proper courtship yet. Lyness, she may not even like me. But there is a chance we were not noticed. Not by anyone who matters." He finally said, "Apollo. *Komm*." The male dog rose and hastily disappeared behind the desk to drop his head into Roman's lap, his unseen tail thumping loud against the floor.

And Lyness realized he could no longer simply stand by.

The other two men had formed the loosest plan around what to do if the rumors proved unkind. The hope that Roman and Emily had not been seen leaving the ball was a naïve one. If Lyness had spotted what was happening from several feet away, chances were very good that others had noticed a baron and an earl's daughter leaving the ballroom and not returning. It was as likely that someone had seen the way Lady Emily had leaned against Lord Hartwell.

At the time, Lyness had been so focused on Emily's distress that he had not paused to consider how best to mitigate what others saw, or what gossip would follow. If he had been thinking clearly, he might have insisted Roman return to the ballroom. But now it was too late. They could not take back what happened.

Hearing Jack's concerns—that the gossip from London would be renewed or remembered in light of this latest incident—compounded the seriousness of it. Perhaps they could explain that Sterling and Lady Juniper had left because of Emily's sudden disappearance, that they had been with her while she felt unwell. But more often than not, it was the dramatic and scandalous version of events people chose to believe, rather than the mundane and plausible.

In truth, they had a limited amount of time to give Emily's absence a harmless explanation. A pleasantly dramatic one, if necessary—anything preferable to scandal.

Marriage to save her reputation stood at the forefront of Lyness's mind. His chest tightened and his hands flexed at his side. The situation distressed him. It would certainly upset her. Perhaps that was why he came at the entire matter with a different sense of urgency. Could he truly allow his brother to announce an engagement to Lady Emily and do nothing?

Athena rose and nudged his hand with her nose, and he gave in at last to scratch her head behind her ears. Thinking.

Roman would always choose the honorable path; it was who he was and had always been. Lyness admired him for that. Indeed, he would never think poorly of his brother's honor. But that did not mean he had to bow before it, either.

Moments after Sterling left and Roman said, resignedly, "It is a very good thing that I admire Lady Emily, and that we are not strangers to one another."

Lyness was silent, taking in his brother's expression, the set of his shoulders, and the slump of his posture. "Do you believe admiration enough to offer for her hand?" he asked quietly.

Roman looked up at him. "Does it matter? We are in this situation now, and I will do what must be done. She is an honorable woman from a good family. I will not allow her reputation to suffer —or her name to be sullied. It is my fault this happened." He leaned back in his chair and stared upward at nothing. "I handed her the cup meant for me. I handed her the poison that will destroy her reputation. I escorted her from the room, when I ought to have helped her to a chair or called for some assistance—anything other than spiriting her away into the night."

Bitterness rose in Lyness even as he smiled. It was difficult to picture his brother "spiriting" anyone anywhere. It was far too theatrical for someone as practical and respectable as Roman.

"I was there," Lyness reminded him. "I was with you, and I am as responsible as you."

"Yes, but," Roman countered, "no one saw you with your arm around her, taking her from the room."

"Perhaps," Lyness said slowly. "But I disappeared at the same moment you did. And you know there are many people in York who confuse us at a glance—until the moment I try to speak."

"I am aware," Roman said with a smirk, rubbing his temples. "I think I could send you places to stand in for me, in situations where nothing is required of me except a body in attendance, and no one would realize which brother they had seen until you spoke."

They could not change what had happened. But what if they recast one of the players? What if it hadn't been Roman who lead Emily out into the night?

The thought struck like lightning. Lyness did not have to accept Roman's plan—nor yield the narrative to it. It had been a crowded ballroom. While the chandeliers and candelabras had offered plenty of light, it would not be difficult to convince people not to trust what they thought they saw: Lord Hartwell escorting Lady Emily from the assembly rooms.

They could persuade the elite of York that it had been the

younger Eastwood brother—Lyness—escorting his beloved out into the night to request her hand in marriage.

The idea turned into a plan. It laid itself out in his mind as clearly as though a map unfurled in front of him. The path he must take already marked.

Roman tilted his head forward again. "You went awfully quiet," he said. "And you look as though you had a thought. Care to share?"

Not ready to reveal his sudden clarity, Lyness shrugged. He bent to give Athena more of his attention, looking into her large, calm eyes. "There is not much I can say that has not already been said. What you ought to focus on now, Roman, is who would have wanted to tamper with your drink. You have made enemies, certainly—but I cannot think of anyone so bold as to drug you. Who would benefit from such a thing? Why dare attempt to destroy the good standing of a nobleman?"

It was the right thing to say and a far better problem for Roman to fix his thoughts upon than Lady Emily's reputation.

Roman sat forward, eyes sharpening with righteous anger. Apollo huffed and moved away from the desk, back to the fire. Roman opened his top drawer, withdrew a small notebook, placed it before him, and took up a pencil. Lyness came closer and realized his brother was making a list of names—names he recognized. Men who stood in political opposition to the York Whig party. Roman had made many political enemies, but they were the sort who spoke boldly against him in public and still sat at his table to dine that same evening.

"What will you do to determine who is responsible?" Lyness asked. "Have you a plan?"

"It will not take long to form one," Roman said firmly. "I will bring my suspicions to those I trust, and with their assistance we can find which blackguard would do such a thing, and ensure he cannot ever commit such an act again."

Roman bent over the notebook with renewed purpose, already scribbling names with the same intensity he brought to accounts and estate ledgers. His focus narrowed to a single, potent point.

"No one endangers a lady in my company without consequence," he muttered. "We will discover who stands behind this."

Lyness watched the familiar crease appear between his brother's brows, the one Roman always wore when he believed he had found a just and noble mission. Good. Let him chase that. Let his honor fix itself on the villain who had dared tamper with his drink.

"That is wise," Lyness said quietly. "Lady Emily is safe for the moment. You may do the most good by finding the culprit who endangered you both."

Roman nodded sharply. "Precisely. Her reputation hangs in the balance, but the source of this attack must be rooted out before any further harm is done." He returned to his list, pencil scratching with grim determination.

Lyness gave Athena one last pat on the head before he stepped back, letting the fire's glow warm his spine. Roman's attention was fully claimed, drawn away from Emily's reputation and pointed squarely toward the enemy he was certain lurked somewhere in York's political shadows.

Nothing could have pleased Lyness more.

His own plan came again in his mind: delicate, daring, and far too easily executed. The ballroom had been dimmer than Roman remembered. The movements quick. The gossip easily reshaped. And Roman, his wonderful and honorable brother, was now thoroughly occupied hunting a different quarry.

Lyness inclined his head toward his brother. "I will leave you to your work," he said, steadying the tremor in his voice. "You have a great deal to consider."

Roman barely acknowledged him, too engrossed in his list.

Good.

Lyness quit the study with a careful, measured step, closing the door softly behind him. And in the quiet corridor, he allowed himself a single, steadying breath.

He would not surrender Emily's future, or his own, to Roman's sense of duty. Not when another truth, another possibility, had begun burning clear as the dawn within him.

# Chapter Eighteen

## August 22nd, 1822

The morning after the ball dawned with a brightness particular to York in August, without fog or clouds to disturb the enjoyment of the day. Lyness Eastwood stood at the window of Hartwell House, in the dining room, watching the faint stir of activity in the street below. Carriages rattled past, servants hurried with baskets of bread or linens, and the distant hum of race-week excitement rippled through the city.

The Sterling family had left a short time ago, all of them exhausted, and Lady Emily leaning heavily on her brother's arm as he helped her into the carriage. Though he had been awake the whole night through like them, Lyness's mind stirred with invigorating ideas.

In a few hours, he would ruin everything.

He pressed his palm briefly to the cool window glass. His thoughts tangled, then untangled, then settled into a single, curving line.

Emily deserved better than fear. Better than rumors. Better than being betrothed for honor's sake. And if he did not act now, Roman would. Roman always chose the honorable path, even when it crushed him.

But Lyness would not let that happen. Not this time. Not with *her*.

Behind him, Roman called from the dining table, "You will keep Mother from fretting, won't you?"

"Of course." Lyness turned from the window with a reassuring lift of his lips. Roman looked pale with fatigue, though his posture remained resolute. He had agreed—after quiet, firm persuasion—that appearing in public today would only fuel gossip. Let York wake with its whispers and no tired baron to confirm them. Roman would send notes to his friends instead and work upon his investigation.

"I worry all of this will distress her." Roman had barely touched his plate.

Lyness nodded. "Mother is more interested in the peonies blooming in Lady Lockwell's garden than any rumors." A half-truth. His mother adored roses, but she loved her sons. She would listen for the gossip as much as Lyness did. She had retired before the Sterlings departed, so at least she would be better rested than most of them.

Roman exhaled. "You will have to take the city's pulse on the matter. I cannot trust myself to react calmly should I hear anything untoward. Or people may hesitate to speak in front of me on the subject."

"I know." Lyness kept his tone even. His heartbeat was anything but. "I will escort Mother to the garden party. I will keep my eyes and ears open."

"Thank you, Lyness. I am fortunate to have a brother such as you."

Lyness bowed and left the study. Hopefully, his brother would still feel that sentiment later.

The hours passed far too slowly for him, but at last the time came to attend Lady Lockwell's annual garden party. She held it every race week on the day of the ladies' purse. Knavesmire was practically outside her front gate, so it was easy enough for the elite members of Society to come and go from her flowerbeds to the Grandstand and back again.

Escorting his mother, Lyness lead her into the gardens with his head held high. Long tables had been set out beneath a striped canopy, laden with pastries, cold meats, and fruit presented in crystal dishes. The guests floated in clusters across the lawns, chattering brightly over their chocolate and tea, women in bright morning gowns fluttering their fans against the rising warmth. Gentlemen discussing the races and how their favorites had already performed.

Lyness walked beside his mother, who was discussing the comparative virtues of herbaceous borders with her usual animation.

"—though I maintain that a row of delphiniums is vastly superior to hollyhocks, no matter what Lady Lockwood insists. Oh! Lady Crighton has brought her niece. Do remind me to ask about her new gardener. The one from Leeds. Absolutely disastrous with roses—"

"Mother," Lyness murmured gently, "you do not need to speak to every gardener in Yorkshire."

"I do if they are *ruining* roses." She sniffed, disdain giving weight to the delicate sound.

He nearly smiled. How easy it was, even in moments of tension, to find comfort in the familiar rhythm of her enthusiasms.

But as they approached the gathering near the refreshments table, the chatter shifted. Faces tilted toward one another. Fans snapped open. Eyes flicked toward them. He knew what that meant.

The rumors had begun.

His stomach tightened. From his left, a familiar figure approached—Mrs. Holly, wearing an expression that suggested she had been born to deliver unpleasant news to others and savor it.

"My lady," she cooed, dipping in polite curtsy, "how *lovely* to see you after such a dramatic night."

His mother paused mid-step. "Dramatic?" She knew as well as anyone how to play the games of Society. She had simply chosen not to take part for a time. "Oh, do you speak of the ball? I suppose the music was somewhat loud. The flower arrangements were certainly overdone. Why does anyone need that many lilies? Their scent is often overpowering."

Mrs. Holly's smile widened. "Oh, come now. One needn't pretend. Due to my connection to your family, through my son's position as solicitor, I have been asked by many if I was aware of the situation. Some were coy with details, of course, but it has not been difficult to piece things together." She lowered her voice a mere fraction, but took on the quality of one sharing a secret. Even if anyone within ten yards could likely overhear it should they wish. "A young lady whisked away from a ballroom by a gentleman —well! It is the talk of the ball this morning. I hear she was scarcely able to walk. Some think she swooned. Perhaps overheated. We all know that Lord Hartwell would come to the aid of a lady in distress. One prays it was all innocent, of course."

Lyness saw the color drain from his mother's cheeks. "Oh? I must have missed that, but then, I did leave early. A young lady of my acquaintance fell ill, you see, so I took her home with me."

That...was not part of the plan. Lyness kept his expression still, admiration for his mother rising. But he had a feeling that story would not be enough.

Mrs. Henry Rothingham had approached, too. A formidable matron in York, even without a title. They owned a great deal of property. "Was it Lady Emily Sterling you took home? How interesting. I heard Lord Hartwell was seen taking her through the servants' corridor."

Before his mother could gather her composure to handle that thread of the story, Lyness stepped closer to her side, smile pleasant, tone airy.

"Mrs. Rothingham, Mrs. Holly," he said without a stutter, thanks to his planning, "you astonish me. You know how quickly tales grow legs during race week." He let out a soft laugh. Practiced.

Light. "I assure you, my brother was not escorting Lady Emily anywhere last evening."

Mrs. Holly blinked, disappointed. "He was not?"

The other gossip wasn't so easily dissuaded. Mrs. Rothingham shook her head. "That is what people saw."

"No indeed," Lyness responded, his hand resting lightly at his mother's back. "People likely mistook us in the low light. It was *I* who escorted Lady Emily from the ballroom."

A ripple went through the surrounding cluster of eager eavesdroppers like wind across a wheat field. Then there was much glancing away and clearing of throats. Someone began a new conversation. Loudly.

Mrs. Holly's brows shot upward. "You, Mr. Eastwood?"

Lyness gave a modest incline of his head. "Naturally. She needed air. As her intended, I did not think it amiss to escort her. The Assembly Rooms grow unbearably hot this time of year. But she was unwell, so I took her home. Mother came as soon as I could get word to her."

The collective gasp was immediate and deeply satisfying.

His mother choked on her breath as she looked up at him. "Lyness—!" But she recovered with admirable swiftness, years of social training snapping into place. She placed a gloved hand on his arm. "Of course," she said faintly. "We had...we had hoped to save the announcement for a more appropriate moment."

Mrs. Rothingham looked as though she had been gifted an elephant and did not know what to do about it. "You are *engaged* to wed Lady Emily Sterling?"

Keeping his expression mild, Lyness lowered his head. Conveying warmth and a touch of bashfulness as best he could. "Yes. Though word has outrun us, it seems. Lady Emily was overcome last night due to the heat." He leaned in slightly, the picture of earnest young love. "I took her into the air for her comfort. Nothing more."

"Oh," Mrs. Holly said, deflated. "Oh."

Wonderful. The moment hung in the warm summer air until a familiar voice sliced through it.

"Mr. Eastwood." Jack Sterling stood a few paces away, his wife at his side. Both wore expressions that suggested they had heard every word.

It was convenient, if unexpected. They had likely attended the event for the same reason Roman sent Lyness. To take the measure of the gossip and decide what to do next.

Nothing could be done about it now. Lyness bowed. "Lady Juniper Sterling, Mr. Sterling."

Jack's gaze was sharp as a blade. "I did not think we planned to announce my sister's engagement in public this soon." His voice was not-quite steady.

The crowd, sensing something dramatic occurring, moved closer.

Lyness met his eyes without flinching. "I apologize, sir. I merely wished to put our friends, Mrs. Holly and Mrs. Rothingham, at ease. They were distressed about Lady Emily's absence last evening. Of course, I was grateful I could be by her side until her family arrived to care for her."

Because he watched them closely, Lyness saw when Lady Juniper's hand tightened on her husband's arm, her smile small but unmistakably genuine. "How kind of them. Thank you, ladies. I will pass your concern to my sister-in-law."

"Yes. Very kind of you both." Jack's jaw flexed. "A private conversation, if you please, Eastwood? A family conversation."

Lyness inclined his head. "Of course."

Mrs. Holly, who had been drinking in every second, seemed to suddenly remember she had other guests to annoy and scurried off, fan fluttering wildly. Mrs. Rothingham wrinkled her nose at them, but then went on her own way, too.

With a lighter heart now that the most difficult part was done, Lyness took one step forward before his mother caught his sleeve.

"Lyness," she whispered fiercely, "what have you done?"

He covered her hand with his own, his voice low and steady. "Something necessary, Mother."

Her eyes searched his face while her own wore confusion, worry, and then, slowly, maternal understanding softened her features. She gave one short nod and stepped back. "I must have that conversation about the Leeds gardener. Do send for me if you need anything at all, Lyness."

"Thank you." He squeezed her hand before letting her go to pursue more pleasant conversation. Doubtless, she worried still, but she also seemed to understand there was a great deal at play. And she had been ready to defend Lady Emily herself. That she trusted Lyness to handle it gave him leave to relax a little more.

He fell into step with Jack and Lady Juniper, on the lady's free side, as they went toward an area in the garden tucked behind a hedge, away from the tables and amusements, where few people stood.

Juniper spoke quietly as they crunched along on the gravel path, barely loud enough for the men to hear. "If you truly care for her, Mr. Eastwood, this is the moment to be brave."

He did not falter in step or mind. Certainly, not in his heart. "And so I shall strive to be, my lady."

And then they stood out of sight of most, in as much privacy as could be found at present, where their private reckoning began, and where he defended not only his plan or Emily's name, but the fragile, powerful hope he had carried for her since the moment he knew was falling in love with her.

EMILY HAD NEVER DISLIKED SUNLIGHT BEFORE, BUT THE THIN BEAM spilling across the carpet and onto her pillow felt as though it had arrived with opinions. None of them helpful. The sun was far too bright and too awake that afternoon.

Unlike her.

She shifted slightly, wincing when her head throbbed, and realized someone had place a damp cloth on her forehead. The scent of lavender clung to it. Juniper's doing, surely.

A soft rustle sounded nearby, and then Juniper's voice, gentle but certainly alert, reached her. "Emily? Are you all right, darling?"

Emily forced her head to turn toward the light. "I cannot tell at present."

Juniper was at her side in a moment, blocking the offending sunlight and smoothing the blanket. She also inspected Emily closely, as though looking for evidence of her health upon her face. "How do you feel?"

Emily swallowed. "As though I was trampled by a horse, then dragged behind it for several miles."

Juniper pressed her lips together, eyes dancing even as she winced. "The doctor said the headache would linger. And the dryness. I suppose we cannot be surprised, then. But you are home and safe."

Safe. How fragile the word felt.

Emily tried to sit up, and Juniper supported her by quickly adjusting pillows behind her back. "Slowly, dearest."

The room swam with less violence than the night before. She breathed carefully until the dizziness subsided. "What time is it?" she asked, knowing her room faced westward. "Have I slept the whole day away?"

"It is to be expected, given you did not sleep at all last night. It is a quarter past two." Juniper moved away to fetch a cup of warm peppermint tea. As she handed it to Emily, she said, "There is something you must know. Something important."

Emily's stomach dropped. "Oh no. Did I do something strange because of that horrible drink? Was I terribly ill-mannered? Did I cause a scene?"

Jack's voice came from the doorway. "No. But someone else created one."

With a sharp turn, Juniper gave him a look full of warning. "Jack, not like that."

Clutching her blanket, Emily tried to ignore the prickle beneath her skin. "What has happened? Please, Jack. Tell me."

His face was unreadable as he stepped fully into the room, but his shoulders held tension she rarely saw. He cleared his throat. "Emily…you are engaged to be married."

Her mind went perfectly blank. She stared at him. Then at Juniper. Then back again.

"I beg your pardon?"

Juniper took her hand. "To Mr. Lyness Eastwood."

The sensation of someone pouring cold water down her spine made her shiver. Lyness Eastwood. Not his brother. Lyness.

The memory fluttered at the edge of her mind—dancing with him, his patience and steadiness, the warmth of his hand against hers. Then everything blurred after the lemonade. Like a story someone had half-erased. But Lyness had hurt her the night before, at his home, had he not? He avoided looking at her and speaking to her, even though everyone else hovered and asked after her health, he stood apart.

"Engaged?" Emily whispered. The word felt foreign on her tongue. "But…how? I do not recall speaking to him about such a thing. Or to anyone else. We were not even courting."

"No. He did not speak to anyone about it either. Until he made the announcement." Jack grimaced. "He declared it this morning at Lady Lockwood's garden party."

Juniper added quickly, "To stop the gossip from harming you. It was already spreading. The implication that you had slipped into the night with Lord Hartwell was circulating. As we feared it would."

"We? But no one told me…" No one should have needed to tell her, Emily realized. She had been so shocked by the events of the night before, so foggy from the laudanum, so exhausted from the ordeal, that she did not once think of the repercussions to the evening. Emily pressed a trembling hand to her mouth. "Oh no."

"It is all right, Emily. Take a deep breath in. Slowly." Juniper squeezed her fingers. "Mr. Eastwood acted to protect you. Truly, your brother discussed the possibility of such a thing last evening. With both Lord Hartwell and Mr. Eastwood."

Folding his arms, Jack said with a deep frown, "This is not exactly what we decided upon, however."

Emily's thoughts stayed on what Juniper was saying rather than her brother's complaints. "Protect me? But how could he...? Without asking? Why did no one speak to me of this first?"

"We thought it best not to worry you while you recovered." Jack said, and when she turned to look at him, unable to say a word for the hurt she felt, he shifted uncomfortably. "It was for the best, Emily. You were not in a position to make any decisions. And now Mr. Eastwood is downstairs. He asked to speak with you as soon as you woke."

Her heart stumbled over itself. "He is here? To see me?"

"Yes," Juniper said softly. "And he is terribly concerned for you." Juniper rose, slowly. "If you are unable to speak to him, I will send him away. If you would like, I can help you dress, too. But you deserve to hear the explanation from him directly, Emily. As soon as possible"

Emily tried to gather her thoughts, but they scattered like startled birds as she realized both her brother and sister-in-law waited upon her decision. She pointed to the door. "Out, Jack. I need to dress."

He gave a stiff nod, touched his wife's shoulder briefly, and left.

The ladies wasted no time in getting Emily out of her night things and into a comfortable day dress. It was not the stunning gown she would prefer to greet the news of an engagement in, but given the circumstances, speed was a higher priority than her appearance.

"What did Jack mean," she said as Juniper fastened her gown at the back, "that this is not what they decided upon? They, who? You? Him? The other men?"

"Lord Hartwell, Mr. Eastwood, and your brother spoke at length last evening," Juniper explained as she finished tying up the ribbons at the back of the gown. Then she gestured for Emily to sit.

They needed to put her hair up. "They were concerned about your reputation. I was only told this before the garden party, but they decided amongst themselves that Lord Hartwell would marry you to preserve your honor. Really, I should not tell you more. But I do think things have worked out better than one could expect." Juniper pulled pieces of Emily's braided hair this way and that, until it looked less like she'd slept in it and more like it was a deliberate style for an afternoon at home. "That is the best we can do for haste."

Standing, Emily smoothed her gown and went toward the door, but Juniper hurried to catch her with a hand on her arm.

"Listen to me carefully, Emily. Before you go in there to speak to Mr. Eastwood."

Turning, Emily looked into her sister-in-law's eyes. "I truly hope you are about to impart something miraculous to me, Juniper. I cannot tell you how addled my mind is, and I feel as though I am being tossed about in the wind."

Without hesitation, Juniper folded Emily up in her arms, embracing her with a gentleness that made tears prickle at Emily's eyes.

"If I could undo everything that happened last evening, I might well try. But we are here now, and the most important thing for you to remember, my dear, is that we love you. Your family. Your brother. Me. You did nothing wrong, and we know that. My advice to you now is that you listen to what Mr. Eastwood has to say, and then you decide what it is you want. Please. Do not think of anything other than your future happiness. If you cannot bear to think of the future he offers, then tell me so. We will find another way."

Even as Juniper's embrace bolstered Emily's spirits, her words did not pierce her certainty that things were moving out of her control. What would her parents say when they heard of the rumors? Of a hasty engagement? It would be terrible. They would be disappointed in her, and those who said their family did not yet belong in Society would be justified.

"Everything will be all right," Emily said quietly, and hoped she told the truth. She parted from her sister-in-law with a weary little laugh. "My head may be spinning at this moment, but what a thing, to become engaged while one is sleeping." She turned and opened the door before Juniper commented, then hurried down the stairs to the sitting room where Mr. Eastwood waited.

When she opened the door, she expected to see Jack standing inside the room with him. But Lyness Eastwood was all alone, standing near Miss Feathersby's cage, facing the door. He appeared pale and uncertain, but braced in that quiet, determined way she had come to admire. He bowed quickly to her, too quickly, as though he had forgotten how to manage it with grace. The little bird in her cage hopped back a touch, wings fluttering.

"Lady Emily," he said, voice rough.

Emily's heart clenched.

Lyness stepped forward, stopping a respectful distance from where she stood near the door. His expression was earnest. Certainly, he seemed more intense than she had ever seen him. His dark eyes kept hold of her gaze, and he spoke slowly and steadily as he said, "First, I must beg your forgiveness."

For a moment, she stared at him, uncomprehending. She had not expected that to be the first thing he said. "Must you, Mr. Eastwood? I was told you had something to explain to me. Perhaps you ought to do that, and then you may beg. If necessary."

That made his lips curl upward a moment, then he shook his head. "It will be necessary. I never meant to take a decision from you. Nor did I wish to put you in a position you did not choose."

"But you *did* take a choice from me," Emily said, quiet but steady. Somewhat impatient. "You made a decision about my future that I should have been involved in. My brother informed me that you declared us engaged. In public."

He swallowed hard. "Yes."

"Why?"

His breath came out in a humorless laugh, on a strange sort of exhale. "Because the rumors were already forming. And they were…ugly. You were being spoken of as th-though—" He stopped, lips pressing closed for a moment. He took in a slow breath and let it out again, more composed. "As though you were compromised. Or worse, that Roman had behaved dishonorably toward you. I could not let that notion stand."

"Why *you*?" Emily whispered. "Why not let Lord Hartwell make the declaration, if he was the one people saw?"

"Because," he said softly, "I would rather the world believe you were promised to me than watch you be sacrificed to duty alone."

Something in her chest twisted painfully.

His voice lowered, he stepped closer as though he could not help himself. "I will withdraw if you command it…but I hope you will not."

Emily's lips parted.

He continued, halting slightly as the words tripped over the edge of his stutter. "I have admired you since the first moment we danced in London. Long before last night. Before any of this, and I cannot deny that truth now. Not when your future happiness and my own hangs in the balance."

A warmth rose beneath her skin, a flush that did not come from fever or laudanum. It sounded like the beginning of a marvelous declaration. The sort she had not dared to hope for. Still, she had to point out, somewhat practically, "But we barely know one another."

"That is true." His tone held no defense. Only sincerity. "But what I do know of you has stayed with me. You are thoughtful. And compassionate. And far kinder than most of Society deserves. You do not hide who you are when someone needs your care. And I…" His voice faltered. "I am your friend, am I not?"

Emily pressed her fingertips to her lips, her eyes stinging. "But you never seemed to want anything *more* than friendship. And your brother—."

"I know," he interrupted gently. "And I do not take this situation lightly. If you refuse me, if you wish to break the engagement after the gossip has passed, your family will stand behind you."

Something in her rebelled at that. "Is it truly so simple to you?"

she asked. "To offer to save my reputation at the expense of your own?"

"Your reputation ought not be destroyed when mine is better suited to bear the weight," he said. "I would rather endure Society's disapproval than watch you suffer again what you endured in London."

She sucked in a sharp breath, startled that he knew of it.

"I was told only enough that I understood what was at stake," he said. "Nothing more."

Emily's throat tightened uncomfortably. "If I were to accept this…engagement…what then? What is expected of me today?"

He straightened, gathering himself. "We must be seen together. At ease and united. At the races this evening, in an hour's time. And afterward at the theater." A tiny wince changed his expression to something almost amusing. "We must leave no room for doubt as to the sincerity of our understanding."

A reluctant, trembling laugh escaped her. "I cannot believe this."

"I can," he said softly. He stepped closer slowly, giving her every chance to withdraw, and offered his hand. "Lady Emily…may I escort you today?"

She stared at his open palm. His fingers were steady, though she suspected his nerves must be a tempest beneath his composed exterior. Hers certainly were.

That made her pulse flutter, to think of being attached to him throughout the day. And yet… "I do not know what I ought to do," she whispered. "I am not prepared for any of this." She looked up into his eyes, uncertain and afraid to make the wrong choice. In her heart, she wanted to put her hand in his. Every moment spent with him had brought her comfort and joy. Every time she thought of him, she could not help but smile and wish to see him again.

He had not denied that their attachment was one of friendship.

His gaze held steady, his smile was slight. "Then let today be simple. Walk beside me. Speak with me. Allow York to see that you are not concerned by what they do or say. Or what they think." He hesitated. "If you are overwhelmed at any moment, I will take you home at once."

She drew a slow breath. "You sound very certain of yourself."

"Not in the least," he said, the words painful in their honesty. "The only thing I am certain of is that I wish to stand with you. No matter what comes."

A long silence stretched between them, threaded with her surprise and tenderness toward him. And the faint dread of the unknown. Then a soft, uncertain note escaped the canary near the window, and Emily glanced at the brave little bird still trying to find its full song.

Perhaps it was time for her to try bravery, too. At last, Emily placed her hand in his. The warmth of his palm beneath her fingers was reassuring, and when he folded in hand around hers she found it dangerously comforting.

"What comes next, we face together," she said as steadily as she could, as though making a pact or a vow.

"First the races," Lyness said. "Then the theater for a play. I already have tickets for this evening's performance."

"You already possess tickets?" Emily blinked. "You seem much more prepared than I am, Mr. Eastwood. What is showing?"

"A new drama from London," he said lightly, lips curling upward. "At the races, we can remain with your family. At the edges of the crowd, if you prefer. Then you need do nothing but enjoy a play. No conversation or performance except what is on stage. For the moment, you only need to look presentable and remain upright."

How she did not laugh at that, she could not say. "Even so little a requirement seems ambitious."

Lyness chuckled and squeezed her fingers, as though it were the most natural thing in the world. "Then lean on me. That is what engaged couples do."

That made her cheeks warm rather unexpectedly. She gazed at Lyness, her hand still in his. "What if I make a fool of myself today?"

"Impossible," he said gently. "I have never once thought you foolish."

Her heart stuttered. "But, Mr. Eastwood—"

With a quick shake of his head, he said, "Lyness. Please. Call me Lyness." A gentle squeeze of her hand gave her leave to relax somewhat.

"Lyness," she repeated quietly, his name leaving her lips with ease. She had thought of him by that name for some time now, so it was almost a relief to finally speak it out loud without needing to correct herself. For the moment, she put her concerns aside. "I suppose I had better dress properly for the races."

At that, his smile slowly widened. "I will return within the hour to escort you, my lady." He bowed over her hand. "And count myself fortunate to do so."

She curtsied, and then she watched him leave, his steps light and his shoulders squared. As though he had all the confidence in the world that this was the right way forward. She crossed to the canary's cage and looked inside at her little bird. "I truly hope he does not come to regret his choice. But oh, Feathers. How will I tell my parents?"

And why did everything hurt?

# Chapter Nineteen

Roman was waiting.

Lyness had barely stepped through the front door when a clipped, unmistakable voice called to him from the study. "Lyness. In here."

He removed his hat, handed it to Thomas the footman, and braced himself. The house was too quiet. His mother must have retired after he returned her home from the garden party. Roman had been at the club earlier, with his list of suspects and the hope of enlisting his friends to investigate. Given the tone of his voice, either it had not gone well or he had learned of Lyness's actions already. Which left Lyness with no chance of delaying what must come.

He entered the study, shoulders squared and head held high.

Standing near the mantel, Roman braced one hand against the carved stone, the other clenched at his side. His jaw tight enough to crack.

"Would you like to explain yourself?" Roman's voice was dangerously calm. "Because I am curious to hear you attempt it."

Keeping his composure, Lyness closed the door behind him. "I take it you have heard the news."

"Heard," Roman snapped, "is far too gentle a word. I was *informed.* At my club. By men who found themselves delighted to congratulate me on my brother's sudden betrothal." He turned, eyes sharp. It was a rare thing, to see Roman shaken enough to let emotion show plainly on his face. He was, in fact, furious. "My brother who, until this morning, had given *no indication* he intended to propose to Lady Emily Sterling."

It took effort to keep his voice steady and his stutter to a minimum. "I acted to protect her."

"No," Roman shot back. "You acted without speaking to me. Did you consult with anyone before you made your announcement?"

"No." His hands balled at his sides, but he told himself to keep calm. He had expected this, but he thought he would be the one informing Roman of the change in plans, not defending himself.

"What were you thinking, Lyness? How could you make such a decision without speaking to Sterling? Without speaking to *her.* Do you have any idea the position you have placed her in? The position you have placed *this family* in?"

Lyness flinched—not at the words, but at the way Roman spoke them, as though Lyness were a reckless boy rather than the man who had helped carry Emily from danger the night before. "I did what I needed to do."

That made Roman glower. "What you needed to do?" He stalked toward Lyness. "I have spent the entire day trying to determine who attempted to drug me, and in the midst of it, I am told my own brother has decided to shoulder a burden meant for me. The responsibility was mine. I am the head of this family, I am the one that must see to it that things are done correctly. You do not understand, Lyness. The engagement ought to have been mine to offer, because I am the one who—"

"No," Lyness interrupted quietly. "The responsibility is mine."

That pulled Roman up short, and his steps halted.

Torn between needing to speak quickly and clearly, Lyness had to fight his tongue for every other word he said. "You speak of responsibility as though I do not understand it. As though running to rescue a lady from scandal is more than I can manage. But Roman, for years now, I have been the one handling the estate accounts. I have ridden through rain and snow to settle disputes between tenants. I have met with the solicitor at every turn while you were here in York, fighting political battles." His voice firmed. "Do not tell me I do not understand responsibility."

Roman's anger faltered by a fraction. A small fraction, but it was enough for Lyness to notice it.

With some relief that his brother was listening, truly listening, Lyness continued, the words finally untangling themselves after years of trapping his tongue. "I have done all of it willingly. Gladly. And I will continue, as it is my duty to our family. But do not lecture me as if I have spent my life idle while you alone carried burdens."

For a long and uncomfortable moment, Roman stared at him. His throat tightened on a swallow. "That is not what I meant."

"Yet it is what you said," Lyness replied, quiet and resolute.

The silence that followed was thick enough to choke on.

Finally, Roman scraped a hand over his face, staring at the floor between them. "Lyness…you should not have claimed a betrothal on impulse. Not for a woman still recovering. Not without speaking to me. Not without knowing—"

"I know what matters," Lyness said softly.

At that his brother looked up, brows drawn together and eyes troubled.

Lyness swallowed. His throat felt tight, but the words would not be denied. They had waited too long already. "I know that I am falling in love with her."

Shock widened Roman's eyes, and his fury melted away.

After Lyness steadied his words with a breath, he spoke with nary a stammer. "I know that when she is unwell, my heart feels as though someone has reached inside and twisted it. I know that every time she looks at me, I feel as though I have stepped into sunlight after standing in the shadows my entire life." His voice softened. "I know that if the circumstances were better, she might never have chosen me at all. But this morning, when gossip was already turning cruel...Roman, I could not bear the thought of her being sacrificed to duty. Or to your sense of honor."

Roman opened his mouth but immediately closed it again, no word leaving his lips.

Carefully, Lyness pressed on. "You would have married her because you believed you must. I declared myself because I wanted to. Because I have wanted to from the first day I met her."

Turning from Lyness, Roman stepped away as though he needed distance to comprehend the words. The fire hissed in the hearth, and the long-case clock in the entryway chimed the hour.

Opening his hands at his side, trying to relax his posture, Lyness thought carefully through the last of what he needed to say to his brother. "If Lady Emily rejects me, then that is her right. I would never force her into anything. But I will not apologize for caring about her. Nor for protecting her when she needed a shield."

Steps away from him, Roman's hands open and closed. His voice, when it emerged, was hoarse. "You should have told me what you planned. Instead you sent me on another path. You encouraged me to focus my attention elsewhere."

"I feared you would stop me."

The lack of denial that followed was as good as an agreement on that statement. Another long moment passed before Roman exhaled, the anger finally bleeding from his posture. "Lyness," he said quietly, turning to face him again. "I have always thought you the gentler of us. The softer brother. But I see now that you are... resolute in a manner I did not expect."

Lyness managed a faint, sad smile. "That makes two of us."

Reluctant acceptance flickered through Roman's expression. Then came something more like the affection Lyness was used to, but felt more brittle than usual.

Circling around his desk, Roman sank slowly into his chair, elbows on the surface, head bowed. For a moment he did not look like Baron Hartwell or the unflappable man who stormed through York's political circles. He looked... tired.

No—wounded.

"This is the third time," he said quietly. Not accusing. Not even resentful. Just stating a truth he could no longer avoid. "Three times I have waited too long. Three times someone else has acted more decisively, winning the hand of a woman who would have made an excellent baroness."

Lyness's heart pinched. He had not thought about that, exactly.

Roman stared into the fire. "I admired her, you know. She is gentle. Intelligent. Steady. I could have been content with her." His voice tightened, almost imperceptibly. "I was not indifferent."

Guilt and relief collided almost painfully in Lyness's chest. "I...I did not realize."

"How could you?" Roman asked, lifting his head at last. His expression softened in a way Lyness rarely saw, stripped of authority, of pride, of all the armor he habitually carried. "I move slowly. Cautiously. It has never served me well where a lady is concerned." He gave a small, humorless huff of breath. "And now it seems that fate would rather hand my chances to you."

Lyness came to stand beside the desk to protest his brother's words. "Roman—"

"No." Roman raised a hand, the gesture brief but firm. "Do not apologize. You acted decisively when I did not. And you did it for the heart's sake, hers and your own. A man cannot resent that." He leaned back, shoulders stiffening as he pulled the mantle of baron back over himself. "I will not."

Lyness nodded, throat tight.

With a steady gaze, Roman asked, "Do you truly care for her, Lyness? You believe yourself capable of loving her?"

"Yes," Lyness whispered. "I have fought against it, especially knowing you wished to court her. But I cannot ignore my heart. Not anymore."

Roman closed his eyes briefly—perhaps bidding farewell to a possibility he'd never claim—then opened them with quiet resolve. "Then you have my blessing."

At that simple statement, Lyness sank into the chair on the

other side of the desk. His whole posture finally loosening. "I had not realized how much I needed to hear that." He passed his hand over his face and tried to smile. It was shaky, at best. "Thank you."

Roman rose from the chair. For the first time since Lyness entered the study, he stepped close and rested a hand on his brother's shoulder. The gesture held both weight and acceptance. And perhaps a trace of grief. "Make her happy," Roman said softly. "Where I might have been content, be joyful. Where I would have been dutiful, be devoted. Let this be the end of disappointment for at least one Eastwood."

"I will," Lyness vowed, looking upward.

With that said, Roman nodded once, the mask of duty settling back over him. "I imagine you have things to do, now that you are an engaged man. I will tell you what happened at the club later."

Rising, Lyness made it halfway to the door before he turned. "I am escorting Lady Emily and our mother to the races this afternoon. Will you come?" Lyness waited, the olive branch extended, and hope in his heart.

Roman turned toward the window, hands braced on its sill, shoulders rigid. But he said, without a trace of bitterness, "Of course. That will show a united front. I will ready myself in a moment."

Lyness bowed his head, then left the room with purpose, the weight of the discussion settling into something almost solemn. An understanding between brothers, and renewed respect on Lyness's part. Roman had ever and always been his closest friend and confident. That he had his brother's blessing, that Roman was not angry with him, was a balm to Lyness's heart.

Now all he had to do was win Lady Emily Sterling's love. Preferably before they married. He could imagine no greater happiness than that.

AT THE APPOINTED HOUR, EMILY HAD BARELY STEPPED INTO THE entryway when the Eastwoods arrived. They came into the cottage, and Lady Hartwell greeted her as though they were old friends reunited after years of separation. Even though they had seen one another before dawn that morning.

"My dear Lady Emily," she exclaimed, taking both of Emily's hands and inspecting her with the air of a florist cooing over a rare bloom. "You look pale, yes, but still as sweet as a daisy after rain."

Emily tried to restrain her smile to something polite, but it proved difficult. "That is kind of you to say, my lady."

"Oh, I only speak the truth." Lady Hartwell squeezed her hands gently, then looked at her sons. "Roman, Lyness—I warn you now, my future daughter-in-law is bound to be my favorite. I will not tolerate anything but the best of treatment for her."

That made Emily's face heat with a blush, and her stomach twisted with sudden nerves. Indeed, a betrothal to Lyness meant becoming part of the whole family. She cast the baron a glance, uncertain how to act for a moment.

To his credit, he bowed and met her gaze evenly. "It is precisely what I expected, Mother. Lady Emily will have my full brotherly support." There was likely much more to his words than what Emily heard and saw. He stepped back with the resigned air of a man well accustomed to his mother's edicts. Lyness, however, stepped forward with a warmth in his eyes that nearly undid her composure.

It surprised her, to react so strongly to him in such short order. "Mr. Eastwood," she murmured with a self-conscious smile. "Thank you for escorting me to the races this afternoon."

"It is my pleasure, my lady. But please. We are with family. Call me Lyness," he reminded her.

Goodness. That made the heat in her cheeks increase. She was likely as red as a strawberry.

Jack came in from a side door, moving more like a soldier than a gentleman at his ease. He bowed to the company. "Thank you for your attentions to my sister, Lady Hartwell. I hope the races prove entertaining this afternoon. We will join everyone later, at the theater."

That pricked at Emily's confidence. She held a hand out to catch her brother's arm. "You are not coming to the races with us? Is everything all right?"

"My wife has a small headache," he said to the others, then made eye contact with Emily. "Juniper is laying down to rest," he said softly. "But she wishes you well on your outing."

"We had best not doddle, then," Lady Hartwell said. "Give your wife my best wishes, Mr. Sterling. I look forward to seeing her this evening." So saying, she slipped her arm through the crook of her eldest son's, while Emily accepted Lyness's escort, and they all walked out of doors.

They were in the carriage in short order. Lady Hartwell ushered Emily inside first, insisting she take the more comfortable corner. The baroness settled beside her. Lyness followed, sitting across from Emily, and then his brother completed their party, arms folded tightly across his chest.

"There. Now we are all perfectly situated," Lady Hartwell said as the carriage lurched into motion. "Lady Emily, if at any moment you wish to rest your head upon my shoulder, do not be shy. I am quite used to delicate flowers wilting during Race Week."

Emily managed a small laugh. "I hope not to wilt, my lady."

"Oh, we all wilt," Lady Hartwell declared brightly. "The trick is finding the person who knows how to straighten your stem again."

Roman made a sound that was half-sigh, half-plea. "Mother." His normal composure disappeared for a moment, a crease appeared in his forehead as he looked at Lyness.

"Oh hush, Roman, it was entirely appropriate." She glanced toward Lyness, then at Roman again. "Do not glare at your brother simply because he has more sense than the rest of us."

That startled Emily. "More sense?"

Lady Hartwell nodded warmly. "Of course. The moment I heard the truth of the matter—that my Lyness declared your engagement because he cared for you—I thought, *Yes. That is exactly the sort of thing a young couple needs.* It is not a conventional start, but it is one built on regard and respect."

The carriage seemed to shrink around Emily.

Lyness went scarlet in front of her.

Roman exhaled sharply through his nose. "Mother—"

But Lady Hartwell was undeterred. "I do not meddle, I merely observe," she said, hands folded serenely over her reticule. "And I have observed that my younger son is at his best when he cares for someone. He is very like a sunflower turning toward light."

Oh dear. Her cheeks would never cool if this continued. She glanced toward Lyness.

He met her gaze for a moment—long enough for her to see the rawness there, the quiet earnestness, the hope within his eyes. Then he turned to the baroness. "Careful, Mother. You may make Emily come to regret her association with us if you begin your flower metaphors too early."

"Not at all," Emily said softly. "You will recall, I have a great interest in flowers of my own. There is nothing to regret." She certainly did not regret her attachment to him.

Though she did not know what she felt, not yet—not through the fog of exhaustion, headache, and shock—but she knew it could not be regret. "I am glad he was there," she said softly. "That they both were."

Lyness's eyes widened a fraction. Roman looked between them, something unreadable flickering across his features—not anger, not quite jealousy. Something quieter. Something Emily did not have a word for. Had she erred in giving them both credit for her rescue?

Lady Hartwell clapped her hands once, delighted. "Then everything will come right in the end. I always say, if young people are going to find themselves in dramatic situations, they might as well come out of them with an engagement."

"Mother," Roman said again, but without force. "When have you ever said such a thing?"

"Oh, hush, Roman. I said it just now, didn't I?" she said, waving a hand dismissively toward him.

The carriage wheels thudded over a rut. Emily braced herself with one hand on the seat, and Lyness reacted instantly—leaning forward, hand half-extended, barely stopping himself before reaching to steady her.

She noticed. Lady Hartwell noticed. Roman noticed.

Emily put a hand to her bonnet to adjust it and smiled faintly at him. "Thank you."

His Adam's apple bobbed above his cravat. "Of c-course."

The warmth that came from his gaze was quiet, small, but unmistakable—like the first stirrings of sunlight warming earth before spring. Perhaps his mother was wrong about who was the flower and who the sun, as Emily felt rather like turning toward him, seeking whatever warmth she might find in that affectionate look.

As the Knavesmire came into view with crowds shifting like bright ribbons across the green, Lady Hartwell leaned in conspiratorially. "When you descend from the carriage, my dear, take Lyness's arm without hesitation. Let people see you are comfortable. Confidence is the best armor you can wear at a time like this." It was the only indication that there was a performance to make, and it immediately brought Emily's mind back to the seriousness of the situation.

Emily gave a firm nod. "I will try, my lady."

"I have every faith in you, my dear," Lady Hartwell said gently. "You are already braver than you think."

The carriage rolled to a stop. Roman stepped out first, then offered his hand to his mother. Lyness moved next, turning back toward the doorway after he landed upon the ground. Emily set her hand into his. He held it firmly, with a confidence she wished she felt on her own.

"Ready?" Lyness asked quietly.

"No," she admitted. "But I am willing."

His faint, amused smile felt like a reward. They stepped out together into the bright swirl of the races, their linked hands a silent announcement that traveled faster than any carriage.

The sunlight struck her with far more enthusiasm than she could muster for it, but Lyness's steady hand around hers kept her from retreating into the carriage. The air smelled of trampled grass and horses, and the faint sweetness of crushed clover beneath the wheels of passing conveyances. People in vibrant race-day attire streamed along the edge of the track like peacocks strutting across a lawn.

Emily's heart fluttered. So many faces. So many glances turning their way.

Lyness stepped slightly closer, not touching her beyond the hand he already held, but shielding her all the same. "It will not be overwhelming once we start walking," he murmured.

She looked up at him. "You cannot know that." It was nearly the same thing Juniper had told her about the ball and dancing. That certainly had turned out the most overwhelming experience of her life.

His brows lifted in a quiet, earnest attempt at reassurance. "No," he said, "but I c-can promise not to let go." He tucked her hand in the crook of his arm as his words landed gently upon her anxieties. She nodded once.

Lady Hartwell called after them, "Do not stray too far, but take your time, my dears!"

It might as well have been an announcement to the entire Knavesmire, given the way heads turned toward them. Emily focused instead on Lyness, on the way he angled their path so the crowds thinned, on the gently increasing pressure of his fingers over her hand whenever the ground dipped or rose.

"You needn't worry about your footing," he murmured. "I will watch the ground for us both."

Something absurdly tender rose in her throat. "I am not quite that helpless."

"I know," he said quickly, a flush rising beneath his cheekbones. "Of c-course not. However, I wish to spare you every unnecessary discomfort."

There it was again. That sincere, charming care for her. She ought not be affected by it as she was. And yet…

They walked along the outer edge of the racecourse, the roar of the crowd gathering near the stands rolling faintly across the open land. Emily inhaled deeply, willing her senses to arrange themselves into order. "I cannot imagine why Society takes such pleasure in horses running in circles."

Lyness startled and made a tiny, coughing sound that became laughter, warm and genuine. "It is not a circle. Well, not exactly."

She glanced up, startled that she had said something so bold. "I did not mean it literally. I merely—"

"I know," he said quickly. "I was not laughing at your words. But it was refreshing to hear my own sentiments from someone else. I come to support my friends and to enjoy the general spectacle, I suppose. But I am not overly fond of the actual racing."

The admission disarmed her. He rarely spoke without caution; rarely allowed himself any ease in conversation. She had never seen his eyes that bright and happy, either.

She slowed a little, turning her head so she could better study him in the sunlight. "You look different this afternoon."

Lyness raised his eyebrows at her. "Different?"

"Yes." It was difficult to find the word for it. "Less…guarded, perhaps."

His gaze darted away, toward the horses warming along the rail. "It is easier when I am not speaking to a crowd. Or expected to hold an entire room's attention."

"You are holding mine." The truth slipped out before she could catch it. He stiffened. She felt her face warm. "I only meant—I did not intend to—"

"I know what you meant." Then, quietly, almost reverent: "It is a gift, to have your attention. I have always felt it so."

Her heart made a wholly inconvenient leap.

They continued walking until the crowd thinned enough that conversation felt private, the hum of the track becoming a soft background murmur. Emily found her breath coming easier.

"May I ask you something, Mr. Eastwood?"

He looked at her from the corner of his eye, his lips tugging upward. "Lyness," he reminded her.

"Very well. Lyness." The name still felt delicate and daring on her tongue. "Why is it that you are so comfortable now—in this moment—when last night you could not bear to look at me?"

His step faltered. The truth of his reaction, the guilt of it, the regret...she saw it all pass through him like waves on sand. Crashing into one another.

"I did not wish to distress you," he said quietly. "You were unwell. And I...when I am afraid, my stutter worsens."

Afraid. The word struck her softly and most unexpectedly. "You were afraid for me?"

His jaw worked. He nodded. After a long moment, he said, "I have stuttered all my life. Some children outgrow such things. I did not." He glanced toward her, then away again. "When Father died, the world expected me to become louder—more commanding, more certain. Instead, I became quieter. The more that was laid upon my shoulders, the more the words tangled when my emotions ran high." He did not quite meet her eyes as he continued. "And last night, when you could not stand, my concern and fear far outran my tongue."

Emily's breath caught in her sympathy. "Oh, Lyness."

He shrugged lightly, as though brushing off a lifetime of hurt was a simple matter. Which she did not believe for a moment. "I do not mind, not usually. It sounds as though you thought me cold and unfeeling. When in truth, I felt too much."

Her eyes stung. She had thought exactly that—that he was distant, uninterested. When all along he had been frightened of failing her in the moment she needed someone.

What could she say to honor the reassurance he had given her? She felt there must be something, some part of her she could offer in exchange for the gift of understanding him. Finally, she said, "Ever since my family's elevation in Society, I have wished to be smaller. Less noticeable. I want to be a good daughter, to not cause worry, to be thought capable. But it has been difficult to feel at ease anywhere." She lifted her gaze to his. "Except with you."

Lyness stopped walking and he turned fully to face her, the murmuring of the racecourse pressing in at the edges of the moment, wind pulling faintly at his coat. His expression cracked wide open—earnest, disbelieving, and something else. Something that looked a great deal like longing.

"Emily," he breathed, her name spoken in a way she had never heard it before.

Immediately, her pulse fluttered like a wild bird and her stomach dipped low. They were standing much too close. Anyone could see them. Anyone could whisper about them. She ought to step back—for propriety, for caution, for the sake of her poor spinning thoughts. But her feet would not obey.

The world narrowed to him and the warmth of his gaze, the tremble of his breath, the gentleness curling at the edge of his smile. His gloved fingers brushed hers.

"I wish…" He stopped, swallowed, and tried again with an intent look in his eyes. "You make me wish I were braver."

Her heart broke and mended in the same instant. The breeze carried the trumpet call announcing the next race. People shifted toward the stands.

"We should—" she whispered.

"Yes." His voice was rough. "But…thank you. For what you said."

She gathered herself as they stepped apart. "It was only the truth."

He offered his arm again, slower this time, as though presenting her with something important. "Walk back with me, my lady?"

Her fingers slipped into the crook of his elbow. "Gladly."

And they returned to the crowd, and she felt the beginnings of something fragile and beautiful growing quietly between them.

# A Letter

## August 27th, 1822

*Benwaith House, London*

My Dearest Emily,

Juniper's letter reached us yesterday, and your father and I have scarcely spoken of anything else since. The very thought of you being unwell—and through no fault of your own—has troubled us both more than I can say. I thank Heaven you were not alone, and that friends acted quickly to keep you safe. I am grateful to have received a letter in your own hand with your account of all of it. My poor darling!

But what joy followed those feelings! Your engagement to Mr. Lyness Eastwood has filled this house with such happiness. Your father declared at once that we will be in York as soon as arrangements can be made, and I confess I could not rest until I put pen to paper. We long to embrace you and congratulate you properly.

Your brothers, Richard and George, speak highly of the Eastwood family. Mr. Eastwood's reputation is excellent, and from all Juniper wrote, he has shown you every care and consideration. That is all your father and I ever hoped for, that you should be cherished. My heart is full knowing you have found a wonderful match.

We shall leave for York shortly. Expect us within the week.

All my love, your mother,

*Margaret*

Countess Benwaith

# Chapter Twenty

## September 3rd, 1822

A late summer breeze drifted through the broken ribs of stone. The abbey ruins and surrounding grounds were not as full as usual. Perhaps the gray sky above made people hesitant to trust their time to the outdoors. Emily had loved the place since her arrival in York. Something about the old stones gave her comfort. On days filled with sunlight, they were warm to the touch and felt like a place to begin an adventure.

On a day like today, Saint Mary's Abbey was somber, quiet, full of wind and old stories. Despite the particularly gothic-like atmosphere, her pulse beat too quickly for serenity. So while everyone in her party sat on blankets and discussed the history of the medieval city surrounding them, she grew agitated.

Her parents had arrived two days earlier, full of joy and eager to meet her betrothed once more. Richard and George had followed shortly after with their wives, Katherine and Susan, turning Jack and Juniper's cottage into a bustling hive of Sterlings. She had missed them greatly, and it was wonderful to have them near.

Emily had laughed. She had smiled. She had told herself everything was well.

And mostly, it was. They had all enjoyed meeting Lyness and Roman again, and Lady Hartwell had been gracious toward Emily's parents and family.

"I think a walk is in order for me," Jack said, kissing Juniper on the cheek as he rose. "Richard. George. Would you like to see more of the old stones tumbling down around us?"

"An excellent idea." Richard rose and dusted himself off. As the eldest brother, he would inherit their father's title. He had undertaken much of the responsibilities of it already. Their father had frequently proclaimed himself too old to learn to be an earl.

His wife, Katherine, tipped her head up and peered at him from beneath her bonnet with a look of caution. "No climbing around on unsteady stones, husband. You are not a boy anymore, and I know you would rather not take up walking with a cane."

"Oh, but think how dashing I should be." He winked at his wife. "Twirling a cane whenever I was not leaning upon it."

George had risen, too. He gave Susan, his wife, an arch look. "No warnings or expressions of care for me, my dear?"

Susan turned a page in the book she was reading. A Gothic romance she had borrowed from Juniper. "If you do not have the sense to look after yourself, I suppose you will suffer the consequences of it." She darted a quick look at him, adorned with a smile. "I am certain your brothers will look after you, should you need it."

"Ah, poor George." Jack clapped their brother on the shoulder. "I recognize the book your wife is reading. She will not put it down. Not until the very end, when they discover the count is really—"

Juniper, Susan, Katherine, and Emily all protested at once, each of them warning him against spoiling the ending, and Juniper threatened him somewhat creatively, though Emily only caught the end of it.

"—back into powdered wigs and brass buttons!"

Everyone went quiet and looked at Jack's wife, who glared fiercely at him.

Jack raised both hands in surrender, and one of the broadest smiles Emily had ever seen upon his face appeared. "I retract even the suggestion that I would dare speak the ending of a book while someone is actively enjoying its pages. You have my sincerest apologies, ladies." He bowed, and the look he gave his wife was full of genuine amusement and a tenderness that made Emily's heart ache.

As they walked away from the ladies and their father—who had fallen asleep a few moments after stretching out on one of the blankets—Emily's thoughts prodded at that ache with curiosity. What was wrong with her? Why was she not happy?

All her married siblings, even the sisters who were not present, had close, affectionate relationships with their spouses. She had not thought they were all so demonstrative as Jack and Juniper, but watching her other brothers tease and laugh with their wives reminded her that such care was expressed in many ways.

And she wanted something like it for herself.

In the nearly two weeks since their betrothal, Lyness had visited her for at least a quarter of an hour every day. He had sat with her in Juniper's company, and he had walked with her out of doors, always behaving properly. Listening to her. Acting much as he had before the trouble at the ball. Like a friend.

"I think I will take a walk with my sketchbook." She must have spoken too abruptly, because the other women around her went silent and stared at her. She cleared her throat. "If...if no one minds."

"Of course not, my dear," her mother said, forehead creased with concern. "I think your brothers have the right idea of it. A little exercise in fresh air is good for us."

Juniper touched Emily's wrist, eyes gentle. "Mr. Eastwood and his family will arrive soon. Do not stray too far, or I will have to send him looking for you again."

The reminder that Juniper had done so before, on the day they rescued the canary, almost made the smile Emily replied with real rather than polite.

But with Lyness running late to their family outing, and the fondness she saw her siblings show their wives, she felt oddly adrift.

Movement would help. She stepped away from the cluster of her family and moved across the grasses toward a low stone wall overgrown with tufts of clover. Opening her sketchbook, she sat down and leaned against the ruined wall. Then she focused on the arch before her—cracked, elegant, and still standing despite centuries of neglect.

Sketching *always* soothed her.

A cluster of voices drifted behind her, familiar ones. It seemed her brothers' walk had brought them to the other side of the wall where she sat. She meant to ignore them—but Jack's tone was taut, unusual enough to catch her attention by accident.

"...I should never have left her side," Jack muttered. "I knew something would go wrong."

"You could not have known," George said as their boots crunched against gravel and dirt. "I have had the story from you, Hartwell, and Eastwood. It was an unfortunate accident."

"It isn't your fault," Richard added. "The real disaster would have been the gossip. At least Eastwood did the honorable thing."

Emily's hand paused over her sketchbook. *Honorable* thing? The graphite in her fingers felt suddenly fragile. She put it down.

George exhaled. "Yes, well...he is saving her reputation. That is more than many men would do."

Jack's reply was not as loud this time, but still sharp with self-reproach. "Emily deserves more than a marriage arranged out of necessity. I fear they are both trapped by duty and the Eastwood sense of honor."

The words struck with the precision of a blade finding an old scar. She had spent her whole life being the daughter who stayed behind—useful, steady, overlooked. Of course this engagement was no different. Of course she had mistaken kindness for affection.

Her heart squeezed painfully. Necessity. Duty. Honor. Of course, she understood the marriage offer came to protect her and her family. But Lyness, the day he stood in her brother's house and told her his reasons for declaring their engagement, had made it sound as though there was more to it. He had said kind things about her, had said he wished to be a man worthy of her notice.

*"I would rather the world believe you were promised to me than watch you be sacrificed to duty alone."*

Yes, she recalled those words perfectly. But what had any of it truly meant? He had not expressed affection for her. Not really. Nor desire, nor that he would have chosen her if there had not been a scandal to contain.

She stood slowly, her breath tight, and slipped farther down the path before her brothers could see her. The ruined walls seemed to tilt around her as though they—or she—had forgotten how to stand upright. She tried to swallow past the ache, but it clung stubbornly to her throat, refusing to be reasoned away. She needed to regain her composure.

She reached a shaded cloister walk—only to nearly collide with Roman Eastwood, who rounded the corner with his brow furrowed in thought, hands clasped tightly behind his back.

"Lady Emily," he said, startled. "My apologies—I was being inattentive to the path in front of me."

"It is quite all right." Her voice came out too thin. She swallowed. "Has your family all arrived, my lord?"

He blinked at her and nodded. "Lyness is making certain our mother is well settled with the other ladies. I am searching out the gentlemen. Have you seen them?"

"Yes, they are over there." She waved in the general direction she had heard her brothers' voices. "But before you find them, my lord, may I ask you something? It is rather important."

Lord Hartwell gave her a hard stare, likely taken aback by her solemn expression. "Of course."

She hesitated and had to look away. It was easier to stare at the moss underfoot. "At the ball… When everything happened…you were the one people saw with me."

"Yes." The word was crisp and given without hesitation.

"And I believed, once, that you might have considered courting me." Her cheeks warmed, but she pushed on. "So why did Lyness offer for me? Why not you?"

The baron stiffened. Only slightly, but enough to betray his surprise.

"My lady," he said, speaking each word slowly and with evident care, " I thought you knew. I would have offered. That was the plan I devised with your brother. You have, and will always have, my admiration. But Lyness acted before I could." He sighed. "I likely should have seen it coming. He tends to shoulder burdens the moment they appear, if he think it will spare me a measure of difficulty."

Her breath faltered. "Burdens?"

"Indeed. In this case, though, he believed himself far better suited to take on the responsibility of your care than I was."

She felt suddenly as though she had been mistaken for a parcel —a delicate one, perhaps, but still something to be handed off to whichever man was willing to bear it.

Without realizing that her heart was crumbling, Lord Hartwell heaved a sigh. "And once Lyness believes something is his responsibility, nothing will dissuade him. He has always been stubborn on that account, I fear." Lord Hartwell looked away, distracted. "He is determined to see this through. You need not fear on that account."

The words fell like icicles from a limb, piercing her heart.

Lord Hartwell had given her more words that weighed heavily rather than gently. Responsibility. Determined. *See this through.*

It was exactly what she had overheard. Exactly what she had feared.

"If you will excuse me, my lady? I think I see your brothers." He bowed politely and continued past her, already lost in whatever thoughts crowded in his mind.

Her throat burned. She hadn't been foolish enough to hope for love—not yet—but she had believed in the possibility. In quiet affection. In the beginnings of something tender. How naïve she had been to think herself someone a man might choose without being forced to it.

Emily stood very still, gripping her sketchbook so tightly her fingers hurt. She turned toward the main green, searching for Juniper—but her vision blurred. Colors blended together. The ruins seemed too bright, despite the gray skies above.

Then a familiar voice called to her, warm and hopeful. "Emily?"

She caught her breath and turned.

Lyness.

He was hurrying toward her across the grass, a welcoming smile on his face. The sight of him—earnest, relieved to see her—did nothing to put her at ease. Not this time.

He stopped short when he saw her expression. "Are you unwell?" he asked softly. "Has something happened?"

"Yes," she whispered. "I mean, no. That is to say…I am not well." But she could not tell him exactly what she was, either.

He stepped closer, concern pulling tight across his features. "Please, tell me what I have—"

"No," she interrupted, the word trembling. "You have done nothing wrong. I simply need some time. To think."

"Time?" His brow creased. "What do you mean?" He reached for her hand.

She tucked it behind her back. It was not a rejection. It was desperation. If he touched her, if he spoke gently, she would shatter, and she refused to humiliate herself in front of half of York. Again.

His hand pulled back sharply, as if she'd struck it rather than removed her own from his reach.

"I only need a moment to myself," she managed, voice shaking. "I think I would prefer to return home. The day does not agree with me."

"Then let me see you to your family. Or to your carriage. It is my duty."

"No," she said, the word firm and stronger yet than anything else she had uttered. Her heart twisted. Oh, she wanted to believe she mattered to him. But she could not bear to hear him speak of duty, not with her heart already bruised by that horrible word.

He swallowed, and it looked painful the way his throat flexed above his cravat. "If I have offended you—"

"You have not."

"Then why—"

"Please, Mr. Eastwood," she said.

Mr. Eastwood, not *Lyness,* and he flinched. His flinch wounded her more sharply than anything her brothers had said. She had never wanted to hurt him. Never. But she could not give him an explanation she herself barely understood.

"I cannot speak of this right now." Indeed, if she did, she would further shame herself by crying in public. She turned away before he could see the tears in her eyes. She started to walk toward the carriages rather than to her family. If one more person asked what was wrong, she would shame herself terribly with a sob.

Behind her, he tried to call out to her one more time. "Emily… what have I done?"

She did not look back. She waved her hand above her head. As though doing so would be enough to brush his concern away. She truly needed to think. She would speak to him—*she would*. But not while her heart was so raw she could scarcely breathe.

Lyness had been late.

He hated being late—his mind had tallied the minutes during the short ride from the house to the ruins—but Roman had needed him, and estate letters arrived unexpectedly, and his mother insisted he change his cravat. All inconveniences he accepted willingly.

But now, watching Emily back away from him as though a wall had risen between them, he wished he had sprinted all the way from their house on Castlegate if it would have changed this moment. Her silence hurt more than any spoken rebuke.

"Emily...what have I done?" he whispered after her, his voice swallowed by the open air and the roar of his pulse in his ears.

She did not turn. Her pale gown vanished behind a crumbling archway, the same arch where she had once carried a trembling canary in his hat.

He remained rooted to the spot, as though any movement might break what remained of his calm. He thought through it again, relived it in his mind—her expression, her tone, the dreadful formality of *Mr. Eastwood.* That had been like hearing a door close. Quiet. Final.

His mother's voice drifted faintly across the grounds as she spoke to Emily's parents somewhere beyond the ruins. Roman stood several yards away with Jack Sterling, both men absorbed in a low, tense conversation. The other brothers listening with solemnity carved into their features.

No one saw Lyness's heart cave in, though his chest tightened painfully. He forced himself to breathe. His stutter, kept in check by sheer, exhausted will these past days, twitched at the edge of his tongue as though every word he wanted to say was doomed to come out in stammers and stops.

He turned away from the path Emily had taken, pressing the heel of one hand to his brow. Something had changed. And it was him she fled from. Had he frightened her? He had seen her every day, practicing restraint, not speaking his heart. Or so he thought. Perhaps he had pushed too much without knowing it. Demanded too much, too soon. He had been cautious—so cautious—but perhaps even his gentleness had pressed too heavily upon her.

Had he been careless? Too hopeful? Too ready to believe—after a lifetime of holding back—that someone as gentle and radiant as Emily might truly want him?

He shut his eyes.

Of course she would reconsider. Of course she would grow overwhelmed. He had announced their engagement with reckless speed in a crowded garden, for heaven's sake. He had dragged her into a life she had not chosen—all under the guise of protection.

He'd meant to shield her. What if he had trapped her instead?

A flicker of memory struck him: her soft voice whispering, *"I am willing."* The delicate weight of her hand on his arm as they walked the Knavesmire. The way she had looked at him before the trumpet call startled them apart.

All of it felt suddenly fragile. Breakable.

Perhaps she had never meant any of it as he had meant it—

No. He would not dishonor her by thinking she spoke false. He lowered his hand and stared at the grass beneath his boots.

She had asked for time, he told himself. He owed her that much. Beyond that, he wanted to give her anything, everything, that she asked of him. But a part of him—small, terrified—whispered that time might not mend this. That she might withdraw completely. That she might go to Jack and say she wished the entire arrangement dissolved.

His chest tightened painfully.

He could withstand society's mockery. He could endure gossip, whispers, even the ruin of his own hopes. But losing her before he had ever truly been allowed to keep her?

He swallowed hard, breath unsteady.

Roman's voice came through faintly, as though through water or thick walls. "Lyness? Are you well?"

He straightened instantly. "Y-yes," he answered, though his voice cracked on the single syllable. He schooled his features, the way he had done since boyhood. He had grown adept at hiding hurt before anyone could call it weakness.

Roman stood almost directly before him and frowned, taking a step nearer. "You look as though you have taken a knife through the heart, Lyness. What has happened?"

Lyness glanced back once more where Emily had disappeared, the image of her retreat carved into his mind like stone relief. He forced himself to speak before Roman could worry too deeply. "I am n-not c-certain. B-but I will f-find out. I n-need a m-moment."

"Of course." Roman stopped, studying his younger brother. "Your betrothed stood here a moment ago, looking nearly as distressed as you do," he said with a tilt of his head. "Lovers' quarrel?"

Roman's attempt at humor landed like a blow. Lyness did not have breath enough to correct him, but he sent a glare at his brother that communicated his displeasure clearly enough.

Raising his hands, Roman stepped back. "My apologies. It is none of my business." He cleared his throat. "I will go check on our mother's comfort." He disappeared down the path and around some rubble.

For the first time since Lyness had dared to hope for a future with her, he felt it slipping through his fingers like sand—fine, impossible to grasp, hopeless to gather. He needed to understand. He needed to speak to her. But she had asked for time. He would give it to her, and gladly. But he feared time might take her further from him rather than bring her back.

He stood alone amidst the ruins, praying that whatever had shaken her would not break him as well.

# Chapter Twenty-One

The upper rooms of Etridge's Royal Hotel smelled of ink, candle wax, and the unmistakable whiff of too many men who had been arguing since tea time. High ceilings, tall windows overlooking Blake Street, and a growing tension made the Whig club feel more like a battleground than a meeting room. The results of Race Week's lower than usual turn out, the Duke of Sussex refusing to attend their party's supper, and other disappointing losses for their members, had all of them looking for someone to blame.

Lyness entered behind Roman, still shaken from the abbey. Emily's retreat haunted him. The way she had stepped away...as though the sight of him pained her. He could still feel the echo of it, like a hand pressed hard against his chest.

Roman, by contrast, looked carved from granite—anger contained so tightly it might crack.

Several men turned at once.

"Ah! Hartwell!" Archibald Kettleburn called. "Come to tell us you have unearthed the villain who meant to poison you with opium?"

Roman removed his gloves with clipped control. "No. That individual remains unfound."

Lyness sat beside him at the table, quiet. His mind kept showing him the image of Emily's pale face, rehearsing for him the trembling in her voice. He forced himself to focus.

Phineas Nelson lounged near the fire. "If someone tried to make a fool of you during Race Week, he is either fearless or stupid."

"Or very sure of his protection from prosecution," Christopher Holly said from his seat nearer the window.

"That narrows it to half of York," Mr. Cooke muttered.

Roman ignored them all, looking over the lists and maps covering the table—the city's wards, voters, patrons. His jaw flexed. "What are we discussing here?"

"Reports on profits and losses from businesses during Race Week. Holly had it in his mind to see if the shops Whigs owned had more losses or similar to the rest," Sir George said as he read one of the reports, making notes. He looked up at Kettleburn. "You could help us go through these. They are most interesting."

"Dashed lot of paperwork." Kettleburn shrugged. "I am more interested in Hartwell's troubles."

With a put upon sigh, Sir George lowered the papers to the table. "We do not even know if the person who tampered with his glass did so because of his politics. It could have been a jealous suitor, or someone who lost money to him gambling, or any number of things. Club matters should remain restricted to the things that have a direct correlation to our political work."

Tapping his glass, Kettleburn did not even look at the older gentleman. "If a servant handed you the drink directly, he belongs to someone wealthy enough to hire carelessly. Or maliciously."

Roman's voice was controlled steel. "I have considered every possibility." He picked up one of the papers Sir George handed to him, scowling at it.

Leaning forward, Phineas shared a crooked grin with Lyness. "One of my cousins bid me to offer congratulations to you, Eastwood, on your engagement. But he was confused, as a few weeks ago, he thought it was Hartwell he saw driving Lady Emily through town."

The room went quiet, and Lyness felt his pulse jolt painfully. Not now, he wanted to say. Not when he felt Emily slipping away from him.

Usually left out of the more social aspects of the club's members, Sir George blinked up at Lyness. " You are engaged, Eastwood?"

Holly smiled as though he had made the arrangements himself. "To Mr. John Sterling's sister. The Earl of Benwaith's daughter."

Roman's expression barely shifted, but a shadow crossed his eyes.

"Yes," Lyness said, steady even as his heart twisted. "We are engaged."

"Excellent!" Sir George exclaimed. "A love match, is it?"

Avoiding the baronet's gaze, Lyness tried to smile. "S-something of the s-sort." Lyness felt heat rise under his collar. How foolish he must sound, how transparent.

Roman's gaze flickered to him—not cold, not angry, but troubled. He said nothing of it. Duty reclaimed him before brotherhood could.

"We are not here to discuss marriages," Roman said. "We are here to discuss the future of our party at a time when blame for everything that goes wrong in this city is put squarely on our shoulders."

At that moment, the older of the Nelson brothers entered the room. Thaddeus Nelson, their father's heir, and the more outspoken of the two. "What goes on here? What riotous gossip have I missed?" He looked at all the maps. "Is this how we will find Hartwell's poisoner?"

With a grumble, Sir George sank deeper into his chair, holding the paper he now examined in front of his face.

"No." Roman rubbed at his forehead. "We are looking at something related to our political goals, Mr. Nelson."

"Oh, good. Because I would hate to make all the efforts here

useless, since I think I have information on the poisoning front."
Thaddeus crossed his arms and swept the room with a bold grin on
his face.

Roman's head snapped up. "Out with it, then."

"My sisters attended a gathering at the Powells' home last
evening. One of them overheard Mr. Patchett speaking with Mr.
Powell, saying the attempt at humiliating 'the baron' had 'failed
spectacularly.'"

Lyness felt Roman go still beside him.

Patchett. Loud, wealthy, aggressively Tory. The son of a magistrate, with family members in high positions throughout the
county. A man whose disdain for Roman's reform efforts bordered
on obsession. But Emily had suffered because of it. That truth
needled Lyness more sharply than any political slight

Though he looked as though he had been pulled into the
conversation unwillingly, Sir George scoffed, "Patchett is a fool, but
drugging a man—"

"I looked into it. That is why I was late today. He has recently
elevated one of his footmen," Thaddeus said cheerfully. "A thing the
other servants are gossiping over, as a more experienced footman
was passed over for the job. If the elevated footman is the same one
who handed Hartwell the drink, it will be an easy matter of
knocking on the door to get a good look at him."

A chill threaded through Lyness. He and Roman exchanged a
look—Roman wanted to see the footman. He rose abruptly. "I
must go."

"To accuse Mr. Patchett?" Sir George sputtered.

"No," Roman said. "To see the footman."

Lyness stood as well. "I am coming."

Something in Roman's face eased slightly. A silent thank you he
did not need to voice. They left the Royal Hotel on foot, walking to
Davygate, and reached Patchett's immaculate town house. The
lion-faced knocker, painted gold, gleamed like a taunt.

Roman lifted it.

Before he struck, the door opened.

A footman stood there. Pale-haired. Sharp-featured. Lyness glanced at his brother but could not tell if Roman looked at the servant with any kind of recognition. But the footman had frozen.

Then he bowed his head slightly. "Mr. Patchett is not receiving today, and the rest of the family is not at home."

"What a shame," Roman said, tone even and eyes taking in the footman. "I suppose we will have to come again." Then without warning he leaned closer and the servant went stiff as a statue. "Your face is familiar."

The footman did not blink. "I have been in Mr. Patchett's service only a fortnight."

"I have never been here before, so I would have seen you elsewhere. Any thought as to where that might be?"

The other man's jaw went tight a moment, but his eyes had widened too. "I do not think that is possible, sir—"

"Lord Hartwell," Lyness supplied with the tiniest of smirks. "He is Lord Hartwell."

"My lord," the man corrected himself with a barely concealed cringe. "If you will leave your card—"

With no regard for proper distance between strangers, Roman stepped forward, voice like Apollo's lowest growl. "You will tell your master that we know what occurred at the Assembly Rooms."

The footman swallowed.

"And," Roman added softly, "you will tell him this—if any harm comes to myself or someone I care about again, I will hold him personally accountable."

This time, fear flickered visibly on the servant's face.

"I will relay your message," the man said.

"Good." Roman turned sharply and strode away. Lyness followed, tension vibrating through him. Protecting Emily mattered more to him than any political rivalry, and he would rather keep his brother out of harm's way, too.

At the corner of the street, Roman exhaled. "That was him."

"Yes. I gathered that."

"And Patchett hired him. Likely paid him to put that cup in my hand." They walked in grim silence until Roman spoke again, his voice rough. "He meant to humiliate me," he said. "He harmed Lady Emily instead."

A quick study of his brother and Lyness knew the whole event had done something to change Roman. His brother would not tolerate harm coming to those he cared for. Lyness's hands curled into fists. "Then we do not give him another opportunity."

Roman cast him a long, assessing look. "No. We will not. Or rather, I will not. This is my responsibility, Lyness. You have taken enough on your shoulders over the years. But I swear to you, if I need your help, I will not hesitate to ask."

That gave Lyness pause. "What do you mean?"

Roman gestured to the street. "Let us make our way back to the others, and I will tell you." They crossed the street, dodging one slow moving carriage before Roman continued his thought. "I have done a great deal of thinking since you announced your betrothal to Lady Emily. And you are right. You have taken on every responsibility I have handed you, and more besides, to the point that you are acting more as the baron than I have been. You manage all the estate affairs, all the tenant affairs, and have acted as steward since we turned out the embezzling fool."

"Someone had to do it," Lyness said with a shrug. "Someone you trusted. You cannot be everywhere and do everything all at once."

"No. But I can certainly spend more time taking care of my family's needs," Roman said with a shake of his head. "I would like to take your future in-laws to the estate at the end of the week. Along with Mother, and you, and your intended. We can stay a few days. Give everyone the tour. And when they leave, you and I need to discuss which matters belong to me and which ought to stay with you. We should probably also discuss your allotment, allowance, and moving into one of the homes we own nearer the estate. Once you marry, I imagine your wife would like a place where she is lady of the house, rather than living with Mother and me always underfoot."

It was an impressive speech, given at such a speed that Lyness could not hope to interrupt it with a single stammered word. But he finally caught hold of Roman's arm, tugging him to stand closer to a building and out of the walking path.

"Roman. It is not nec-necessary. All of it. It is too much."

"No, Lyness." Roman put his hand on Lyness's shoulder and held his gaze. "It is precisely what I should have done ages ago, instead of handing more and more things to you to manage while I played at politics and pretended myself the champion of this city. I piled responsibility upon you, thinking myself indispensable everywhere but home." He shook his head. "You do too much. And soon you will have a wife and a household of your own to manage. Of course," he said with an amused tilt to his head, "I still want you to act as steward. But we both know you have always preferred the country to the city. This will give you more time to build a life of your own, a family of your own." He clapped Lyness on the shoulder. "You know I am right. I am always right."

Slowly, Lyness shook his head, unable to keep in his chuckle. "Almost always," he corrected.

"Indeed. Now. We have work to do before we go home and tell Mother she is hosting a brief house party."

Though they went back to finish the club meeting, they did not stay long. The sun was still shining, casting long slant of light through the streets of York, when they returned to Hartwell House.

Lyness and Roman had returned with tired minds, both silent as they shed their hats and gloves in the entryway. Roman retreated to his study with a mutter about answering correspondence. Lyness meant to follow, mind still churning with political danger and—far worse—the memory of Emily's stricken expression at the abbey.

But his mother appeared at the base of the stairs, her eyes sharp despite softness of her smile.

"Lyness," she said gently. "Will you walk with me a moment?"

He had never denied her anything. He nodded and followed her out the door into the small rose garden.

Autumn would soon creep along the edges of the petals; some blooms already sagged under the weight of their final days. The garden was small—nothing like the sprawling grounds at the country estate—but Lady Hartwell tended the blooms with the devotion of a queen guarding her jewels.

His mother brushed one with her fingertips, then turned to him. "Lady Juniper sent a note this morning," she said. "Emily left the abbey rather early yesterday. Before anyone expected her to."

Lyness exhaled slowly. "Yes."

"Why?" Lady Hartwell asked without a note of accusation in her voice. Simply concern.

He looked down at his shoes on the paved walk, uncertain how to speak to his mother about this matter. It had been years since he had come to her with the troubles of his heart. "I do not know," he said at last, words slow to minimize the stuttering. "Sh-she was distressed. Something troubled her. She asked for time, and I did not wish to press her. I still do not." His throat tightened. "But I fear…I fear I have somehow harmed her."

His mother studied him with the kind of steadiness he had not seen since his father's death, when she had leaned more heavily on Roman in her own grief. It was a look that carried so much: a mix of love, worry, and a knowledge of all his quiet hurts.

"Did you quarrel?" she asked softly.

"No." His voice cracked. He stuttered over nearly every word he tried to say next, but trusted she would understand. "That is the worst part. If she were angry, I could amend it. But this felt like losing her without knowing where I mis-stepped."

Lady Hartwell touched his sleeve with a light hand. "My son. You carry your worries with such a sensitive heart. You always have. But you always pretend it does not hurt you. Even when I can see it does."

He looked away, blinking hard. After he kept hold of his composure, he managed to say, "I would like to send her something. Flowers, perhaps. Something that might convey—" He broke off helplessly.

"That you care for her?" his mother offered.

He nodded once.

She turned back to her roses, inhaling the fading scent. "Roses speak nearly every sentiment, depending on their color. And I have taught you what I know of other blossoms and their meaning. But Lyness..." She plucked a small, near-withered bloom and held it between them. "Emily does not need a message chosen from a gardener's dictionary."

He frowned at the dark and dying bloom. "Then what do I give her?"

She smiled, a touch sad, a touch fond. "My heart has always spoken in petals and blossoms. Your heart speaks in strokes of ink and beautiful words, my dear."

"My stammer—"

"She does not seem to mind it, that I have noticed." She lowered the bruised rose and regarded him with drawn eyebrows. "Use the talent that you love, the gift you have, to tell her how you feel. At least as a start."

His heart squeezed and he shook his head. "A letter?"

"Not merely a letter, Lyness. You are a calligrapher before you are anything else. Your heart speaks in lines and flourishes, as well as beautiful words. If you wish to reach her—write to her. Not out of duty or courtesy, not copying the poems of other men. Use your words. Tell her what is in your heart." Her fingers brushed his arm. "Tell her the truth."

Lyness closed his eyes. "What truth?"

"That you care for her," she said simply. "That you are not indifferent. That you wish to understand what troubles her. These are sentiments a woman needs to hear from the man she is to marry. Tell her how you feel about the future you will build together."

He went still as he once more remembered Emily's pale face. Her trembling voice. Her retreating figure. All of it had wrapped around his heart like a thorned vine, prickling and painful.

"And Lyness?" his mother added, stepping close enough to straighten the line of his cravat the way she had when he was a boy. "You deserve joy. You deserve love. I know you doubt that. I can see it."

A soft, choked sound escaped him. He shook his head.

"My only hope and my greatest joy," she whispered, "is to see my children happy."

Lyness bowed his head, eyes burning. "I want to be worthy of her."

"You are," she said firmly. "But she needs to know how you feel. And that must come from your own hand, not my gardens."

He nodded slowly. "I will write to her," he said. "Tonight."

His mother squeezed his hand once, then put her arm through his and walked with him through the garden, showing him her favorite blooms, and giving him time to order his thoughts.

# Chapter Twenty-Two

The morning light in the herb garden painted everything a pale gold, warming the stones edging Juniper's neat beds of lavender, chamomile, and rosemary. Dew clung to the leaves like jewels on a duchess, turning each plant into a treasure both delicate and lovely. Emily had always loved the early hours before expectations stirred, before anyone asked anything of her.

This morning, she wasn't alone. Her parents kept her company.

She moved slowly along the path, the basket at her elbow filled with cuttings she intended to dry or press. Her parents followed a few steps behind, her mother stopping every so often to admire a blossom, her father muttering about missing country mornings while living in London.

"Well now," her father said at last, folding his arms and looking about with narrowed eyes, "you have an excellent garden." His tone tried for gruff indifference, but she recognized the effort he made. He hated titles and hated having to wear his best coats so regularly. But he loved his children. He tried, every day, to prove it.

"It is lovely, Emily," her mother murmured, brushing her fingers over the head of a chamomile plant. "I had worried you would not find your footing in a new place without us, but this feels like you."

She smiled and adjusted the bonnet she wore. "Drying flowers and mixing salves again. I am glad you haven't left your old skills behind."

Emily returned the smile, but the corners of it faltered. "It has been comforting," she admitted, arranging the sprigs in her basket unnecessarily.

Her father grunted. "Good, good. Better than all that nonsense in London, with ladies fluttering about like jeweled pigeons." He shot a look at her mother. "This place makes me miss the farm. At least cows don't whisper behind fans."

"Cows have their own opinions," her mother said with her usual air of peacefulness. "They are merely less concerned about sharing them." She nudged Emily's elbow. "Now show me what you have concocted."

Emily led them inside to the small stillroom she and Juniper had made out of a kitchen pantry. They had made it useful, adding more shelves, hooks, and creating a pleasant orderliness that belonged fully to Emily. Bundles of lavender and mint hung from thin cords, drying in patient rows. A mortar and pestle sat where she had left them last night. Small glass jars, neatly labeled in Lyness's careful hand, glinted in the morning light.

Her mother's breath caught softly. "Oh, Emily. This is perfect."

Her father stepped inside with the wariness of a man entering a ribbon shop. He picked up one of the jars, squinting at the label. "Comfrey salve. Hmph. Your mother swore by this when any of you scraped a knee."

"And it worked every time," her mother said, taking the jar from him as though he might drop it. "I hoped you would come back to this work someday, my dear. It is good for you. Good for others too." She inspected the label and her eyebrows raised. "This is beautiful penmanship. Is it yours?"

"No." Emily's throat tightened unexpectedly. She busied herself with the basket again, taking out the herbs to arrange them on the narrow table beneath one of the shelves.

After putting the jar down, her mother stepped closer. "You

have done well here, Emily. And your letters always sounded so content." She paused. "But something is troubling you now."

Emily kept her gaze low. "Nothing is wrong, Mama."

Her father made a disbelieving sound. "Child, we have raised six children before you. Of course we know when one is chewing on something unpleasant."

"She does not want to worry us," her mother said gently, brushing a curl behind Emily's ear. "But worrying is part of loving, Emily. Tell us why your smile looks borrowed and ill-fitting this morning."

A breath caught in Emily's chest. She stared at the drying herbs —her refuge, her familiar work—yet even here, her thoughts were tangled with yesterday's words. *Duty. Honor. Responsibility.* Cold little stones settling inside her heart.

She swallowed. "I cannot... I do not want to cause any worry or trouble. Not after London. I thought, foolishly it seems, that if I could be perfect here, if I made no mistakes, you would not have to bear any more humiliation on my account."

Her father let out a quiet, pained sigh. "Emily. Forget about London and perfection. I care little for Town and less for people who claim what only God can attain."

Her mother touched her hand, warm and patient. "It sounds as though you are carrying a weight, child. Something is pressing on you."

Emily's fingers tightened on the edge of the table. "I do not want to trouble you. Not again." But the ache behind her ribs pressed harder, demanding she set it free.

"What nonsense is this? We are your parents," her father said. "Children are supposed to trouble us, vex us, and worry us. How else will we know we have them?" He stood on the other side of her, a hand on her shoulder. "Come now. Let us hear it."

Leaning into her father's shoulder, she looked down at the bottles with Lyness's neatly written labels. Perhaps it was time to admit defeat.

"I have tried to be everything lady ought bye be," Emily said quietly. "Since London—since everything—I have worked at it. To be a good daughter, the one who does not make trouble, who never embarrasses anyone." She twisted her fingers together, knuckles whitening. "I have studied every book of etiquette in my possession. I have worked until my head aches to make myself someone you can be proud of, and above all that miserable London gossip."

Her father's brow drew down at that, but she didn't stop.

"And still," she whispered, "I failed. In London, I did not understand the situation with Mr. Waldegrave, and the rumors grew until a *duke* stepped in. I came here hoping I could make things better."

Her mother's hand pressed lightly on her arm. "Oh, Emily…"

"But now," Emily said, voice cracking despite her efforts, "this betrothal feels like a consequence Lyness must pay because of one small accident. Because something had to be fixed. Because honor demanded it." She swallowed hard. "I keep thinking Lyness only offered for me because he had no choice. That I am, once again, trouble to be managed."

A soft, distressed breath escaped her mother. "Darling—"

However, her father made a low, irritable sound—one he usually reserved for obstinate livestock or foolish neighbors. "That is utter pigswill," he said flatly.

Emily's eyes widened. "Papa?"

"Richard," his wife gasped out. "We do not use that word anymore. It is uncouth."

"It is a perfectly good word. But fine. I s'pose the nobility would say nonsense. Whatever it is, I will not have you speak it, Emily Sterling." He fixed her with a fatherly frown as he put his arm around her shoulders. "The threat of rumors did not *cause* the engagement. Even I can see that. They were just the excuse the lad needed."

Her heart thudded painfully as she tilted her head to look up at him. "What do you mean?"

The Earl of Benwaith, her father, looked at her with exasperation and love mixed together in a uniquely paternal way. "Emily my girl, I have lived long enough to know what a man in love looks like. I have seen it in my sons. Even in your brother Jack. Saw it in myself, long before your mother saw fit to look my way."

Her mother smiled faintly at that.

"And I saw it yesterday," her father went on, firm as a hammer strike. "Plain as the nose on your face. Lyness Eastwood is besotted with you."

Emily stared at him. "Papa—no, he cannot be. We are good friends is all."

Her father snorted and released his hold on her. "I have been wrong about the price of oats a time or two. But this? I am not wrong about this." He put his hands on her upper arms and looked down into her eyes. "The boy looks at you as though you are an angel walking on the earth."

Heat crept up her neck. "He is kind, yes, but kindness does not mean—"

"Emily," her mother interrupted softly, "your father is not given to fanciful notions. If he says Mr. Eastwood's affection is real, I would not dismiss it lightly."

Emily looked between her parents, trying to fit their words into the hollow ache within her heart.

"But no one noticed me," Emily said quietly. "Not until after the title, anyway. And even then, I think it was only because of the marriage settlement that horrible lawyer told you to give me. Then everyone in Town found out about it, and Mr. Waldegrave was one of them. Why would Lyness care when no one else ever has? I am five-and-twenty. Most women my age are married or resigned to never be so."

That declaration brought a strong reaction from both parents as they exchanged glances and looked at her with wide eyes.

"What do you mean, no one noticed you?" her father asked. "You mean suitors? Before we had the nobility foolishness fall into our laps? Emily, you never seemed interested in that sort of thing. I told a few fellows they were welcome to court you if you wanted it, but none of them had any encouragement for you. They went on their way."

To Emily's surprise, her mother was nodding along with him. "I am afraid that is the truth of it, darling. you never showed the interest in courtship and marriage that your sisters did."

"They were the pretty ones," she said quietly. "Everyone wanted to court Mary and Anne. They were always going to dances and picnics."

"Those two could never sit still," her father grumbled. "They wanted their independence from each other as much as they did from our household. They went after husbands with a single-mindedness that nearly drove your poor mother mad."

"I was rather exhausted by the time both of them wed," the countess admitted, a wry smile on her lips that Emily had inherited. "My Emily, I would have done all the same things for you that I did for them, but you seemed so content."

Her father hesitated, then added in a gruffer tone, "You were happy in the quiet. Or so we thought. You'd wander the fields, help your mother mix her herbs, sit with the neighbors' little ones. We believed that was where you wanted to be." His voice softened, almost uncertain. "We didn't mean you to feel neglected, Emily. Not ever."

Her breath caught.

Her mother slipped an arm around her shoulders. "You have always been our steady one. Our gentle one. We cherished that about you. I never thought to ask if there was more you wanted. I am sorry for that, my darling."

Emily shut her eyes, overwhelmed by the weight of love and misunderstanding, of years spent assuming she had been the forgettable child—useful, dependable, and easy to set aside. The child not meant to stir up trouble or call attention to herself. She had pressed herself into that role. To hear they did not mean for such a thing to happen…she would have to think on it. At that moment, there was too much in her heart to study it closely.

But hearing her father's admission—he had *seen* something in

Lyness, something tender and unmistakable—shifted her thoughts in that direction.

"Besotted," she whispered, as if examining the word. "Do you really think so?"

Her raised both his eyebrows at her. "I am quite certain. The lad is in love with you. The only fools in this situation are the ones who won't speak plain to each other." He fixed her with a stern look. "You are as much in love with him as he is with you, my girl. Time to tell him."

Emily pressed a trembling hand to her mouth, unsure whether to laugh or cry.

Her mother drew her gently into a full embrace. "Oh, my darling girl. You do not have to be perfect. You only need to be yourself. That is all anyone who loves you ever truly needs."

# Chapter Twenty-Three

## September 5, 1822

The rain returned to York, fine and misting, the sort that left the windows filmed with gray and the garden blurred as though one looked at it through a veil. Emily sat on the settee in the sitting room, Miss Feathersby's cage on the table beside her, sketchbook open and entirely ignored in her lap.

The canary hopped from perch to perch, trilling the occasional uncertain note, as though trying to decide whether a song was worth the effort.

"I know precisely how you feel," Emily murmured. "Everything seems…muddled."

Her family had gone out. Her parents to call on an acquaintance of her father's, George and Richard to attend some entertainment or other with their wives, and Jack to a meeting with Lord Hartwell about the poisoning. At least he promised to bring back whatever news he learned.

Only Juniper remained home to keep Emily company, but at present she was in her room penning a letter to her elder sister, Lady Ivy Dunmore in Ireland.

That left Emily alone with her thoughts. A dangerous state for her, of late.

Lyness's face rose in her mind—his quiet, earnest gaze at the races, the way his voice had turned rough when he said *I will withdraw if you command it...but I hope you will not.* And then Roman's words, Jack's, her father's all echoed in her ears, too.

She pressed her hand to her sternum, trying to steady the ache there. What was she supposed to believe? What was she supposed to do? Every book she possessed advised ladies to conceal more passionate feelings, to modulate everything from their voices to the beating of their hearts.

And what if Lyness only saw their friendship and nothing more? Her father might be wrong. It had certainly happened before.

A knock sounded at the front door, startling Emily enough that she jumped in her seat. Miss Feathersby fluffed her feathers indignantly and gave a scolding chirp. The sound of voices in the entryway followed, indistinct at first. A servant's and then Juniper's, low and surprised, and another voice, quiet but unmistakable.

Lyness.

Emily's heart tripped over itself. She stared at the sitting room door, suddenly torn between the urge to flee and the knowledge that running away from him was the worst sort of cowardice.

A moment later, Juniper appeared in the doorway, her expression carefully composed. She must have read something of Emily's distress in her face, because her eyes softened at once.

"You have a visitor, Emily," Juniper said, voice gentle.

Emily rose and put her arms around herself. "I am not receiving callers today."

"Emily." Juniper stepped inside the room and lowered her voice. "You know exactly who is here. Lyness Eastwood. Your intended." Her gaze steadied. "You are at liberty to refuse seeing him. If you like, I can tell him you are resting. But I think you ought to speak to him. He looks rather miserable."

"Miserable?" she repeated, then glanced at the window. "Very well. I will see him. He did come through this dismal weather."

"I think that is a wise decision." Juniper came forward, taking Emily's hand to offer a gentle squeeze of encouragement. She looked directly into her sister-in-law's eyes. "I know you are troubled. You have been for days. You needn't see him alone, if that gives you pause. Shall I stay?"

The question immediately steadied Emily. She did not need anyone to protect her from Lyness, or the feelings he stirred in her. This was something she had to work through with him, on her own. She shook her head, throat tight. "No. But thank you for asking."

"I will not be far," Juniper promised. "If you call for me, I will come at once." She withdrew, leaving the door partly open.

A heartbeat later, Lyness appeared on the threshold, hat and gloves in one hand, the other arm bent close against his side as though holding himself together. He wore his usual dark coat, but his cravat had been tied with even more care than usual, and his hair was shorter. It also looked as though he had raked his fingers through it a dozen times before deciding there was nothing to be done about it.

"Lady Emily." He bowed deeply, eyes on the ground. "Th-thank you for—" His throat worked. "For seeing me."

Her breath caught as watched him, her fingers curled into her skirts. "Good afternoon, Mr. Eastwood."

The faintest wince crossed his features at the formality.

"I will not keep you long," he said. "I only—" He held up what he carried in his left hand. Folded, thick cream paper, sealed with dark blue wax. Her name, written in his elegant script, scrolled along the center of it.

Even at this distance, she could see the beauty of his penmanship.

"I have never been particularly adept at speaking without..." His jaw clenched. "Without difficulty. So I hoped you would allow me to offer you this first." His gaze lowered briefly, then rose again. "If, after you read it, you wish me to leave, I will. Without another word."

The room seemed to narrow to the few steps between them.

Emily's palms prickled, and she rubbed them along the fabric of her gown to ease the sensation. "You could have sent it by messenger," she said, mostly to fill the air.

"I could have." His fingers tightened on the letter. "But I did not want you to think I had written it to escape your answer. Or that I was a coward, unable to bear seeing your reaction."

She looked at him for one long moment. Then, slowly, she extended her hand.

He crossed the room and placed the letter in her hand with reverence, as though entrusting her with something of great importance. The paper was smooth and heavy—far finer than anything she had ever purchased for herself.

She sank back onto the settee because her knees did not feel entirely reliable. Lyness remained standing a little way off, near Miss Feathersby's table, hands clasped behind his back.

The canary hopped once, tilting her head toward him, as though she, too, was curious about his visit.

Emily broke the seal.

Inside, the sheet unfolded to reveal careful lines of script, each letter shaped with exquisite precision. Flourishes swept just enough to be graceful without rendering anything difficult to read. It was the sort of hand one might see in illuminated copies of treasured works, orderly and beautiful both. Gentle sweeps along the edges of the letter suggested flowers and vines, and there was not a single word crossed over or smudged.

Her name crowned the top of the page, each letter a work of art.

*Emily,*

*I fear that in attempting to do what was right, I have caused pain I never intended. I have made decisions that should have been yours, without giving you the time or the freedom to offer your thoughts on matters. For that alone, I owe you an apology I can scarcely frame in words.*

*But I hope this letter will convey to you the truth of why I acted as I did, why I do not regret it, and the truth that I carry in my heart.*

*I cannot deny that duty has guided my actions. Duty to your name. Duty to your family. Duty to my own conscience. But if duty were all that bound me to you, I would never have presumed to make my declaration in so public a manner. A sense of obligation might have compelled an offer in private, where it could be refused quietly and forgotten. What I did that morning was born of something I have not had the courage to name aloud until now.*

*The truth is this: My heart chose you, Emily. Long before the ball.*

Her thumb caught on the edge of the paper. Everything was silent save for the soft tap of Miss Feathersby's claws on her perch and the patter of rain on the windowpanes. And the room felt suddenly too small to contain the words he had given her.

*From the first time we danced in London, you have remained in my thoughts. I have admired other women in my life, but never as I have admired you. You are gentle without being weak. You are kind without being foolish. You care for people others overlook. You speak when you ought, and you remain silent when others would rush to judgment. You saved a little bird in the ruins because you could not bear to leave her alone. You listen—truly listen—in rooms where everyone else only waits to speak. Being near you has always made me want to be kinder and a better man.*

*I did not mean to tell you any of this in such a hasty, clumsy manner. I had thought, foolishly, to ask my brother's blessing first. To earn the right to court you honorably, to see you smile at me as someone more than a friend. Necessity overtook my plans, and fear for your good name pushed me to act hastily. If I erred, it was in letting that fear convince me before I knew your heart.*

*I understand that this may be of little comfort to you. You have been subjected to gossip. You have watched your family maneuver within a world that too often values advantage over affection. It would be natural to suspect that any man who offers for you in such circumstances does so for convenience's sake alone. I swear to you, on all the honor I possess, that where you are concerned, my affection for you is why I made the decision to claim your hand for my own.*

Her breath came unsteadily now. She cupped one hand to her mouth and read the final lines through a blur.

*If you wish to end our engagement, you have only to say so. I will bear whatever people say of me and will not allow any blame to attach itself to you. I will speak to your brother, to my own, to anyone who listens, and I will tell them the dissolution was made without resentment, and that I alone am at fault.*

*But if there is any part of you that can believe me, any corner of your heart that has felt even a portion of the regard I hold for you, then I ask most humbly to remain your betrothed not by necessity, but by your choice.*

*I do not ask that you love me today. I only ask that you allow me the chance to prove, with the rest of my life, that I chose you freely. And that I would choose you again, and again, in any circumstance. My heart is yours, as is my devotion and my love.*

*With deepest respect and unshaken affection,*

*Lyness Eastwood*

When she finished, the ink swam before her eyes. She lowered the letter carefully into her lap, pressing her fingers to its edges until they stopped trembling.

He had not sat. He still stood by the canary's cage, shoulders straight, gaze fixed on the far wall. His jaw worked once as he swallowed. His hands, now visible at his sides, were curled into tight fists, as though he were bracing himself for a blow.

"Emily?" he asked at last, not quite looking at her. "If you w— wish me to go, I will."

Her heart hurt. "Lyness," she said on a breath.

His head jerked. His eyes flew to hers.

"I have read your letter," she said, fingers tightening on the page.

"I understand what you mean to tell me." The words scraped on the way out. "But I need to hear you say it."

The silence stretched, fine and tense.

Color climbed his neck to his cheeks, but he nodded once, as though accepting a challenge. He took one slow step toward her. Then another. He stopped a pace away, enough distance left that she did not feel crowded, and yet near enough that she could see every flicker of emotion across his face. Slowly, he lowered himself to one knee in front of her.

"I chose you," he began, the first words catching slightly. "L-long before th-that night. L-long before I had any r-right to." He exhaled, his gaze never leaving hers. "I will not pret-pretend it w-was easy. To adm-admit that to myself. I th-thought...if I kept my distance, I w-would spare us both complication. And then..."

He closed his eyes tightly for a moment and opened them again, clearer.

"And then someone put a d-drugged cup into your hand," he said, voice low. "And I felt the ground g-go from under me. I thought I had lost you. Before I had ever truly been allowed to claim you, even in my thoughts."

Her eyes burned.

He continued haltingly, but with growing resolve. "Where you are conc-concerned, Emily, I have only ever wanted to do what would keep you safe and happy. I acted r-rashly so that I could see to those th-things myself. If that has harmed you, I will reg-regret it every day I draw breath."

She swallowed. "My brothers think you are shouldering a burden that should have been shared. That you tied yourself to me to relieve their consciences."

His mouth twisted in something like pain. "Do you think me so unfeeling that I would of-offer you a lifetime, a shared lifetime, of cold obligation?"

"That is what I feared." The confession slipped free, raw and honest. "I have always tried to be useful. As a daughter. As a sister. As...as a lady. And I thought—perhaps that is all this is. Another useful arrangement. Another way for me to be a problem solved, rather than a person someone wanted." Her voice trembled. "I have never been anyone's first choice. Not truly."

He flinched as though she had struck him.

"Emily." Her name left him on a breath. He reached for her hand, taking it gently in his own. "Look at me."

She did.

"From the moment I met you, I wanted to know everything about you," he said, the words rough but determined. "You were a miracle. To dance with you and speak with you was like a dream. I hated leaving London because I kn-knew others would see you and want to c-claim your heart, and that I would never have that chance. When you came to York, I had such hope. Every time you laughed, my heart soared. You have never been a burden to me. Not in any sense. You are the reason I want to be brave."

She drew in a trembling breath.

"And if you tell me now that you do not w-wish to marry me, I will accept that. I will release you. I will protect your name as best I can. But do not ever think," his voice broke as he leaned nearer, "do not ever think that you were forced upon me. I went to that garden determined to cl-claim you, selfishly, even if only with my words. I have wanted to ask for your heart since the m-moment I realized I had already given you mine."

The tears she had been holding back spilled over.

Slowly, as though afraid of startling her, he reached into his coat and took out a smaller square of paper—scrap from his drafts, its corner filled with a small, intricate drawing in ink. A sprig of chamomile, each petal perfectly etched.

"I d-did this," he said, voice gentling. "The night after the ball. I could not sleep. I kept seeing you with the blossoms in your hair. It seemed a p-poor substitute for having any right to keep the real thing."

She looked from the simple drawing to his face. He held her gaze, love in his eyes. Her heart, which had been twisting in confusion and fear, settled suddenly with a sense of rightness so profound it made her light-headed.

"I want this," she said, voice hoarse. "I want you."

For a brief, stunned moment, hope flared so bright in his eyes she hardly dared to breathe. His hand trembled as he lifted it, hovering beside her cheek, not quite touching. "May I—"

"Yes," she whispered.

His gloved fingertips brushed her cheek with exquisite gentleness, as though she were delicate and precious. The touch was barely there, and yet it steadied her more than any firm grasp could have done.

"I love you," he said, the words certain, each syllable careful and deliberate. "I have been a coward about admitting it. But I do. And if you will have me, not from obligation, but because you want me, then I will spend the rest of my life proving that you are my first choice. Always."

She laughed then, the sound edged with tears. "You have put the most beautiful words on paper," she said, lifting the letter slightly. "But this...this is what I will remember."

He looked startled. "Even with the..." He made a small, helpless gesture near his mouth. "The st-stumbles?"

"Especially with them," she said, fiercer than she meant to be. "You could have sent this"—she touched the letter—"and spared yourself the difficulty. Instead, you spoke the words of your heart out loud. For me." Her throat tightened. "Lyness," she said, tasting his name with new certainty, "I choose you too. Not because I must. Not because it is the sensible thing. Because I have not stopped thinking of you since our first dance in London."

His eyes widened, a smile tugged at his lips. "You too?"

She nodded swiftly, her eyes tearing up and her lips curling. "One of the reasons I agreed to stay with Jack was because I knew you would be here. In York. And I wanted to see you again. But I thought I had to make a practical match, and your brother was showing interest, and I doubted if you would care for me—"

"Emily," he said again, her name a prayer.

At last she let the words escape her, giving them to him with her full heart. "I love you, Lyness."

Something broke in his expression, a dam, perhaps, or a carefully constructed wall. Wonder flooded through, unguarded and reverent.

She did not know which of them moved first. Only that one moment she sat before where he knelt, staring into his eyes, and the next his hand cupped her cheek more surely, and their lips met in a kiss that was sweet and utterly right.

It was not like the dramatic embraces in gothic romances, all thunder and tempest. It was a soft, trembling touch, careful and sweet. His lips were warm and hesitant, hers still salty with tears. His hand slid to the back of her head, fingers threading lightly through her hair, holding her as though he feared she might vanish.

She leaned into him, free hand laying against his chest, feeling his heart pounding against her palm. When they parted, barely an inch, their foreheads rested against one another. He was breathing as though he had run the length of the Knavesmire racecourse on foot.

"I am going to m-make a mull of this," he murmured, a shaky smile tugging at his mouth, "if I attempt to say anything clever now."

She smiled through the lingering dampness on her cheeks. "You do not need to say anything clever. Only stay with me. Tell me you love me as often as you like"

His thumb brushed away the last of her tears. "That," he said softly, "I can promise. I love you, Emily." He pressed his lips to her forehead in a lingering kiss. "I love you."

From the table, Miss Feathersby let out a bright, hopeful trill. Her simple song the perfect underscore of their soft confessions.

# Epilogue

## September 22nd, 1822

A pollo and Athena draped themselves lazily across the sitting room of Hartwell House, and Emily stepped over the large dogs carefully as she made her way back to the table where she and Lyness were sitting together. Outside, the city hummed with its usual bustle, but inside all was calm and perfectly comfortable.

She sat at the small writing table Lyness had commandeered for her, pressing it up against his own—because she preferred a place near the windows, and because he liked to be where she was. Half-finished sketches lay scattered before her: herbs, apothecary jars, flowers newly dried from Lady Hartwell's garden.

Across from her, Lyness bent over a sheet of ivory paper, carefully shaping calligraphy labels for more herbal bottles. His brows furrowed in concentration, lips pressed together as though each stroke of the quill mattered more than the last. Emily suspected, with a warm flutter in her heart, that to him it did.

"You write 'elderflower' more beautifully each time," she teased lightly.

He glanced up, eyes shining. "I have a very important patron to please." His smile grew crooked. "Also a very lovely one."

Heat spread through her cheeks and pleasure bloomed in her heart. She pretended to examine her sketchbook to disguise the obvious signs of her affection. She was not yet used to being openly adored, but she doubted she would ever tire of it.

Roman sat nearby in an armchair, reading the York Gazette, though Emily suspected he was truly watching the two of them over the paper's edge. He hid it well—Roman hid everything well—but she'd learned to spot the telltale crease near his temple that meant he was listening. It was strange, but now that she knew he would be as a brother to her, she had a much easier time interpreting his expressions and silences.

Lady Hartwell swept into the room then, her gown rustling like the petals of one of her own prized roses. "Children," she announced, because she seemed determined to call them that until the end of time, "we must discuss the wedding. Again."

Folding her hands in her lap, Emily looked up with a smile. "Of course, my lady."

With a sigh dramatic enough to shake the curtains, Lady Hartwell sat upon the chair that matched Roman's. "I simply cannot understand why Christmas." She clasped her hands. "Think of the roses I have at this moment ready for a September wedding! White roses, Emily. I have none in my glasshouse. They will not be available in December."

Lyness looked at Emily, waiting for her to answer. Trusting in whatever she said. The thought made her heart warm.

Emily folded her hands atop her sketchbook. "We are waiting because we want time for a proper courtship." She darted a shy glance toward Lyness. "I want to enjoy this season of learning one another. Without rushing to the end of it."

Lyness's quill paused. He lifted his gaze to hers, that quiet, earnest warmth she had grown so attached to shining in his dark eyes. "As do I," he said. "Very much."

Lady Hartwell pressed a hand to her heart. "Well. The two of you make planning terribly inconvenient, but I suppose you make up for it with your sweetness."

Roman cleared his throat and rose abruptly. "I must leave you all to your discussions." He folded his newspaper with meticulous precision. "I believe the dogs need a walk."

"They are asleep," Lady Hartwell pointed out.

"Then I need a walk," he corrected.

Emily gave him a gentle smile as he bowed slightly to her, then to his mother, and departed the room. Athena and Apollo, roused by the hint of departure, scrambled after him with cheerful clamor.

As the door closed behind them, Emily looked at Lyness again. He had resumed his lettering, but his smile had deepened at the edges. One chestnut lock of hair fell across his forehead and she itched to smooth it back, though propriety demanded restraint with his mother present.

Someday soon, she would not have to restrain herself at all.

"December is not so far away," she said quietly.

"No," he agreed, lifting his eyes to meet hers. "But long enough to savor everything before it."

She traced a line in her sketchbook, her heart full. "I never thought happiness could feel like this."

Lyness's voice softened. "Nor I."

The sun shifted. The room glowed. Emily's world, once an uncertain jumble of expectations and missteps, now felt as steady as his presence beside her, and warm as the look he gave her every time she spoke his name.

She closed her sketchbook and let herself enjoy the quiet of the moment.

She was loved.

And she had found her home.

Roman stepped out into the crisp September air far more briskly than the dogs, though Athena and Apollo trotted at his heels eagerly enough. The street was quiet, with sunlight flickering through the branches of the lindens lining the walk.

He inhaled slowly.

It should not have caught him off guard, the sight of his younger brother alight with happiness, that soft, private smile Lyness wore now in Lady Emily's presence. Roman had always known Lyness capable of great feeling, if given room to express it.

But knowing and witnessing were not the same.

A few weeks ago, he'd thought Lady Emily's gentle kindness might be something he could grow into. Something steady, sensible, and that an affection would blossom between Roman and Emily in time. He had admired her. He had respected her. He had even wondered, once or twice, whether a future with her might hold more comfort than duty.

But now? He saw the truth plainly. She and Lyness fit together.

"I am glad for them," he murmured under his breath. And he meant it.

Apollo nudged his hand in his insistent, hopeful way. Roman scratched behind the dog's ears.

But he wondered when he would find his own contentment. Lyness had earned every ounce of his happiness. And Lady Emily deserved a man who would walk through fire for her without hesitation. Roman's affections had always been careful and measured.

Athena pressed her large head against his knee, sensing some shift in his mood. Roman exhaled, long and slow.

He had responsibilities. Duties. Enemies still to contend with and political battles to wage. There was more than enough in his life to keep him busy in the city that he loved.

Still. He wondered what it might feel like to be looked at the way Emily now looked at Lyness. The tenderness and affection she held for Lyness had done wonders for his brother's confidence.

Continuing toward St. Helen's Square, he said to the dogs, "Someday."

Athena barked once, sharply, as if in agreement. Roman smiled despite himself.

Today belonged to his brother. And Roman, for all his quiet yearning, found himself rather proud of the man Lyness had become.

IF YOU ENJOYED THIS STORY, PLEASE CONSIDER LEAVING A REVIEW.

If you can't get enough of these characters or this kind of gentle tale, make certain to read the Clairvoir Castle Romances, in which Lyness, Emily, Roman, Jack, and Juniper all made their first appearances!

You should also sign up for Sally Britton's newsletter here: https://geni.us/AuthorSallyBritton You'll get all kinds of great updates about her books, characters, and sales.

Have a lovely day!

# Acknowledgments

Thank you for picking up *Mr. Eastwood's Match*. I am so delighted to finally begin a series centered in the beautiful city of York. After multiple visits and much exploration, I'm thrilled to share its historical texture with you.

This series has been a long time coming, and people have been waiting for more of Roman and Lyness since April 2022, when they appeared in Sir Andrew and the Authoress! Your patience is much appreciated.

**On the Nature of Historical Fiction:**

As a writer of historical romance, my focus is always on emotional truth and the messy, human struggle for happiness. This sometimes means placing story and character arc above a strict adherence to every single social rule.

An author friend once put it this way: "In two hundred years, people will look back at our speed limit signs and insist everyone *always* drove exactly 65 MPH on the highway." We know better. We know people, then and now, drive faster, slower, and make exceptions based on circumstance and who is watching.

My aim is to give you a historically plausible, immersive setting, but always in service of the tender, hopeful romance at the center. I hope you enjoyed Lyness and Emily's journey to choose an imperfect, genuine love.

**Now, the fun part:**

To my incredible author friends and critique partners who cheered me on and helped me untangle the complexity of Lyness's quiet heart and Emily's inner struggle—your support is invaluable.

And to my own patient, loving family and the beautiful, complex romance of my life: thank you. You are the foundation that allows me to tell these stories of love, self-worth, and courage.

Thank you again for reading. I am forever grateful.

*Sally Britton*

# Also by Sally Britton

## Castle Clairvoir Romances:

A Duchess for the Duke | Mr. Gardiner and the Governess | A Companion for the Count | Sir Andrew and the Authoress | Lord Farleigh and Miss Frost | Lady Ivy and the Irishman | A Gentleman for Lady Juniper

## Gentlemen of York:

Mr. Eastwood's Match

## The Inglewood Series:

Rescuing Lord Inglewood | Discovering Grace | Saving Miss Everly | Engaging Sir Isaac | Reforming Lord Neil

## Return to Inglewood:

Romancing the Artist

## Devoted Hearts:

Martha's Patience | The Social Tutor | The Gentleman Physician | His Bluestocking Bride | The Earl and His Lady | Miss Devon's Choice | Courting Miss Ames | Penny's Yuletide Wish

## Stand Alone Romances:

The Captain and Miss Winter | A Haunting at Havenwood | A Mistletoe Mismatch | An Unsuitable Suitor | Mistletoe for Felicity

## Love Unawares

His Unexpected Heiress | Her Unsuitable Match

## Hearts of Arizona Series:

Silver Dollar Duke | Copper for the Countess | A Lady's Heart of Gold

# About the Author

Since Jane Austen isn't releasing any new titles, Sally decided to try her hand at writing a few stories set in the Regency period. Those attempts led to a happy career doing what she loves most: telling love stories.

Sally Britton, her husband, their four incredible children, their dogs, the cat Willow who tolerates them, and a snake named Basil live in Oklahoma.

Sally started writing on her mother's electric typewriter when she was fourteen years old. Reading her way through Jane Austen, Louisa May Alcott, and L.M. Montgomery, Sally fell love with the elegant, complex world of centuries past.

In 2007, Sally earned a bachelor's in English Literature. She met and married her husband not long after, and they're quite busy living happily ever after.

All of Sally's published works are available on multiple retailers and you can connect with Sally and sign up for her newsletter or visit her website, AuthorSallyBritton.Store